Ms. Renfield and the Deadly Puzzle

ISBN: 978-1-944736-58-3

v00004082026a

Ms. Renfield and the Deadly Puzzle

Just A Nerdy Woman Solving Murders with Her Impossible Vampire Boss

Immortal Boss

Book 2

Annika Martin

Cinnamon Crane & Dagger

Chapter One

Harriet

The basement of Cleveland First Shepherd Congregational Church has the same linoleum tile and drop ceiling as every church basement I've ever been in. Alexandru and I bypass the folding table with the Mr. Coffee and the Styrofoam cups and swizzle sticks and take our seats in a circle of metal folding chairs with fifteen or so people from all walks of life.

A woman with a name tag that reads "Doreen Facilitator" stands up. "Welcome, everybody! We're so glad you're here." She projects a mix of confidence and cheerfulness, but not too much cheerfulness, because this is a crime victims support group, after all. She glances nervously at Alexandru, the standard response to a six-foot-something man in a three-piece suit who radiates danger. "And welcome, new members."

I push my glasses up and give her a warm smile to hopefully balance him out. My smile says, nothing to see here! Please ignore every instinct telling you that my impeccably dressed companion would happily drain your blood!

Look instead at his harmless, slightly nerdy companion! She seems friendly and safe with her glasses and curly mop of hair, right?

Doreen manages to tear her gaze away from us, hopefully having taken my intended message. "Just a few ground rules. Number one: no cross-talking. Number two: no advice-giving unless specifically requested. Number three: what's shared in this circle stays in this circle." She smiles hopefully. "Does anyone have questions?"

Nobody has questions.

She casts another nervous glance at Alexandru. A lock of dark hair has tumbled over his brow. I don't know how he always looks so elegant, like he just wandered in from the Paris opera house and decided to stay among the rabble.

There's some more meeting business, and then Doreen announces that we'll go around the circle for introductions. "Just share your first name and, if you're comfortable, why you're here. No pressure for details. We are here for each other's healing, and you get to decide what form that takes." She presses her clipboard to her chest. "I'll start. I'm Doreen, and I facilitate this group because my brother was killed by a burglar eight years ago."

There's a chorus of "Hello, Doreen."

Doreen nods to the man on her left, and we begin around the circle. Identity theft, hit-and-runs, a stabbing outside a bar, a carjacking. Some people take an angry or defiant tone. Others sound exhausted, like they're repeating the same thing for the umpteenth time.

I catalog it all: ages, types of crimes, how long ago the incidents occurred. The information arranges itself into tidy categories like it always does. I can't seem to look at a room full of people without my brain turning them into orderly data. Who knows, maybe it'll be useful someday.

But mostly I can't help it.

Alexandru and I are here to find a woman we know only as Elaine99. She joined the *Northern Ohio True Crime forum* a little while ago and promptly began to rant that her neighbor was murdered, and that the police arrested the wrong guy, and she knows who really did it.

Which was interesting to Alexandru and me.

Very interesting.

Because Alexandru and I happen to be searching for a murderer. Any murderer. Rather desperately.

As a vampire, Alexandru feeds on human blood—to the death, and he can't go longer than a month between meals. I don't recommend pushing it to the deadline, because that's when he enters what I have privately labeled "beast mode."

Anyway, that month is halfway over. If I don't help him find that victim, he'll go after anybody. Even my friends and family.

Why is this my job, you might ask?

For starters, it's my fault he's here in Ohio instead of brooding away back in his weird ancient castle in Karsovia, a microstate that borders Romania. A place with torchlit hallways, no cell service, and a business empire run on handwritten ledgers and trips to the post office. It turns out that my biological father, who I met only once (don't ask), was his longtime servant, as were generations of Renfields before that.

After his death, I was summoned to what I thought was his memorial service. It turned out to be part of Alexandru's warped hiring process to replace him with a new "Renfield"—which, for the record, is not my last name.

It was fun to meet my European half-siblings, less fun to discover we were imprisoned there by a vampire with scary super strength and the ability to not be harmed by knives.

When he declared I'd be his new Renfield servant and my half-siblings would be slaughtered, I made a bargain: I'd work remotely from Ohio, and everyone would live.

Alexandru eventually decided he wasn't a fan of remote work. He relocated to the quaint Ohio tourist town where I live, having intention of feasting on my friends and neighbors. We made another bargain: I would work with him at his refurbished Gothic hilltop manor if he agreed to feed only on murderers we nab.

If we can't find a murderer before the month is up, he'll go beast mode and drain just anybody.

Hence the desperation.

Elaine99 didn't respond to my private messages on the forum, but she once mentioned she lives in Cleveland and goes to a crime victims group.

So here we are, hoping that this is the group she attends. We need to see if her story has any merit. Nobody in the circle has mentioned a murdered neighbor, but we're only halfway around.

Suddenly it's our turn. Alexandru gives me a look that means *I'm waiting, Ms. Renfield.*

Even though Doreen said we weren't required to share the crime we're here to heal from, everyone's been telling all, so I decide to go for it. We do qualify—last month Alexandru and I investigated a string of staged wedding accidents, and some masked figure tried to steal my tablet full of investigation notes.

They didn't get it, and we caught the wedding killer in the end; Alexandru handled the aftermath—with his fangs, presumably. That killer is currently a drained corpse at the bottom of Lake Erie.

But it was technically a mugging, though we're still not sure who did it.

I clear my throat. "Hi. I'm Harriet. And we were, uh, mugged at gunpoint last month—me and my—" I pause. How do I even describe Alexandru? Employer? Overlord for life? "Me and my boss," I finally decide.

There are murmurs of sympathy.

Alexandru shifts beside me. Is he annoyed I called him my boss?

"It was pretty scary," I add. "They wanted my tablet."

"Unfortunately, the perpetrator escaped." Alexandru's cut-glass English accent surprises people. "I looked back at Ms. Renfield here and saw her stumbling. At that moment he fled and I did not pursue, choosing instead to determine if she was shot."

"Wait, the mugger shot at you?" a man in a turtleneck asks. "Shot at you and ran off?"

It does seem odd. What kind of mugger shoots at a person and then runs away? The answer would be a mugger who puts a bullet in a guy's chest and the guy keeps casually walking toward him like the Terminator. That's the kind of mugger who shoots and runs off.

"Yeah. We were lucky we weren't hurt," I say.

Alexandru says, "The man disappeared by the time I was

able to determine that Ms. Renfield was unhurt. A faulty decision in retrospect."

People disagree. "You did the right thing." "You had to help her."

Alexandru brushes an invisible spec from the sleeve of his gray cashmere suit coat. "Indeed. She is of no use to me injured. Rest assured, I will find this man. I will make him regret ever raising a weapon against someone under my protection. There are so many ways to make a man sorry. Far more than most people presume." His voice lowers to a dangerous rumble. "No one threatens my Renfield and lives to tell the tale."

"I know you're new," Doreen says gently, "but we don't condone vigilante justice here, so I might ask you to avoid that kind of talk?"

"He doesn't mean it," I say quickly. "It was a very emotional experience."

Alexandru makes a low sound, but Doreen moves on to the next speaker—a woman whose house was burglarized twice. She's thinking of moving.

Finally we get to a woman in her mid-forties, blonde hair pulled back in a severe ponytail, navy blazer buttoned over a white T-shirt.

"My name is Elaine, and I'm here because my neighbor was *murdered* three years ago, and the police completely botched the investigation."

Bingo!

I feel Alexandru's attention sharpen beside me.

"They put away her husband, but I *know* it wasn't him. I knew her husband. We'd talk every Saturday doing yardwork, and he'd go out for a jog like clockwork at three in the afternoon rain or shine, and that's when my neighbor was murdered—during his jog, and I know he was on that jog because he loves to jog—he told me once that jogging was his lifeline and if there's one thing a person never gives up, it's their lifeline. Think about it, that is the thing they throw from a boat to rescue you from the water. It's his *lifeline*." She pauses to look around at the group for emphasis. "It was completely circumstantial, what they put him away with. What's more, there's this guy who runs a butcher shop a few blocks out and he has this food truck where he does smelly sausages and jerky and stuff and he's always had a thing for my neighbor. I've seen the way he looks at her. I told the police about it—"

"Okay," Doreen interrupts. "Thank you, Elaine." Her firm yet patient tone suggests to me she's been through the Elaine experience before.

"No, but my point is that I told the police and they barely questioned the butcher." Elaine's voice trembles with outrage. "I *watched* from across the street—they actually shook his hand after they spoke! What kind of police officer shakes a murderer's hand? I've confronted the butcher of course—"

"Elaine—"

"Not aggressively! Just asked where he was that day, questions the police should've asked, and he was evasive. Now he's watching my house. Following me."

"Okay, thank you," Doreen says. "Remember, this is not a place to relitigate cases or rehash police investigations. This group is about working through your own emotions and what you can control going forward."

"But how can I go forward when they framed a husband and let the murderer go free?" Elaine grits out.

I glance at Alexandru, who looks faintly weary. I don't need his empathic abilities to tell me this woman is unhinged.

We finish the circle. A teenage girl talks about her best friend's death. An older man mumbles about getting scammed.

Then comes open discussion. Elaine's hand shoots up again.

"I've been documenting everything," she says, pulling out her phone. "I have a detailed timeline—"

"Sorry, we're not doing the timeline," Doreen says. "Let's let others share."

Elaine huffs, crossing her arms.

I stare at the ceiling. If only Elaine had shared a little bit more of her reasoning with the true crime forum, we wouldn't have wasted this trip.

The teenage girl wants to read a poem she wrote, and we all settle back to listen. It's long and earnest and full of pain.

Alexandru grumbles softly beside me.

"We have to stay," I mumble under my breath. Alexandru has batlike hearing—he can pick up the faintest whisper.

Alexandru grumbles again. He is not used to constraints of any kind.

When I next look over at him, he is glaring at the far wall, which is festooned with colorful banners. He seems to be fixating on one that says "...and the meek shall inherit the earth." Like he's outraged by the very concept.

Chapter Two

Alexandru

I sometimes fail to understand Ms. Renfield's motivations. Why she thinks we must now sit and listen to this female's maudlin poem about a friendship bracelet and a picture in a locker is beyond me. The girl weeps as she reads. She rambles about "the empty desk where you should be." Several others begin to weep.

Humans are so sentimental. It really is a wonder they've managed to survive all these years.

And truly. The banners upon the far wall are preposterous, if not downright offensive. *The meek shall inherit the earth?* A remarkable delusion. I have walked this earth for a thousand years and the meek have inherited nothing but early graves.

There's another that says, *Humble yourself before God.* Having spent three centuries in chains, I find this notion particularly grotesque.

True, humans are mere livestock, but surely even livestock do not voluntarily humble themselves.

The man who spoke earlier about a hit-and-run goes next.

He drones on about his meditation practice, about learning to "sit with his feelings" and to "breathe through the anger," when a far better solution would be to hunt down the driver and put an ice pick through his eye. But apparently that is frowned upon here at the crime victims support group. Humans are so quick to settle for self-soothing, but then, they are a helpless lot.

Finally, the leader announces there will be a snacks break. Ms. Renfield rests her small hand upon my arm and squeezes. I'm startled by the contact, but then I realize that she wishes to communicate something. I watch her stroll over to the leader. She has a fighter's build, this Renfield—compact and sturdy. So very capable, if not formidable. She tilts her head as she thanks Doreen for the meeting and makes excuses about the long drive back, striking, just the right tone. She can be a pleasing ally.

"What a waste of time," I grumble as we speed down the dark highway. The headlights pierce the night, illuminating the nothingness of this American Ohio road.

"At least Elaine's unreliability was obvious." Ms. Renfield turns to me. "What did you get from her?"

Ms. Renfield, always so curious about my empathic abilities. She would love nothing more than to chart them on one of her spreadsheets, to reduce centuries of hunting to columns and categories. But what I perceive cannot be captured onto her electronic ledger. It is not data; it is the way the shark senses blood.

I consider how to explain. "Elaine believes what she says, but she is a boat with no anchor. Drifting senselessly through her obsessions with the husband and the butcher."

"Right. Well, we have seventeen days left. I'm confident that we'll find a nice, tasty killer for you." Ms. Renfield likes to project optimism, but she can't hide the tension that she feels now.

At least not from me.

"I would highly suggest not taking each and every one of those seventeen days," I say.

She nods, remembering, no doubt, the state I was in when last I went too long without feeding. When the world narrows to blood. Warmth. The drive to consume another's life force.

"Things really are popping with your business in Brussels!" she says, maneuvering her old car expertly off the major highway onto the two-lane road that leads to Silverton Valley, where the village of Ashwood sits.

People say that Ashwood is "picturesque."

I suppose it is pleasingly picturesque in the sense that it is full of well-fed, unwary villagers who would be easy to stalk and kill—or they would be, at any rate, if Ms. Renfield's moral sensibilities had not taken them from my dinner menu.

It is full dark by the time we reach the gravel drive that leads to Kingston Manor, solemn and silent, its Gothic spire pointing up at the starless sky. It is nothing like my castle back in Karsovia, but after an evening spent among weeping humans, the sight of it is a balm.

I climb the steps and fling open the great carved door. Gregor's head dips as we enter.

"Gregor! Tell me you haven't been standing there the whole time waiting for us to return!" Ms. Renfield says, coming in after me.

I hand Gregor my coat. "The affairs of my household are not your concern, Ms. Renfield."

She shoots me a withering glance—the kind that would

wither a lesser man, at any rate—spins on her heel, and disappears down the corridor to her wing, radiating indignation with every step.

I climb the stairs to the library and select a volume at random—a treatise on siege warfare that I have read perhaps forty times. Gregor follows without being summoned and busies himself at the hearth, shuffling the embers back to life.

I have not needed warmth in many centuries, but I find I like the flicker and crackle of a fire. I like the shadows it casts. Perhaps it touches some human memory.

I settle into my chair, but I do not read so much as listen to her movements in the wing beyond. The faint slide of drawers, the creak of the bathroom door, the swish of curtains being closed.

I have grown accustomed to her presence. It is...tolerable. Much more so than her father's presence, with his fits of melancholy and his regrettable tendency to wander the halls weeping. He so vexed me at times; I would be forced to send him to the dungeon to count grains of rice in the darkness until he collected himself. And he was not the worst. Bartholomew James Renfield would bow and scrape so excessively I once locked him in a closet simply to be free of his fawning. Jonas Renfield, once a noble, grew so obsessed with the ledgers that he became nearly useless at times. Thaddeus Wilbur Renfield, whom I took from a monastery where he served as a record-keeper, went about clawing at the walls until his fingers were pulpy stumps. He ruined many a business ledger.

It is the way of things that a Renfield serves me. They owe a debt that can never be discharged—not in any century. Not in any universe.

Harriet Renfield is even more organized than her predecessors, something I would not have thought possible. And she works with newfangled tools. I have seen her command her electronic ledger with her voice alone. A useful redundancy, should she begin to claw the walls as her great-great-great grandfather did.

I turn a page. The sounds from her wing have quieted. Perhaps she is asleep. I cannot hear her sleep breathing from up here, but if I were to go down to the foyer, perhaps I would.

The night passes quietly.

Around five, I hear her stir again. She pads to the kitchen. The familiar clatter of her morning ritual begins: the grinder, the kettle set onto the stove.

I can picture her bent over the kitchen island, scratching and tapping on her electronic ledger with her white pencil that has no lead, as is her way, raven curls wild from sleep, glasses perched on her nose, dressed only in undergarments, though she insists they are not undergarments but rather "T-shirt and leggings."

I listen to the pouring of the coffee, the impatient tap of her spoon against the mug. Another tap on the ledger.

She brings her coffee to her office, where she conducts her morning communications with my European team—property managers in Brussels, solicitors in London, bankers in Zurich. There seems to be some problem with what Ms. Renfield terms as "red tape."

I smile as I listen to her breach one barrier and then another, and then I focus back on my book. Her voice recedes into a muffled rhythm.

Until I hear a sound that freezes me: a sharp gasp.

I straighten.

Her heartbeat has quickened. Her chair scrapes.

"Something's happened," I murmur.

Gregor stirs in the corner, where he's been slumped for some hours.

"Go to her office," I tell him. "See what's the matter."

He turns to obey, but before he reaches the door, Ms. Renfield bursts in, wild-eyed and holding her ledger.

"There's been a murder in town," she says. "One of the Snag Tooth Riders—you know that motorcycle club? One of their members was killed with a crossbow."

"A crossbow." I close my book. "Exquisite."

Ms. Renfield frowns. "A man is dead. That's never exquisite."

"Yes, fine. A tragedy of great proportion." I rise from my chair. "And now we have something to investigate that does not involve weeping females reading maudlin poetry."

She makes a sound of exasperation but does not argue further. Within minutes she is dressed and ready, and we convene in the foyer.

I settle my wide-brimmed hat atop my head. Contrary to myth, vampires do not perish in the daylight, but our skin is exceedingly sensitive to the sun, so I never go out uncovered.

Gregor hands me my day-walking gloves. I ease my fingers into the first glove, feeling the warm leather yield and then tighten around each knuckle as I press deeper.

Ms. Renfield's eyes track every movement. I have noticed this before—this fascination with my hands as I don my gloves.

Curious.

I draw the glove fully on, flexing until the fit is absolute, and her pulse quickens.

I take up the second glove and repeat the process with the same unhurried care, working into the warmth of the leather. I adjust the cuffs, taking my time. Her breathing grows shallow.

She seems to enjoy the process, and I find myself oddly pleased by this.

Until I remind myself that she is a Renfield. What do I care of her pleasure?

"Get the car. Make haste, Renfield."

Ms. Renfield guides her car down North Commerce Street, hands stay fixed at equidistant points on the wheel. Sunlight slides across her raven hair, limning her curls, one of which has escaped to caress her cheekbone.

I look away. That sun would pain me if not for the smoked tint Gregor applied to the windows.

Ms. Renfield informs me that this murder was done by crossbow right out in front of the hardware store, which is near Ms. Renfield's family's antique store. A motorcycle gang member named Razor Johnny was felled like game.

There is no suspect as of yet.

No suspect. I find myself oddly pleased by this development.

Ferreting out murderers is a time-consuming way to dine, but there is a certain sport in it that I rather enjoy. The centuries tend to blur together; thus a fresh puzzle is not unwelcome.

"The villagers here are indeed benighted and dull in their thoughts," I say to her. "Nevertheless, I find it odd anyone would name their child Razor Johnny."

"That's not his real name—that's his motorcycle gang name," she says.

"Your favorite people."

Ms. Renfield snorts. "Yeah, not so much."

I smile, remembering her righteous fury last month when they'd thundered through town on their Harley Davidson motorcycles. *It's called a muffler—look into it!*" she'd shouted, a lone, indignant voice into the roar like Don Quixote at his windmill.

So very Ms. Renfield.

She maneuvers the car into a space that seems impossibly small, but not for her. Up the street, yellow tape cordons off a section of sidewalk. The hapless villagers are scattered around in groups. Even from here I can smell the sharp copper tang of blood.

"Let me do the talking," she says. "Maverick is going to be territorial about this."

I feel a growl begin deep in my throat. *Officer Maverick Cooper.* "Your former suitor."

She checks herself in the mirror, adjusting the clips that hold back her hair. "You can't antagonize him."

"I have no reason to antagonize him. Unless he antagonizes me."

"His entire existence antagonizes you."

"What antagonizes me is the fact that he so desperately wishes to bed you. It is intolerable. You are my Renfield."

"Maybe you should just pee on my leg and get it over with."

I examine her expression as we exit the vehicle, uncertain what she means by this. Vampires do not urinate.

"Kidding!" she says.

We make our way toward the cordoned-off area. The crowd parts around us instinctively.

Beyond the tape lies a body beneath a sheet, and what I presume is the shaft of a crossbow bolt, tenting the fabric upward.

A village official of some sort crouches, examining something on the sidewalk next to the body.

Officer Maverick Cooper presides over the scene, orange hair bright as a warning flare, copper-freckled face set in what he likely believes is an authoritative expression, chewing gum in his usual aggressive rhythm.

A pair of men duck under the yellow tape and engage Maverick in conversation.

"That's the county medical examiner," Ms. Renfield says. "They'll be taking the body away for further examination. I wish we could've gotten a look at it."

"Further examination," I say. "I find that whatever is sticking out of a body is typically what killed them."

"It's protocol." She winces at something she spots on the other side of the cordoned-off crime scene in front of the antique store.

It's her grandmother, Granabelle.

Granabelle wears a bright yellow outfit with a bright yellow hat that has a giant plume sticking out of it, and she has her rectangular phone set up on some kind of tripod.

"Good grief, is she interviewing crime scene gawkers?"

"It would appear so."

"I'll deal with her later. Let's see what Hardware Sam and Pilar know." She nods up ahead at the hardware store that sits right in front of the cordoned area, its door propped open. A heavyset man in his sixties stands in the entrance, his frizzy hair dusted with gray, conversing with some peasants. Beside him stands a compact woman of similar age, eyes sharp as a raptor's, watching the scene.

A sign above them reads "Hardware Sam's."

"They would've had a perfect line of sight to the murder," Ms. Renfield says. "And if they didn't see it, they'll have heard every version of it by now. Sam and Pilar know everything that happens in town. Sam is every guy's buddy, and Pilar is the central hub of gossip."

"Ah."

"You remember Josie, my best friend in the world whose blood you thought about draining when you first came to town? Pilar is her aunt."

I follow her down the sidewalk, past gawking peasants, including a woman pushing a baby carriage from which an annoying wail erupts. "To be fair, I think about draining most everybody's blood."

"So egalitarian!" she says brightly. "See those chairs in front? Pilar and Hardware Sam put them there on purpose and let people have free coffee. Pilar randomly bakes these mini-hot cross buns they sell for a dollar, and nobody knows when she'll bring them out, so people always loiter around. And they get to talking."

"The village well." My gaze drifts over the hardware store's windows on either side of the doorway, displaying wares that the peasants likely use to maintain their various hovels.

Small villages are all the same, whether in this century or ten centuries past. Different tongues, different tools, but the same humans being born, raising their broods, and dying all within the span of decades.

Ms. Renfield's urging me forward. "Sam! Pilar! How are you holding up?"

"Harriet." Sam's voice is steady, but there's a tremor there, and plenty of adrenaline. "We're fine. Just... a shock."

Ms. Renfield shakes her head sadly. "Right here on the street. Unbelievable. Did you actually see it?"

"I heard it," Pilar says. "I'm sorting an order of hinges and Sam's up at the cash register and suddenly this shout. It was horrible. You could tell it was a man but sounded...I don't know. Gutteral."

"Like an animal," Sam puts in.

"Oh my goodness." Ms. Renfield casts a dark look at the street, then turns back to them, and the three of them seem to share some wordless togetherness. Ms. Renfield has a way of making her fellow villagers feel tended to.

"We rush out and there he is," Pilar continues. "Just on the other side of the walk, blood spreading out from under him. A couple of tourists were already there, kneeling by him. We went over and it was obvious he was dead."

"Very obvious," Sam says.

"I put in the call," Pilar adds.

"Did the tourists see who did it?"

"No," Pilar says. "They were getting in their car when they heard Razor Johnny cry out, and then a thump and there he is, face-first on the pavement. They think it came from the alley next to Gable's."

I study the alley in question. Narrow. Good sight lines. A hunter's position.

"Bigass crossbow bolt sticking out his back," Sam says.

"So we heard," Ms. Renfield says.

We stand together and watch Maverick scold a man for getting too close, then he and another official clear a path for those bearing the stretcher.

"Medical examiner," Ms. Renfield says.

They hoist the body onto the stretcher.

"Is a crossbow bolt a type of bow-and-arrow thing?" Ms. Renfield asks

"Certainly not," I say. "The crossbow is no gentleman's weapon. Compact. Heavy. Unforgiving. The bolt flies slower than an arrow with great force. I have seen it pierce a knight's breastplate as easily as a needle through wet parchment, the warrior toppling like a statue, blood filling his steel shell like wine into a cup."

People stare at me as if I've just grown a new head.

"Okay!" Ms. Renfield presses a hand to her heart. "Strong opinions on the crossbow. Somebody's been watching the History channel again." She tries for a smile. "I'm so sorry. Where are my manners! Have you two met Alexandru?" She makes introductions, as is her way. This man's name is Sam Washington, but he informs me that I'm to call him Hardware Sam.

"Nice to finally meet the fella that rehabbed Kingston Manor," says Hardware Sam, shaking my gloved hand enthusiastically. "Hell of an undertaking, that."

"Indeed it was." I extract my card and hand it to him.

"Oh," he says, looking at it. "Alexandru Miramonte, princeps." He turns it over, as if to see if there is more on the back.

"So nice to meet you, Prince Miramonte," Pilar says, giving my hand a squeeze. "Pilar Galindo."

"Please, call me Alexandru." I hand her a card as well.

"Oh!" she says.

"Yeah, he's not really a prince," Ms. Renfield explains. "It's an ancient title...kind of a relic."

"What does princeps mean?" Pilar asks.

"There's not really an English word for it," Ms. Renfield says, and then quickly changes the subject. "So nobody saw anything?"

"Nah. Doesn't matter, though," Hardware Sam says. "Everyone knows who did it."

Ms. Renfield straightens, surprised. "Really? Who?"

"Dooley Brogan," says Hardware Sam. "Remember him?"

Ms. Renfield narrows her eyes. "Why does that name sound familiar?"

"Dooley Brogan is the one who went down for killing his business partner...Benson something maybe what..." Pilar looks up at Sam. "...fifteen years back?"

"Something like that," says Hardware Sam. "With a big ol' crossbow. The two of them owned Silver Wheels Automotive. Pretty decent garage up on Highway Five. Dooley Brogan got thirty to life. But guess who just got released on a technicality."

"It was prosecutorial misconduct," Pilar corrects. "Apparently the prosecutor withheld some fingerprint evidence."

I frown, confused. "You are telling me that you had a murderer in prison and intentionally freed him?"

"Sometimes if they find out that the rules for a trial weren't followed correctly, then they let the person out or have a different trial." Ms. Renfield turns to Pilar. "What was the fingerprint evidence?"

Pilar says, "A partial print on the crossbow that wasn't Dooley's. They never turned it over to the defense."

Ms. Renfield's eyebrows go up at that. "So somebody else handled the murder weapon."

"Dooley did the crime," Hardware Sam says. "Everyone knows it."

"Not everyone," Pilar says. "People always had doubts."

I am thoroughly confused. "He was imprisoned for murder and then let out. Due to a *fingerprint*."

"Because the prosecution hid evidence," Ms. Renfield says. "If the trial isn't fair, the verdict doesn't stand. The principle of a fair trial is more important than putting any one murderer away."

"I'm guessing you don't do that where you're from?" Hardware Sam says.

"No." I scowl at Maverick strutting around self-importantly. "If the town fathers let a murderer out of jail, the peasants would stone them in the village square."

"Well, in the past, maybe," Ms. Renfield says.

Ms. Renfield. So concerned about appearances. I turn to her with a significant look, raising my eyebrow slightly. "A murderer, walking free."

Hardware Sam nods vigorously. "And he's already back to killing."

Ms. Renfield doesn't seem to comprehend my line of thinking. "So a known murderer is running free this very instant."

"Unless the authorities picked him up," Sam says.

"Ms. Renfield, it has come to me that I have that pressing dinner engagement. Should we not attend to that?"

She smiles. "I haven't forgotten, but there's still plenty of time."

Does she not get my meaning? Dooley Brogan is the perfect next meal for me, but I can hardly drain his blood if he's behind bars. Or at least, not without copious bloodshed.

"Best to get out ahead of these things," I say.

She simply shrugs.

"You call her Ms. Renfield?" Pilar says.

"Inside joke," Ms. Renfield says. "That was my dad's last name and Alexandru just can't get enough of it."

Shouts go up from the alley next to Gable's Grocery. A police officer carries a large crossbow in his gloved hands.

"There's the weapon," Pilar observes.

"What is the security camera coverage like out here?" Ms. Renfield asks.

"Spotty," says Hardware Sam. "Definitely nothing covering that alley. We've got a camera on the front of the store, but the angle's wrong."

Ms. Renfield's friend, her "bestie," Josie Galindo, appears and everybody hugs and repeats information and agrees it is terrible. Ms. Renfield tugs on the lapel of her jacket and jokes that Josie is in city councilperson mode.

Pilar beams at Josie. "Have you heard anything?"

"They've gotten no witnesses," Josie says in a confidential tone. "But I'm pretty sure he sent somebody to pick up Dooley for questioning by now. Do we know if he's living in town?"

"Living with his sister up on Greentree Ave.," Hardware Sam says.

"Very nice girl," Pilar adds. "She's a nurse up at Creighton General. Two sweet little kids. Personally, I wouldn't be bringing Dooley Brogan into that house, brother or not, considering the Snag Tooth Riders might be out for vengeance."

"I didn't even think of that possibility!" Ms. Renfield says. "But it's a bit much, don't you think? The man gets out of prison, grabs a crossbow, and goes shooting someone?"

"Some people aren't right in the head," Hardware Sam says, a notion with which I heartily agree.

"Do we know what his beef with the victim, this Razor Johnny guy, was?" Ms. Renfield asks.

Hardware Sam sniffs. "Most everybody's got a beef with the Snag Tooth Riders, what with all that protection racket and petty crime."

"But to get out of prison and instantly murder someone using the same bizarre method..." Ms. Renfield says. "It seems farfetched."

"Killers are not known for their brilliant ideas," Josie says.

Ms. Renfield gazes across the street where her grandmother seems to be interviewing another one of the villagers. "I need to put a stop to that."

Nobody asks her what she means.

"Best not forget about those meal arrangements," I remind her.

"There's time. See you guys later!" She starts off, circling around the crime scene tape to get to the opposite side of the street.

I match her stride. People's heads turn as we pass. The villagers here do like to stare. "We must locate this Dooley Brogan before the police or any brigands do."

"Just because somebody got killed with a weapon Dooley Brogan used fifteen years ago, that doesn't mean it was him. In fact, he'd have to be a madman to think that was a good idea."

"Perhaps he is a madman."

"Maybe, maybe not," Ms. Renfield says. "But anybody can grab a crossbow and shoot somebody."

"Hardware Sam seems to think he's guilty. He was convicted at one time."

"We need to be sure the person's guilty," she says.

Somewhere in the vicinity, a baby shrieks.

"I think you are adding a lot of caveats to our agreement that I drain only murderers."

A voice rings out. "Prince Miramonte! Yoo-hoo!" Granabelle waves frantically.

Ms. Renfield casts her eyes upward. "And what am I? Chopped liver? It's all about you?"

"As it should be."

"Prince Miramonte!" Granabelle Morgan sweeps toward us, wielding her tripod-and-phone contraption.

Ms. Renfield's grandmother has fashioned herself into a sort of minor celebrity on an entity called Instagram. She is a seventy-something influencer, according to Ms. Renfield. This influencer status seems to involve wearing a rotating collection of hats and outfits from the family antique store and filming and photographing herself and others.

"I'm here with one of our town's most illustrious residents, Prince Alexandru Miramonte," Granabelle announces breathlessly.

"Granabelle, you shouldn't be livestreaming a crime scene," Ms. Renfield says.

"Nonsense! It's the people's right to know!"

"The people's right to know isn't a thing."

Granabelle plants herself beside me, angling the phone camera so our faces fill the little screen, excluding Ms. Renfield entirely. "Prince Miramonte, do you have any comment on the tragedy that has befallen our peaceful town? I hope it won't tarnish our reputation. Such a crime is *not* typical of Ashwood."

I incline my head toward the small rectangle with the image of us. "I assure you, madam, I am untroubled. Why, the week before I left Karsovia, a man was stabbed through the neck. Compared to that, your village seems a haven of serenity."

Ms. Renfield groans softly beside me.

Granabelle beams at her audience. "I suppose you're right, Prince Miramonte. There is crime everywhere, and the real test is how the citizens respond. How well they pull together. Ashwood Strong!"

"Granabelle," Ms. Renfield says sternly. "I need to talk to you. Off camera."

"This cannot wait?"

"Definitely not!" Ms. Renfield says.

Granabelle fiddles with the apparatus. "What is it? I have several other interviews to do."

"You're not a newscaster."

"No .I'm something better. Is this what you had to tell me?"

Ms. Renfield glances over at officer Maverick Cooper, who is standing around inside the crime scene tape talking to yet another civil servant of some sort. "What have you heard?"

"Pretty much nothing. Maverick flatly refused an interview," Granabelle says. "He is paid with our tax dollars, but apparently, he's forgotten that. I got the tourists to talk, but they were spectacular deadbeats considering they were right there. Not that I was asking them to divulge the gruesome particulars, but…"

"But you kind of were?" Ms. Renfield puts in.

"Harriet!" Granabelle scolds.

I give Granabelle a small smile. "You always know more than you let on." I lower my voice. "Have you spoken to anybody who talked to Maverick? Are there any other suspects?"

I can feel Ms. Renfield's eyes on me. Surprised, perhaps, that I would pursue this. But, for all her foolishness, I have noticed that Granabelle does know how to gather intelligence.

Granabelle slants her gaze toward the scene. "I think they're going to tread carefully. I have no doubt it stings, seeing a man walk free on a technicality. No lawman likes that. He's not going to get it wrong this time."

"It was prosecutorial misconduct," Ms. Renfield tells her. "They withheld fingerprint evidence that could've cleared Dooley!"

"Maybe they withheld it because it wasn't important," Granabelle says. "Dooley Brogan should never have been let out, if you ask me. A leopard doesn't change its spots. Though Razor Johnny was no prize in his day. You know he tried to shake us down a few times."

Impatience rolls off of Ms. Renfield. She adjusts her glasses. "Yes, you've told that a zillion times."

"But has the prince heard?"

Chapter Three

Harriet

There's no stopping Granabelle once she gets going about the day Razor Johnny swaggered into our family's antique store and faced off with my mother.

Granabelle says, "He took this Korean War-era naval officer's sword down from the wall—a very nice piece—and he told us how much he'd like to have it. Well! Harriet's mother, Lorna, told him to check the price tag. Suddenly he's hinting around how it might be good if the store had 'protection' and how tragic it would be if the front windows 'accidentally' shattered, but he could see to it that no such thing happened.

"Well, Lorna was having none of that. She was in the army, you know and she stepped right up to Razor Johnny and asked him to tell her what exactly he meant. She's a wee one, but fierce as all get-out." She gives me a squeeze. "Well, a man like Razor Johnny's not interested in talking plainly. He just went on about threats to the store and how important it is to have friends like him. The man seemed to think he was in *The Godfather!*"

A few other people have gathered around by now.

Granabelle is on fire. "Meanwhile, I grabbed this Hungarian hussar cap that hangs behind the register. There was a fuzzy spider pinned to it! I put it on at a jaunty angle, held up my phone and asked him a few questions about the fascinating skull embroidery on the back of his motorcycle jacket. For example, did he ever consider bedazzling it? And he set the sword down right then and there, mumbling something about being back. Well, did he come back? No, he didn't!" This last as if she has no earthly idea why he would've fled my tough cookie of a mother and my grandmother wearing a military hat with a large spider fixed to it.

Alexandru's voice drops to something scary and cold. "You will alert me if such a thing ever happens again."

I look up at him, surprised. I've noticed he has a strange protective streak over me, but I didn't know it extended to my family.

"Why, thank you, Prince Miramonte," Granabelle declares, "but I do believe we have it under control."

"Nevertheless," he says in a grave tone.

I've heard that tone before. It was during our last mystery, moments after Alexandru rescued me from a man holding me at knifepoint. The man was lying in a heap in the corner, and Alexandru touched the tender part of my throat, tracing the scratch the man had given me. "For this he must die," he'd rumbled.

And then he'd taken my hand, turned it over, and pressed his lips to my palm.

The heat of it had gone through me like a current, and

every rational thought I had just...vanished. That had never happened to me before.

Berky appears at my side, jogging me out of my Alexandru fugue state. She nods at the other side of the street where a woman seems to be pleading with the medical examiners and Maverick. "That's Razor Johnny's mother."

"Oh no," I say.

"He was not a bad sort," she says in her French accent. "His silly protection racket. He wanted money at first, but I told him he could have a cookie." She shrugs. "A cookie is no big thing, and I do not want trouble."

"What was his favorite cookie?" I ask.

"Sprinkle explosion." She pronounces the words in a very French way. "Those motorcycle boys, they are not so fierce as they wish us to believe."

"So we could've given him a couple pieces of saltwater taffy?" Granabelle says.

I look over at Razor Johnny's weeping mother. One of the police officers is putting her in the car, probably for her to go to the morgue to identify the body. Whatever he became later, Razor Johnny was a little boy once, looking forward to birthday parties and dreaming of dump trucks and fire engines. And that poor mother...

"Not the most effective criminal..." he begins.

"Later!" I say, and I drag Alexandru away from the little group before he can say more obnoxious things.

We stop at a nearby light pole.

Alexandru flexes his gloved hands, causing the leather to loosen and tighten around the contours of his muscular fingers.

His knuckles. A large and comely thumb. It's like a man hand symphony.

His gloves, hat, and charcoal-gray cashmere suit keep the sun at bay, but his dangerous hotness burns at full strength. And I do mean dangerous. Vampire beauty is a trap—an Italian-menswear-model-looking trap designed to catch the unwary.

Best to keep that in mind.

"Ms. Renfield," he bites out. "Are you listening?"

"What?" I tear my gaze away from his hands and scan the crowd again, taking in the gawkers.

"We must talk to this Dooley."

"We will. The police probably have him right now, though." My gaze catches on a young man standing apart from the others with his bicycle propped beside him. Dark hair. Intense gaze. Dressed for serious cycling.

Jerome.

My stomach does an uncomfortable flip.

Alexandru turns to me, because of course he caught my emotional discomfort with his vampire senses. "Ms. Renfield?"

I push up my glasses. "Nothing. Just someone I know."

Alexandru follows my gaze to Jerome, and his voice goes low and dangerous. "The one with the bike. What did he do to you?"

"Nothing! It's what I did. He was on the high school newspaper during the blowup where I made us lose our big swim team scoop."

"Ah yes. I remember. You demanded additional documentation. They felt it was excessive."

"It *was* excessive. I was being a jerk, and I blew their big story."

"You were being a Renfield. Your hereditary obsession with order and your drive to impose structure on chaos is a great strength. You were simply too young at the time to manage the powers that you possess."

I look at him, surprised. He's probably the only one in the world who sees my organizational diligence as a power, except maybe my old boss, Serena.

"Anyway, Jerome worked on the paper back then. He wasn't as mad as Sloane and the rest of the crew. Actually, he's been nothing but nice in recent years, but I still feel weird around him. I bet you anything he's gathering information for his Substack."

"His Substack?"

"It's a newsletter that people read on their electronic ledgers," I explain.

"Ah."

Alexandru has a lot of amazing powers as a centuries-old vampire, but being up on tech is not one of them. At the castle in the Carpathian Mountains where he used to live, they were still in the carrier pigeon communication era.

"Jerome's Substack is called *Silverton Uncovered*," I add. "It's local news with some gossip mixed in, so this murder is definitely something he'll cover. I can probably get him to tell me what he knows."

Alexandru is silent for a moment. "His shining purple garments... he presents himself in public this way? Deliberately?"

"It's cycling gear. Aerodynamic. Let's do this."

We make our way over. Jerome's expression shifts when he spots us—surprise, then something else. He looks pale, honestly. Shaken. "Harriet," he says when we reach him. "Long time no see."

"Too long!" I give him a quick hug and introduce him to Alexandru.

Jerome takes a good long look at Alexandru. "The prince with the mansion everyone wants to get a look into."

"Not the least of all Granabelle," I say. "She'd give her favorite flowered hat for a chance to do a livestream in there."

"Is it true you're living there, too?" he asks.

"Well, yes!" I say.

"She attends to my affairs," Alexandru puts in.

I gesture at the crime scene. "Did Maverick take off?"

"Yup," Jerome says. "I'm guessing he and Officer Wright went to pick up Dooley Brogan for questioning."

It's right then that I hear it: the roar of motorcycles rising up from the north.

"Just questioning?" I muse. "No arrest?"

"That's what I hear." He squints. "It's all just such a mess. They found the weapon behind a dumpster next to Gable's."

"We heard."

The three of us watch as ten or so Snag Tooth Riders motorcycle gang guys roar up. They park their bikes on the far side of the taped-off scene. One of the officers left behind goes up to talk to them.

"Here we go," Jerome says.

Right then, I notice Alexandru studying Jerome with that unsettling intensity he gets sometimes. Something about Jerome has tweaked his senses.

What?

Jerome tears his attention from the gang and nods in the direction of Hardware Sam's. "Saw you over there. Did Sam and Pilar have anything interesting to say?"

"Well, I didn't know about the prosecutorial misconduct that got Dooley sprung out of jail."

"Yup." Jerome nods. "Withheld that partial print."

"Hardware Sam says there isn't any camera coverage in that alley where the shot came from. He thinks it was Dooley, but killing somebody with the weird method that put you away, not the smartest move if it was him."

"It wouldn't be smart at all," Jerome says distantly.

I turn to Jerome right then, remembering something. "Didn't you and Razor Johnny have some beef? Like he blamed you for that story that helped send him to prison? And he was riding over your grandmother's tulips or something?"

"A few years back, yeah. Real piece of work. I hear he tried to shake down your mom and Granabelle and she beat him back with a flowered purse and a livestream."

"So she says. But I think he realized they would be more trouble than they're worth."

Jerome checks his phone. "I gotta go and put something out on this. Anyway. Good seeing you, Harriet. Nice to finally meet you, Alexandru."

Alexandru watches him leave with more than his usual predatory focus. It is only when Jerome turns the corner and disappears out of sight that Alexandru finally speaks. "He is terrified. There is something he is not telling you."

I turn to him. "Excuse me?"

"Your Jerome. He is fearful. Hiding something."

"Jerome!? No way. Are you mad that I hugged him?"

"He reeks of guilt and fear and dark secrets."

"What?"

Alexandru shrugs.

"Are you suggesting he's the killer?"

Another shrug.

"No! I've known Jerome for years. He's a standup guy who cares about this town and he cares about doing what's right. You have this one wrong, Alexandru. He's probably just upset like everyone else. Someone got murdered. Of course he's frightened."

"Ms. Renfield," Alexandru says wearily, adjusting his cufflinks. "Even the newest, greenest vampire knows how to distinguish the terror of the innocent from the terror of the guilty. The terror of the innocent is so much sweeter."

"Well, isn't that lovely," I say. "But maybe Jerome feels guilty because he wishes he'd gotten back to town ten minutes earlier, so he could've stopped it or something. You don't know it's not that."

He doesn't bother to answer.

I turn and we start back toward the car. "He's a friend."

Alexandru catches my arm.

I turn.

His grip is firm, unyielding. My pulse jumps beneath his fingers. We're close enough that I can see the precise line where his collar meets bare skin. I lift my eyes to his. Something tightens low in my stomach, which is incredibly inconvenient right now.

"I have lived many centuries, Ms. Renfield." The rumble of his voice hits deep. "I may not know your SubStacks and such, but I have an intimate acquaintance with human nature. Your friend Jerome carries a terrible secret. Take heed; he may be the killer."

His gaze drops to the hollow of my throat where my pulse pounds out of control, showing him everything I'm feeling, which at this point ranges from outrage to "why is this hot?"

"Well…" I stammer, "umm…you're not a psychic!"

"Do I understand correctly that Jerome had a quarrel with the victim?"

"Razor Johnny blamed Jerome for sending him to prison many years ago. If anything, that would give Razor Johnny cause to kill Jerome, not the other way around."

"What of the grandmother's tulips?"

I'm acutely aware of the feel of soft leather against my skin. "A man riding a motorcycle over someone's tulips doesn't drive a person to murder. And Jerome is a journalist. If he wanted to fight Razor Johnny, he'd do it with journalism. Words and pictures are Jerome's weapon."

"I am telling you what I sensed from this man."

"You're letting your vampire instincts run wild."

A muscle jumps in his jaw. The space between us feels charged. "Take heed," he says quietly. "I will not permit harm to come to what is mine, Ms. Renfield."

"I'm not a possession."

"You entered into a contract. You are bound to serve me." His gaze drops again, and for one reckless second, I think he's going to kiss me. Or drain me.

The draining would be bad. The kissing would be worse, probably. Or different kinds of bad.

He lets me go.

I suck in a breath. "Well! The villagers shall harm me at their own peril. Now that that's settled, let's focus on this Dooley Brogan situation. It sounds like the police have him in for questioning, but I think we should go and talk to his sister."

We walk back to the car in silence, him brooding and me doing my best to ignore the tingly warmth on my arm where he held me.

Chapter Four

Harriet

Tilly Brogan's house sits on a quiet corner of Oaktree Lane, a tidy ranch with yellow shutters and a swing set in the yard. Two bikes lie on their sides near the front steps—one with training wheels, one without.

I hesitate on the walkway. "Maybe we should've called first."

Alexandru adjusts his gloves. "The unprepared are more honest."

He has a point, I suppose. I step over a bike and knock.

The woman who answers wears nurse's scrubs printed with cartoon penguins, and her brown hair is pulled into a neat ponytail. Her eyes flick nervously to Alexandru, then back to me. "Can I help you?"

"Tilly Brogan?" I ask.

"Yes?"

"I'm Harriet Morgan, and this is Alexandru Miramonte. We're—we're looking into what happened on Commerce Street this afternoon. The incident with Razor Johnny."

She looks exhausted, and now her brother is in trouble. I feel bad for bothering her like this. "You're reporters?"

"No, not reporters. My family owns Mrs. Morgan's Curios, which is sort of near where it happened, and we were just down there..."

"Wait, you're Granabelle's granddaughter?"

"Yes. That's my grandmother."

"Love her reels."

"She would be thrilled to hear that," I say. "We heard Dooley was brought in for questioning, and we wanted to hear your side of things and see what was going on."

She studies me for a long moment, wary.

She should be wary. The fact is, we're here to see if her brother is somebody that Alexandru could maybe drain like a Capri Sun.

Uhhh. How is this my life?

"Well, if you really want to hear our side." She steps back and motions us in. "Dooley is absolutely not guilty of killing anybody. And he never was. He's got big dreams and a good heart and it's just not in him."

"You two are close?"

"Very." She grabs a stuffed elephant and a child's jacket off the couch. "Sorry about the mess. The kids are at my neighbor's right now, but..."

"You have nothing to apologize for," I say, settling onto the couch. "So was Dooley here this afternoon?"

"No, he was out on a walk. I know how that sounds, but you wouldn't think it was weird if you knew him. He always hated to be confined, and suddenly he's free from jail like that? He's been wandering all over."

"I can imagine," I say.

Tilly perches on the edge of an armchair and looks up at Alexandru, who has remained standing. "I'll tell you this: Dooley doesn't have it in him to kill. He was innocent when they sent him away and he's innocent now. Why would he get out just to turn around and do another murder? And with the same weapon? No way. This last week he's been just—" Her voice catches. "So happy. A kid in a candy store, trying all the foods he missed. The new video games. Roaming around the forest, fixing my car. And now..." She looks like she's going to cry.

"So...he's been free for a week?" I ask.

"Just over a week." She picks at a loose thread on her scrubs. "You should see him with my kids. They play cards for hours on end. He has these big dreams to open another garage. Denny Cole hired him for some handyman work the other day. Denny never thought he was guilty."

I nod. "Denny's a good guy."

Alexandru shifts his weight. No doubt tracking Tilly's heartbeat, her breathing, and who knows what else with his mad skills.

"Do you know if Dooley was acquainted with the victim?" I ask. "Razor Johnny?"

"He doesn't know him. Dooley wasn't involved in that world."

"Even when he was in prison?"

"No way. He never thought much of the Snag Tooth gang." She lifts her gaze to mine. "I hope you believe me. And I hope you'll tell people that. He's a good guy. I know it looks bad."

Clearly, she believes in her brother, but I think that's pretty common for a family member. "If he didn't do it, somebody needs to figure out who did," I say.

"And fast," she says.

Alexandru stands there looking out of place in the sweet little ranch house, expression unreadable.

What would be most helpful is for him to interview Dooley. It's not as if he could look into Dooley's mind or anything, but he can sense deception and fear, and all kinds of other emotions that are helpful in crime solving.

He's a pretty good investigation partner, and I think he finds the investigations entertaining at times. A sort of Wordle for vampires.

Or more like one of those snuffle mats for dogs that makes them work for their food, actually.

There's a knock at the door.

"Oh—finally." Tilly hurries over and opens it.

Her neighbor, another tired-looking woman in scrubs, ushers in two small kids. "Sorry, Tilly. I'm running late." Her eyes flick to Alexandru, and she freezes for a moment. "Um. Wow. Hi. Okay, see ya!" With that she's gone.

Tilly sets a hand on her kids' shoulders. "Simon and Kiki, this is Harriet, and this is, uh... Prince Miramonte."

Simon is skinny and serious. Kiki is younger, dressed head to toe in a pink princess outfit. They both stare unblinkingly at Alexandru.

I smile. "Hi!"

Nothing.

"Where are your manners?" Tilly says. "Say hello to Prince Miramonte."

The kids just stare.

"They're usually not like this," Tilly explains.

"It's okay," I say.

"Simple prey response," Alexandru says.

I snort. "I don't know when I'm going to get used to your European sense of dark humor, I really don't!"

"Oh my goodness, like when they killed off that guy in *Downton Abbey*?" Tilly says.

Simon is glaring at Alexandru, now. Kiki clutches her wand with both fists.

"Why don't you check the cookie jar?" Tilly tries. "One each."

No reaction.

Kiki lifts her wand and gives Alexandru a shaky wave of the tip. "No, no, no."

Alexandru gives her a strange smile. "It seems your weapon is inadequate."

Tilly groans. "I don't know what's gotten into them—come on." She steers them out of the room.

Once they're gone, I exhale. "At least they're not crying," I whisper.

"They're old enough to recognize that stillness is a superior response. It would at least give them a chance in the wild. Unlike a *crying baby*," he adds with the utmost disdain.

"Seriously, dude, remember our talk about trying to fit in?"

"Oh, I remember it," he says, bored.

He remembers, but he doesn't care. That's the part he's not saying out loud.

Tilly returns, brushing stray glitter from her jeans. "I think they're just tired."

"Of course." I smile. "Kids are unpredictable."

Her phone chimes and she grabs it. "Dooley's on his way back!" She tucks it away. "He's probably pretty worn out."

"We really would love to talk to him," I say.

She leans back on the built-in buffet behind her. She's not so sure if she wants us to stay.

"I need you to know, we really are interested in getting to the truth of things. I'm on this true crime forum and justice is a passion of mine."

I can see the moment it clicks about James. "Right. Of course you would be."

I can feel Alexandru's gaze rivet to the side of my face, wondering what she's talking about.

I haven't told him how my little brother, James, disappeared twenty years ago.

The James thing makes people look at me differently, just like Tilly is doing right now. I'm the girl who left her brother alone in the playground at a time when the Cuyahoga Killer was snatching young kids. And then disappeared.

Everybody thinks the Cuyahoga Killer got him, and that he's for sure dead now. I don't believe it. I won't.

People also say that my mania for bringing order to chaos, for organizing the world on spreadsheets and databases is another coping mechanism. Like if I can organize the world enough, I'll find him.

I say, "I think justice should be everybody's passion."

"Of course," she says too quickly. "Absolutely! Everybody should be interested in such things!" She glances toward the door. "It's a good sign that they're letting him come home, don't you think?"

"I think it is," I say. "Though to be honest, it could just

mean that they don't have enough evidence to hold him. Do you know if he called his lawyer?"

"I'm guessing that he did. He was slow to call one last time around and I think he's learned his lesson."

Tilly heads to the kitchen to check on the kids. A few minutes later, the door opens, and Dooley Brogan bursts in.

Chapter Five

Alexandru

Dooley Brogan has the overwrought look of a man fresh from battle. He closes the door behind him but does not step into the room. "Are you... friends of Tilly's?"

"We have a mutual interest in recent events," I say.

The female rushes in from the kitchen and hugs her brother. "They let you out. Thank goodness. How did it go?"

"We have visitors?" Dooley says.

"This is Granabelle's granddaughter. From that antique store down on Commerce, and this is Alexandru. He just moved here. Don't worry, they're friends."

"Okay, well, I guess I'll take all the friends I can get." Dooley collapses on the couch. "So yeah, they let me out. I don't know why; I don't have much of an alibi. I was out for a walk, which is exactly what guilty people say."

"All you can do is tell them the truth," the sister says.

"Didn't work so well the first time around," Dooley says bitterly.

Carefully, Ms. Renfield asks, "Did anybody see you taking this walk?"

Dooley frowns. "I don't understand. Are you guys investigating this?"

"We are. We don't want to see anybody wrongfully convicted." Ms. Renfield tries for a smile, emotions unfolding like a symphony. Guilt at the half-truths she's laying out for him. Compassion and dread, too—she doesn't want Dooley to be guilty, but she knows that he might be. And beneath it all, her drive for answers, for order, to make sense of the world in her charts.

Dooley gazes at the ceiling. "People saw me on my walk, but would they remember me? I guess the cops are checking it out right now. I can tell you they are suspicious. Why go on a long walk to nowhere, right? But if you've been inside for fifteen years, you know why. Rambling aimlessly around is very underrated," he says with a lopsided smile.

"I can imagine," Ms. Renfield says. "Did they ask about a specific timeframe?"

"Yes, 1:20. That's when the murder happened."

She nods, enjoying the specificity of this detail. She marks it down. "And where were you at that time?"

"That's the thing. I don't know. And no, I didn't bring a phone. Who would I call? I took off from here at around eleven and wandered up Kempton and then all the way down Old Bluff Road, down through Gazebo Park and down to the river. I watched them cleaning the big paddle boat." He stares off in the direction of the river. "They didn't have paddle boat dinner cruises and a floating lantern festival and flower baskets hanging from old-fashioned lamps and all that when I went in.

Anyway, at some point I was up on Commerce Street. I went into Berky's to look at those cookies she makes, though that's not something we're spending our funds on right now," he adds with a look at the sister. "I used to dream of those peanut butter sprinkle ones, though. The kid there asked me if I wanted a sample, but it seemed like a dick move to get a bunch of samples and then walk out."

"So you wandered into a patisserie and denied yourself even a morsel," I say.

Dooley appears startled by my question. "Yeah. And then I looked in the windows of that new paper shop. And then I went and checked out the new park benches. Those weren't there when I went inside, either. Ashwood got a glow-up, I guess you could say."

The sister smiles. The two of them are quite close.

"After that I hit Gable's Grocery, again, not buying anything. No morsels, but it's nice to look at all that food after you've been eating prison slop. My lawyer says that the cops will probably try to pull security footage, but I don't know how much of that there is. After that, I cut through the alley and headed up Greentree and on up back home."

"Did you do it?" I ask. "Did you kill Razor Johnny?"

Three pairs of eyes rivet to me.

"Alexandru!" Ms. Renfield says.

I keep my gaze fixed on Dooley. "It's a simple question."

"No, I'm glad you asked. I'd rather have people ask than just suspect me. The answer is no, I didn't do it," he says. "Why would I do it?"

I say, "We have been told that the shot came from the alley near Gable's."

"Well, I don't know where I would've gotten a crossbow. Was I carrying one around? I think people would've remembered that. Did I know this guy who got killed? No! Did I murder my business partner fifteen years ago? No!" He shoots a glance at the sister. "Tilly's always telling me to try and have compunction and show the parole board compunction for that murder, but I won't show compunction for something that I didn't do. Suddenly, I get this second chance at life, and I feel like somebody's trying to frame me or something. A crossbow? Do I look like a moron?"

Ms. Renfield watches my expression, trying, perhaps, to gauge my assessment of his truthfulness. This Dooley seems truthful enough, though some murderers believe their own lies. And sociopaths lie without effort. And there's something more there with Dooley. A secret.

The sister sees something out the window and her alarm spikes. "Some guy's been sitting out there in a parked car this whole time since you got home, Dooley."

Dooley's up out of the couch like a shot. "I guess I shouldn't be surprised they put a tail on me. I wish they had one on me all day and they would know I didn't do it." He sits back down with a huff.

"Why did the female think you would have a particular passion for solving crime?" I ask Ms. Renfield as we settle into her car.

She turns the key and the engine rumbles to life. "That's the question on your mind? To delve into my passion for solving crime when we're racing the clock to figure out whether Dooley did this murder?"

"I am able to entertain several lines of inquiry at once. You have a secret. You will tell me."

"Oh, now I have a secret?"

"Indeed you do. You will divulge it to me."

She maneuvers onto the road. "You're entitled to my secrets? I must have missed that clause." Her eyes stay fixed ahead. "Are you requesting to amend the contract?"

"I am not. You are my underling, my servant. Thus your secrets are my property, and I am requesting access to what is already mine."

"Whatever happened to a certain vampire saying that the inner lives of Renfields are no concern of his?"

I am annoyed that she would remind me of this. Yes, I said that once. Indeed, I have come to regret it.

In truth, I never cared a whit about the interior lives of Renfields, despicable creatures that they are, but I must know this secret that she keeps. I have sensed its presence before; I can sometimes feel it lurking inside her, dark and shameful. And there was no mistaking the surge of painful emotion within Ms. Renfield's breast when the sister commented that *of course she would be interested in justice.*

Why?

We pass through a neighborhood of modest homes with tidy squares of lawn. The villagers have attempted to distinguish their plots with small statues: a ceramic frog here, a woman frozen in prayer there, or most preposterous of all, a white goose. Many have enshrined a white goose. A goose is a vile, ill-tempered creature with no redeeming qualities whatsoever, and these people have chosen to immortalize them on their lawns as though such hostility were a virtue. Between the geese and Ms. Renfield's obstinance, my patience is wearing dangerously thin. "Your inner life is yours to maintain. Your *secrets* are another matter entirely. They could affect your management of my business affairs."

She turns down another prettily arranged street, heading up to Bluff Road. "Number one, secrets and inner lives are the same thing. Number two, Ms. Renfield is not my name. Number three, did you think Dooley was lying or not?"

I glower at her. Never has a Renfield maddened me more!

No matter. I will know all in the end. In the game of cat and mouse, the cat wins eventually.

"The male was full of nerves and fear. Bewildered. I did not detect deception, but it is always possible that he believes his own lies. There is something he is not telling."

"Like what?"

I shrug. "If I could talk to him when he was in a calmer state, I might sense more."

Ms. Renfield makes a small sound of assent. "He really did seem a bit freaked out. The man just got out of jail and endured an interrogation."

"What does all this matter?" I ask. "The man would be convicted of murder but for the blunder of a civil servant. Even the shopkeepers are convinced of his guilt. You will call Dooley and tell him that we have found evidence. You will suggest we meet secretly by the river, and I will take him as my meal."

"Wait, what?" Ms. Renfield twists in her seat, nearly careening off the road. "We can't do that!"

"I will simply drain his blood. It's not as if I'm breaking him on a wheel."

"But he said he wasn't guilty of the original crime, and you just said yourself, you didn't sense deception. What if he's innocent of both crimes?"

I sigh, frustrated. "He is seen by many of your kind as a murderer. I sense a secret. What more do you require?"

"A lot more!" Ms. Renfield jerks the vehicle to a halt before Berky's Patisserie. "I'm thinking we should follow his footsteps and construct a timeline. We know that the murder occurred at 1:20 in the afternoon."

"But the police would have already done this."

"Yes, but they don't have your empathic abilities, do they? Or your powerful hunter's senses. And it's my belief that their goal is to gather enough evidence to put him back in jail. We'll be approaching this with an open mind, working off hard facts and hard facts alone."

I tug on my gloves, ensuring full skin coverage. It is just like a Renfield to be painstakingly thorough. It is typically a formidable advantage, but it has been too many days since I've taken a meal, and there are limits to my patience. I can feel the feral edge of it now—the way my senses sharpen whether I will it or not. The way her pulse beats, bright and steady. The way her warmth radiates like a hearth in winter, beckoning.

I look away at once.

Berky emerges from the back of the patisserie, wiping her hands on her apron. Her tight dark curls are bound beneath a blue scarf, and she brightens when she sees me. "*Bonjour*, Prince Miramonte! Had I known you were coming, I would have prepared a *millefeuille* for us to share."

"No need. The *baba au rum* lives on my tongue even now. A legend," I say—in French, of course.

Ms. Renfield steps up beside me. "Bonjour! We'd like six plain croissants, please."

Berky instructs her helper to gather the pastries.

Ms. Renfield leans in. She has refreshed her lipstick—a vivid red that catches the light. "I hear you had a notorious visitor recently."

"*Mais oui!*" Berky wipes, her hands on her apron. "The crossbow murderer himself! He stared at the cookies, making love to them with his eyes. So very unseemly." She motions at another underling who wipes her hands on her apron just as Berky did. "Come, Monique. You will meet the prince and tell him about the scoundrel."

Monique seems to be Berky's granddaughter, fresh off the boat from France. "And you remember Harriet Morgan, of course."

Ms. Renfield smiles at the girl. "Were you the one who spoke to Dooley Brogan?"

"*Mais oui!*" she says, mimicking Berky in every aspect. "He was staring at the peanut butter sprinkle cookies, putting his fingerprints all over the glass. And when I asked him if I could help him, he said he did not need help. No, he was shamelessly consuming those cookies with his eyes. He did not need help with that!"

"Shamelessly," Berky says.

"Do you have a sense of the time he was here?" Ms. Renfield asks.

Monique says, "That's what the police wanted to know, but I didn't remember. We were finishing with the lunch rush, that much I know."

Berky says, "A busy Monday lunch in May, that's when you know the tourists have arrived."

"Was he carrying anything?"

"A small pack, I believe," Monique says.

"Did the police talk to any of the customers?" Ms. Renfield asks.

Berky sniffs. "Why would they? The man was seen in Gable's Grocery soon after, and it is my understanding that the shot came from the alley next to Gable's."

"We would like to establish a reliable timeline," Ms. Renfield says. "Can you tell me who was in here when Dooley was here?"

The French girl names a few customers, and Ms. Renfield notes the names upon her electronic ledger with her white pencil.

She does not know it, but she looks exactly like her father when she does this—the careful recording, the quiet intensity. Ms. Renfield's father had a nearly mystical connection to his ledgers. He worked for me nearly a century, a fact that seems to greatly disturb her.

"Did you do something to him to make him like you?" she once asked.

I informed her that her father was not a vampire and certainly nothing like me. He did, however, beg me to extend his life, so great was the honor of serving me. An attitude that his daughter has yet to cultivate. Well, *the night is young*, as these humans like to say. She has served me only a short time, and there has never been a Renfield whom I cannot break into utter submission.

My hands tighten inside my gloves. No. That is not entirely true.

The memory comes unbidden—stone beneath my knees, iron biting into my wrists, a dark-eyed smile striking wild rage into my heart. A Renfield smile.

I steady myself.

Never again.

"...Percival was here, and there he is, still at his table!" The girl nods at a man in the corner, hunched over his own electronic ledger, pretending to look into the square rectangle of light, but his attention is on us. "He teaches branding and media relations up at the music conservatory."

"Yes, three hours later and still he is here. He thinks it is his office," Berky says, eyeing me strangely. "You have my permission to bother him. I doubt he noticed anything."

We stroll over. Percival looks up, eyes wide. He has a thick, blond mustache and the rounded eyes of an owl. "Can I help you?"

"You were here when the murderer came to the counter," I say, in no mood now to be careful with people. "What time was it?"

"Are you the police?"

"No, sorry," Ms. Renfield says. "We're just looking into some things related to the tragic events today."

"I don't have to tell you anything," Percival says. "Even if you were the police, I wouldn't have to tell you anything."

I lower my voice. "You will answer."

Percival straightens, thrumming with excitement. "I will not."

Such impudence. In Karsovia, this man would not have dared to meet my eyes. But this is America, where the peasants fancy themselves kings.

Ms. Renfield takes the seat across from him. "You'll have to excuse Alexandru. He's from Europe, and a personal friend of Berky's, and he has a very keen interest in this case. I know that Berky would greatly appreciate it if you helped out with anything. To know that you're looking out for the place."

"Answer's still no."

A voice from the next table. "The guy left here at 12:50."

I turn to see a girl with purple-dyed hair munching on a one of the giant cookies.

"Percival's been talking about it all afternoon," she adds.

"Seriously?" Percival bites out. "They come in here like that and you're helping them?"

"Dude, they're out here taking an interest in things and you're gatekeeping something stupid like that?" She takes another bite of the cookie.

Percival says, "I'm not gatekeeping, I'm standing up for myself and my rights as a citizen not to be aggressively questioned by other citizens."

"And I'm keeping my rights to say what I want," she says.

They continue to argue. I walk out of the bakery.

Ms. Renfield follows behind me. "Hold up!" She falls into step next to me. "What's going on?"

"These villagers are infuriating."

"But we're doing an amazing job of establishing the timeline," she points out. "And guess who we're going to speak with next?"

"I tire of these games."

"We're going to visit your biggest fan!" She tips her head at Aster Press, the stationery shop owned by a female by the name of Sloane, whom Ms. Renfield's calls "frenemy."

Letterpress. Archival. No pixels, the sign reads.

It was from Sloane that I purchased my calling cards, which serve a dual purpose: reminding me of civilized times and irritating Ms. Renfield.

The bell rings as we walk in.

"Prince Miramonte! What a nice surprise!" Sloane wears her hair in a haughty twist that puts me in the mind of society women. She turns to Ms. Renfield with a pretend frown. "And here's *Harriet...*" This with theatrical pity.

Ms. Renfield straightens her spine and smiles brightly, every inch the warrior. "Hello, Sloane."

"Can I help you?" Sloane asks with a look of the cat that has just swallowed the canary.

"Did you hear what happened down near Hardware Sam's?" Ms. Renfield asks.

Sloane says, "Dooley Brogan. Not the brightest bulb."

I settle my gloved hands up upon the counter. "I am given to understand that this Dooley Brogan stopped to look at the window. Did you notice him?"

"Oh, Prince Miramonte, please don't tell me poor Harriet has looped you into another ridiculous investigation."

I smile. "I find these investigations to be diverting, if not nourishing on a certain level."

I feel Ms. Renfield stiffen behind me, unappreciative of my *double entendre.*

Sloane clasps her hands, posture erect. "I'm sorry, but I can't answer that. I like to afford my customers a certain measure of privacy."

"The man was looking in the window," Ms. Renfield says. "He wasn't a customer."

"A window shopper is a customer," Sloane says.

Ms. Renfield's annoyance spikes. "A customer is somebody who buys something."

"A monetary transaction is only one part of the journey of being a customer of Aster Press. Before even approaching this counter, my customers dream of improving their lives with beauty and vintage flair. Dooley Brogan was partaking of that dream."

Ms. Renfield sucks in an almost indiscernible breath. "I think *somebody* here is dreaming."

Sloane smiles prettily. "Agreed. It seems somebody here is dreaming that Maverick has deputized them, and they're running around playing sleuth."

"Did Maverick come in and talk to you?" I ask.

Sloane gives me a mischievous look. "Perhaps he did, Prince Miramonte."

Ms. Renfield sighs.

I cast a glance around her shop. My gaze falls on a display case in the corner. "Are those carrying cases for calling cards?"

Sloane prickles with excitement. "They are."

"The calling cards I ordered from you are truly first rate, but one can hardly carry them around loose in one's pocket, and my hapless underling, Gregor, neglected to pack the case I used in Karsovia. I would ask to see your very best one, please."

Ms. Renfield bristles. "Alexandru, there's no need."

"Of course there's a need," Sloane says as she moves to the case and brings back a velvet-covered tray with five cases on it. "You don't want those cards damaged! A calling card case is a terrible thing to forget."

"I assure you, he was punished roundly for his oversight."

I do not have to look at Miss Renfield to know that she is casting an annoyed glance in my direction, but Sloane laughs, and tells me about each of the five cases. She picks up a golden one with a filigree design on top. "This one is particularly exquisite. This is gold filigree." She opens it up and shows where the calling cards would nestle.

Ms. Renfield looms behind me, a teapot ready to burst. She hates the idea of bribing Sloane, but I've known many people like Sloane through the years. The easiest way to do business with such a one is bribery. And I do, in fact, desire a carrying case for the calling cards that I purchased here.

"And if I were to inform you that the information we desire might very well help clear the name of one of your aspirational customers..."

"Well, when you ask like that, I suppose I could tell you that Dooley Brogan was mesmerized by the vintage reproduction postcards. He stood here for at least ten minutes, just staring at those old pictures. Who knew he was on his way to commit murder?"

"Allegedly," Ms. Renfield says.

"Seriously?" Sloane says. "Maybe you need to wait until he

kills somebody right in front of your eyes. But even then, you might want to check it out some more. What if it was an optical illusion? Maybe you'd have to check for nearby mirrors and track the exact angle of lights on a spreadsheet."

"That is quite *enough*." My voice cuts like a blade.

Both females turn to me, surprised by my vehemence, perhaps.

I care not. While I share Sloane's annoyance with Ms. Renfield's sometimes overly methodical ways, I will not abide her being spoken to in such a manner. She is my Renfield. Mine to command. But also mine to defend.

"What time was it when this man stared into your window?"

Sloane regards me suspiciously. "You two aren't an item now, are you?"

"We are not," I say.

A smile tips Ms. Renfield's glossy red lips. "Alexandru would not marry one such as myself even if the alternative were to be chained to the bottom of the sea and slowly consumed by eels."

I frown. Yes, I did once say that. Ms. Renfield takes strange delight in repeating it.

The sentiment pleases Sloane. Like most females, she finds me inexplicably alluring.

Ms. Renfield produces the small black square which she calls the "estate credit card." Sloane completes the invisible transaction of money and wraps the gold case in pale blue tissue paper and places it in a pale blue bag with little strings. "He was staring in this window between 12:55 and 1:05, I would guess. I always have my lunch just after one o'clock, and I remember wondering if he was going to come in here and make me eat late."

"Was the man carrying anything?" I ask.

"Not that I could see."

We emerge onto the street. Ms. Renfield takes in the scene —the line forming at the steakhouse next door, the park with its Victorian lampposts and wrought-iron benches, and finally, the ice cream shop on the other side. A bolt of guilt strikes her at the sight of the ice cream shop, as it always does.

I asked her about it once, and she quipped that it was the scene of a "butter brickle binge," but the taste of her guilt tells a far darker story. Another secret she thinks she can hide from me.

"Your beloved ice cream store," I point out.

She sets off walking in the other direction, pretending not to hear.

What is it about the ice cream shop?

And what do I care?

She is a Renfield. Let her keep her miserable little secrets.

We near Gazebo Park.

"No comment?" I pursue.

"My comment is that I can't believe you bought her overpriced piece of junk. You know she would've told you eventually."

"It is the easiest way. Sloane is transactional."

She snorts. "She's interested in having *some* kind of transaction with you, that's for sure."

"Ah, yes, that goes without saying," I say wearily. "Like

most females, Sloane is aware of my superiority on a deep and utterly primal level, and she intuits my vast sensual abilities, intuits the excruciating pleasure that I could bring a woman."

"Well, you *are* excruciating," she says lightly, but I hear the skip in her heartbeat. I smell the warmth rising to her skin.

Chapter Six

Harriet

Naturally Sloane had to use the most excessive packaging imaginable for Alexandru's ridiculous calling card case. I toss out the be-ribboned bag and tissue paper into a garbage bin and shove the bubble-wrapped thing into my pocket, because of course Alexandru doesn't carry his own purchases.

Some kids have set up some kind of obstacle course in Gazebo Park. They're screaming and laughing. A few adults cluster around a picnic table nearby. The scent of burgers reaches my nose.

I want to ask him if he really punished Gregor for forgetting to pack a calling card case, but I'm afraid to hear the answer. Alexandru can sometimes be weirdly charming or stick up for me in a way that I'm not used to, but then he'll reveal some disturbing moral opinion, or he'll make Gregor scrub the dungeon with a toothbrush, and I'll remember that he's a very bad guy.

Correction: not a guy. He's a beast, a monster, and his good qualities make him all the more dangerous.

"The timeline is not looking so good for Dooley so far," I say. "The murder took place at 1:20 and he's heading for Gable's Grocery just after one. But he obviously wasn't carrying a crossbow, or people would've noticed."

"Agreed," Alexandru says. "But he could have hidden it in the alley beforehand."

True enough.

We head into the brightly lit world of Gable's Grocery. I'm glad to see somebody I know is on duty—Marcy from history class in high school. I introduce her to Alexandru and ask about Dooley.

"Officer Cooper and Officer Wright were just here a little while ago asking about that," she says, confused. "Do you know Dooley or something?"

"A little bit," I say. "We're just checking things out, is all."

Marcy glances over at Alexandru like she's not so sure about him. Like he might do something unexpected, which is a pretty sound instinct. "Once a journalist, always a journalist, huh?"

"Something like that," I say.

"Well, I can tell you what I told them. Dooley came in here just after one o'clock. The man wandered around. I knew who he was of course, and I kept a good eye on him. I can tell you that he stared at the apples for a long time. Talked to one of the produce boys. I went over to make sure things were cool, but basically, he just wanted to know how many varieties of apples there were, and he was all kinds of impressed about that. I don't know. Maybe they don't have different apples in prison or something."

"And his demeanor?" Alexandru asks. "Was there anything unusual in his bearing?"

Marcy blinks at the English accent coming out of this six-foot-something man in a wide-brimmed hat.

It's a surprisingly good question, given that Dooley would presumably be about to kill somebody at this point. I find myself studying Alexandru's profile—the sharp line of his jaw, his dark lashes—as Marcy goes on about apples and then something about the freezer section and different kinds of ice cream.

"...he seemed really interested in the oat ice cream. He wanted me to tell him why they would make ice cream out of oats, and I explained about the whole non-dairy thing. Fifteen years away, I guess you miss a few things, like the non-wheat, non-dairy, non-groundnut thing."

"The non-wheat, non-dairy, non-groundnut thing?" Alexandru asks, astonished. "What do you mean?"

"You know, all the people that don't eat bread and cheese and sugar and nuts and all?"

"I do not understand. Eating is one of the few pleasures afforded to humans in their short and pathetic lives."

"Um..." Marcy looks confused.

"Alexandru is from a microstate in Eastern Europe, and they haven't caught up to the allergen thing."

"Well, it's a thing," Marcy says. "Like I told the police, Dooley left a bit after one. I was busy with a return, and nobody was really paying attention. And no, I didn't see which way he went."

"Anything else you can tell us that we have not asked," Alexandru says.

Another good question. There were times in our last investigation when people didn't tell us things we could've used, just because we hadn't asked the right questions.

"He did ask if we had any job openings. I told him no. It's the truth, but I don't know that Mr. Gable would hire him even if we did have an opening, what with his murder record. But then again, Mr. Gable does take a chance on people, so who knows. And then Dooley looked at the bulletin board for a while." Here she lowers her voice. "You didn't get this from me, but when Maverick and his partner were over there, looking at the board, I could hear them saying that he was probably just pretending to look at the board, but really scoping out the sidewalk for a victim."

We wander over to the bulletin board, which is ruffled with flyers and business cards advertising everything from pet sitting to psychic readings. I point to a flyer for a summer nature camp —"BAT NIGHT AT SKELLY PEAK! Bring the kids to learn about Ohio's flying friends!" "Look, Alexandru! Bat night! Right up your alley!"

Alexandru grumbles. He has informed me in no uncertain terms that he does not transform into a bat and that vampires truly have nothing to do with bats. He really has a thing about it.

"Ohio's flying friends," I repeat.

He ignores this. "One could do worse, as a vantage point for selecting a victim."

"Speaking from experience?"

"I have never required a bulletin board." He says it like that would be an insult.

The alley next to Gable's yields nothing of interest—just a few dumpsters. The police found the murder weapon behind one of them.

"It all seems really straightforward so far," I say once we're in the car heading back. "Almost too straightforward. If Dooley did it, it's an incredibly stupid way to commit murder. And if somebody's framing him, it's just so ham-handed." I drum my fingers on the steering wheel. "We need more data. We have to find out if he had a relationship to the victim that nobody is seeing."

Alexandru's gaze drifts toward the window. "Are you suggesting a visit to these Snag Tooth Riders? Do they have a lair of some sort? A den?"

"They have a clubhouse, but I don't think we can just waltz in there."

"Why not?"

"Because it's private, and these are not people who welcome drop-ins."

Alexandru turns to look at me, something almost like amusement in his dark eyes. "They would not be able to bar me; I would allow no harm to come to your person. Not even an untoward stare."

"No untoward stares? What would you do, pluck the offending eyes out with your super vampire speed?"

"With relish."

"There are other ways to talk to the motorcycle gang," I say, suddenly very interested in the road ahead. "Kip's bar, for example."

"Yes, where they consume the repellant nachos plate known as the Widowmaker," he says.

"Also known as the beard greaser. So gross." I look over and find him smiling at me, which is strangely unsettling.

"Such is the way of fighting men," Alexandru says. "In every age, they find the most repulsive thing on the table and devour it with pride."

Alexandru told me once that he was born in 1003, and that he was at one time a soldier. Was he one of the men who consumed repulsive things? Did he actually see men in armor get pierced by crossbow bolts, bleeding into their suits like tin cups like he told Hardware Sam? He so rarely talks about his past, and then he'll come out with these statements that feel very firsthand knowledge-y.

I tease him when he goes all medieval, but a thousand years is a lot to carry around in your head. I shouldn't laugh when he calls my iPad an electronic ledger or asks, in complete seriousness, where the scribes who do the writing and ciphering are. Sometimes when he uses a word like laptop, I'm not sure he fully understands what it is.

And he won't stop asking about the ice cream shop. He knows there's something there. I keep thinking maybe I should just tell him the whole thing, how my little half brother vanished when I was twelve, how it was my fault because I was there at that ice cream shop, flirting with a boy instead of picking him up at the playground and walking him home like I was supposed to.

The mistake that separates before from after.

But sometimes I like that there is this one person who

didn't automatically see me as the girl who left her eight-year-old brother to be stolen by the Cuyahoga Killer.

One person who doesn't see me as the girl who never recovered from it, like I'm driven by damage. Like my spreadsheets are a trauma response, my hyper-organization "compensatory" instead of simply the best way to do things. As if every system I build is me trying to undo the past.

Then again, my BFF, Josie, knows my history, and she doesn't see me as hopeless and damaged. Mom and Granabelle don't look at me like that.

Maybe I should trust Alexandru with the truth. We aren't exactly friends, but we are partners of a sort.

It's dark by the time we're back at Kingston Manor. Gregor is in the foyer, as usual, awaiting our arrival. Alexandru hands him his hat and then begins to remove his gloves, tugging the leather over one finger after another with lazy precision. The motion shouldn't be compelling; it's just a man removing gloves. But there's something about the way the leather slides over his knuckles, the glimpse of skin beneath, the flex of tendons in those large hands that makes it impossible to look away. I'm still staring when he pulls the second glove free and passes it to Gregor.

"What is it, Ms. Renfield?"

This jolts me out of my stupor. "I'm gonna call Kip's bar and try to see if I can find out if the Snag Tooth Riders might be in tonight. Maybe we can get a sense if they have some information on why Dooley Brogan would go after Razor Johnny. I'm thinking if they go in there at all, it'll be late."

"Good. Then you will dine with me in the great hall

beforehand, and we will discuss next steps. Gregor, you will prepare something for Ms. Renfield."

"He doesn't have to go through a lot of fuss. I can just whip up some spaghetti with the noodles and tomato sauce he made the other day." I give Gregor a smile. "You could join us with your...gruel."

This of course, earns me a stern look. "Gregor does not wish to join us."

"It's customary to allow members of the household to speak for themselves."

Gregor casts a wary glance at Alexandru, who says, "Gregor does not want to join us for a meal."

"How do you know? Maybe he didn't want to join you in the past, but people change their minds on things."

"I will not change my mind, milady," Gregor says. "Such things are not for me."

"How do you know they're not for you if you don't try them?"

"Gregor does not have to try things to know that they are not for him," Alexandru bites out.

"It is true, milady," Gregor says, eyes downcast.

I glare at Alexandru. What else could Gregor say? He's obviously terrified of Alexandru.

"Gregor, see to it that she has fresh bread and fresh butter to accompany her meal."

"Yes, overlord." Gregor makes a small bow and leaves the room.

"Well, ummm, thanks in advance, Gregor!" I say. Because obviously Alexandru isn't going to thank him. I give Alexandru one last disgusted look and head to my wing down a hall lined with wall sconces that flicker with actual candles. They cast long shadows across the oak paneling and the horrific portraits of hunts and battles I try not to look at too closely. Needless to say, I did not do the décor on the hallway to my part of the mansion.

I don't know what's going on with Alexandru and Gregor. The man's been Alexandru's servant for around 500 years, but he's obviously not a vampire, but did Alexandru do some creepy life extension on him like he did for my father? And why does Gregor tolerate this treatment?

I feel like he has Gregor brainwashed into thinking that he could never hope for a better life than this. It's not okay.

I call Kip's bar, a.k.a. the Muddy Pint, and I'm happy to find myself talking to a bartender there, or "barmaid" if you are a certain archaic somebody who my mom knows. "Just out of curiosity, do you think that the Snag Tooth Riders might be in tonight?"

"I'm pretty sure, yeah. Doing a lot of prowling, if you know what I mean. They're like a stirred-up wasp's nest since the killing."

Good. That's a perfect place to interview the members.

I answer a few emails related to Alexandru's worldwide real estate and financial empire. It's almost five in the evening in Ohio, which means it's the middle of the night across Europe, but he does have San Francisco holdings, and Asia is waking up.

I sometimes wonder how my father managed all of this on his old-fashioned 1950s accountant's ledgers.

I saw those ledgers the one and only time I ever met him when I was seventeen. I tracked him to a tiny café in Karsovia on spring break, expecting...I don't know what I was expecting. Not what I found: a harried man muttering nonsensically about "the master" and obsessing over a table strewn with ledgers. Not just the business ledgers, but these other much weirder ledgers with black covers and mystical symbols all over the place. I looked through one of these more mystical ledgers and asked him about it, but he was barely aware of my existence. At one point, he plucked a fly out of the air and gobbled it up.

Not exactly the father-daughter reunion I had hoped for.

I saw those ledgers again at Alexandru's castle when he imprisoned my half-siblings and me for his process of choosing a new Renfield. I got a little too absorbed in them. I might have even lost time.

Which was scary.

I was not thrilled to find them in a box in my wing of Kingston Manor when I moved in there. I could feel their dark pull immediately. I told Gregor to have them sent back to Eastern Europe, but Alexandru wasn't having any of it. He has them in the mansion. Somewhere.

I dream about them sometimes. I think about them a lot. One time I found myself randomly doodling some of the symbols I saw on those pages.

I think about my father a lot, too. Did he start out normal? Did he have a job and a favorite pub in London and people who knew his name before all of this consumed him?

And who came before him? That would have been my grandparents. Scratching away in that old castle with just Alexandru and Gregor for company. What a miserable existence.

My phone pings. A text from my former boss at InovaSpire.

Serena: do you have a few minutes to hop on a Zoom with the team? Need your institutional knowledge on a Rayburn thing quick.

Me: of course!

Quitting InovaSpire was the last thing I ever wanted to do. It was a great job, and I loved being the organizational whiz, helping to put my brilliant boss, Serena's, vision into action.

But living in Alexandru's mansion and working for him full-time was the only way to stop him from using my town as hunting grounds.

Luckily, the InovaSpire gang still needs my knowhow. I go in for consulting once a week and I'm always up for a call.

I hop on with the four of them, all of us in our little squares.

"I know you're dropping by tomorrow," Serena says, "but the Rayburn contract is coming up for renewal, and you set up the original Rayburn relationship three years ago. We need to ask about some of the contingencies."

"I popped it into our shared box," Malik says.

I answer the team's questions one by one.

Malik and Varla are my replacements. Malik seems to be in a great mood. Varla is silent, and uncommunicative toward me —enough so that I wonder if I said something to offend her. KC, our overeager former intern, who is now on staff, is in one of his oppositional moods, where he makes faces like he's not quite sure he agrees with me on things. At one point, he outright objects to one of my answers, insisting my interpretation conflicts with his assessment.

He explains what he means, but I patiently explain why his way doesn't hold water, and we move on to the next question, and then some budget allocation stuff.

I forgot how nice it is to be able to arrange all these moving parts into a perfect, well-oiled machine, and to make everything make sense. Unlike my life with Alexandru, where there is so much that is inexplicable, if not downright frightening.

I get off the call and tidy up my wing, which consists of a sitting room, an office, and the grand bedroom, all exquisitely furnished. There are two fireplaces and floor-to-ceiling windows with sweeping views of Silverton Valley. My wing is separated from the main house by that hallway, but even from here I can smell the glorious tomato garlic pasta sauce that Gregor is cooking up.

My stomach rumbles excitedly.

I finish up and wander out into the ridiculously baroque grand foyer, underneath a grand curving stairway with a serpentine railing that is best not inspected too closely, head for the kitchen, thinking again about telling Alexandru about James.

We *are* working together, after all. There are times when he shows signs of humanity. Maybe the human he once was, bursting through.

What's more, he has my back in his own weird way. And more communication is always better than less.

I stroll into the kitchen area. "What am I smelling? Gregor! Yum! And are you baking fresh bread?" I look around for him.

His voice comes from the direction of the little scullery room at the far end. He sounds out of breath.

As I draw near, I hear a rhythmic *thunk-splash, thunk-splash*. I stop in the doorway.

And there is Gregor, his dark green coat buttoned all the way up despite the warmth of the kitchen, vigorously pushing a long wooden plunger up and down in a tall wooden cylinder. *Thunk-splash. Thunk-splash.*

I stare for a moment, my analytical brain trying to process what I'm seeing. Wooden cylinder. Cream-colored liquid visible when he lifts the plunger. Repetitive motion. Kitchen setting.

"Are you..." I squint at the contraption. "Are you *churning butter?*"

"Yes, milady," he gasps.

My jaw drops. "Dude, it's the twenty-first century! We could just buy it at Gable's Grocery."

No answer. Gregor's knuckles are white around the wooden handle. There's a sheen of sweat on his tall forehead. How long has he been at this?

"In sticks. Pre-churned."

"I am aware." *Thunk-splash. Thunk-splash.*

"Not to demean or discount the very hard work that you're doing. I'm sure it will be delicious but—"

He turns his hooded, heavy-lidded eyes to me. "It is my task."

"Did Alexandru ask you to make butter like this? I don't want you to go through all this trouble just for butter for me."

"It is my task." The plunger moves faster.

Did I upset him? Is he angry?

"Well," I stammer, "I bet it will be unbelievably delicious." I get out of there and stomp back out and up the grand curved staircase into the dining hall, which features a stupidly long wooden table under a weirdly pugilistic iron chandelier.

There's a hearth off to the side with two cozy chairs. Alexandru sits in one, book in hand, relaxed and at ease.

"You're making Gregor churn butter?"

Alexandru sighs wearily. "Yes, I heard you carrying on about it."

"Carrying on about it? Yeah, you could say I was carrying on about it. Why give poor Gregor an unbelievably laborious task that takes whatever long it takes when we can just buy it for like, so cheap? It's obviously very hard for him."

He simply shrugs, like it's beneath his notice.

"What?!" I demand. "Do you like hearing him suffer? Is that it?"

"The rhythmic churning *is* a bit soothing."

I snort, disgusted. "This from the man who once made poor Gregor scrub the dungeon with a toothbrush. I guess I shouldn't be surprised you'd make him churn butter."

"I am pleased that you understand," he says in his infuriatingly composed English accent.

"No, I don't understand. It's horrible. Why give him such a needlessly inefficient task?"

"Efficiency is a human value."

"As opposed to your superior vampire values of murder, and cruelty, and boasting about your sexual prowess?"

"If anything, I am under-reporting my sexual prowess." Alexandru turns a page in his book. "As for Gregor, each and every task reminds him of what he is."

"What he *is* is a human being with dreams and desires and a right to dignity."

Sort of a human being, I amend to myself. *Human-ish,* considering he's over 500 years old.

"Debatable," Alexandru drawls in his English accent.

"Tell me, what did Gregor ever do to you?"

"Gregor is not your business."

"Gregor's not a Renfield or I'm sure you would've told me. Is he some other enemy of yours?"

"Perhaps he is not an enemy at all."

I cross my arms, unsure what to think. But this opens the door to a question I've been circling for a while. "You said my dad came to work for you in 1921. Did he *want* to work for you? Or did you force it like you did with me? And then slowly drove him bonkers?"

Alexandru looks up, finally. "The latter, I would say."

"And before that? What was he before that?" I'm hoping he can't hear the eagerness in the question.

Alexandru closes his book. "Your father was a London-born lawyer. Quite a good one, I'm told."

"And you just snatched him up?"

"His mother, Eleanor Vivian Renfield, summoned him when it was time."

"So that's who worked for you before him?"

"Yes. Eleanor was with me for over a century. She had been a lady's companion earlier in her life, but her skills were rather wasted in that position. She instituted an elaborate filing system for my correspondence. Truly remarkable."

"I don't get it. She actually had a baby while she was working for you? And she sent for him to replace her?"

"As I have told you, it is one of the primary duties of a Renfield to replace themselves. Eleanor had several children, all placed in appropriate homes. She was honored to serve one such as myself and desperately hoped that privilege would transfer to one of her own rather than a cousin or some such. And indeed, your father proved quite sufficient. Until the end."

"What was my father like when he first started working for you?"

"Methodical. Precise." Alexandru stares into the middle distance. "He was accustomed to finer things, so the castle did not suit him at first, but he settled into his role soon enough."

"Because you basically imprisoned him?"

"If you want," he says casually.

Grr.

"And before my grandmother Eleanor?"

"That would be Bartholomew." A faint smile crosses his face. "He worked for the East India Company for some time before he came to me in 1702. He was the nephew of Millicent Renfield, once a lady-in-waiting to a German princess." He pauses and folds his hands over his book, looking thoughtful. "Before Millicent was Thaddeus Wilbur Renfield, a monastery recordkeeper. I brought him to me in 1502. Then there was Jonas, and before him, Edmund, who developed my first cataloging system."

"And who was before that?" I ask.

He takes up his book again. "I tire of this line of inquiry."

"Oh, come on. You were born in 1003. There had to be Renfields before Edmund."

Alexandru looks up at me, and for a moment I see something behind his eyes that makes me wish I hadn't asked. Something hot. Ancient. Like maybe fury.

It hits me then. Somewhere in those missing three hundred years was the Renfield who wronged him. The one who created a debt so vast it cursed my bloodline in his eyes forever.

The *first* Renfield, perhaps. The one who started it all.

Who was he?

Or she?

Just then, Gregor comes in with a tray bearing an Orangina and a selection of cheeses and olives and crackers, and a small bowl of Bugles.

I go and take my place at the far end of the table. If there were any mercy in this world, Alexandru would not join me. It's not like he eats, anyway.

No such luck. He settles into one of the chairs at the side, laying his book in front of him.

I thank Gregor, and make much ado of the Bugles, even though I have a box of them in my desk drawer. I inform Alexandru that the Snag Tooth Riders are expected at the Muddy Pint bar tonight, probably around ten or eleven. We go over our plan, which is pretty simple: to find out if Dooley knew Razor Johnny or if Dooley had any kind of beef with the Snag Tooth Riders.

Maybe he did. Alexandru did sense some secret he was keeping.

Gregor brings out freshly baked bread along with freshly churned butter, and it is indeed delicious. More than delicious. It's a warm, creamy, soft wonderland of tastes. Then comes the spaghetti. I don't even want to ask if he made the noodles.

Chapter Seven

Alexandru

The Muddy Pint is a squat brick building on River Road. Its small windows blaze with neon signs, and motorcycles line the curb in diagonal formation. Across the street is the much-ballyhooed river walk, now empty. Perhaps it is the hour, or perhaps it is the specter of the Crossbow Killer, which, according to Ms. Renfield, is "all over the news."

I pull open the heavy door and the scent hits—grease and stale ale. The peasants huddled around scarred wood tables go quiet as we enter, gazes lifting one by one. Ms. Renfield greets the barmaid, with whom she appears to share some history, and orders two beers.

And there in the far corner, as promised, are the Snag Tooth Riders, sprawled across two tables, leather vests bearing their club's insignia: a skull with one unaccountably large, crooked tooth.

Good. We have come to see if Dooley Brogan knew Razor Johnny.

"Lucky for us nobody wants to sit next to them." Ms. Renfield nods to the empty table that seems to be the buffer between the bike pack and the villagers.

I take the seat nearest to the pack; they'll be no trouble for me, and I have no doubt Ms. Renfield would prefer to face them and see all. I do not need to see them to know their movements.

The barmaid delivers our ales, and then the Snag Tooth Riders order three plates of Widowmaker nachos.

Ms. Renfield widens her brown eyes and elongates her red lips, forming what I have come to know as her WTF face, because she'll often whisper those letters to accompany the expression, which should be displeasing, but somehow isn't. "Not the 'gross beard nachos'!"

A strange thrill of pleasure runs through me. I raise a brow.

Ms. Renfield leans in. "I'm not sure exactly how to do this. I don't think people just normally talk to these guys. And they seem a little riled up."

Indeed they are. Their pulses beat fast, adrenaline high. I stand and turn to the men. Eleven pairs of eyes turn upward. The man at the head—older, perhaps fifty, with gray in his beard and patches on his jacket, seems to be the leader. I meet his gaze. "Your brother was slain," I say simply.

"What's it to you?" the leader barks.

I can feel Ms. Renfield's alarm behind me. I say, "The town speaks of Dooley Brogan."

Another pause. The younger ones shift in their seats. They wait for the leader. The leader simply watches me.

"What do you make of it?" I ask.

He says, "What I *make of it* is that Razor Johnny rode with us for twelve years and that coward shot him in the back with a crossbow."

A younger man stands up beside him, all lean muscle and coiled energy. "And that coward is a dead man."

Grunts go up from the table.

"We'll see." The captain keeps his gaze fixed on mine. "Question is what *you're* making of it. You a cop?"

Ms. Renfield speaks up here. "We're just wanting to know what happened."

"Why is that?" one of the men barks at her, this one with mottled skin and a scar bisecting his eyebrow.

I give him a look, and he stills like a rabbit.

The leader studies me with new interest. "You're that guy who bought Kingston Manor. The castle up on the hill."

"I am."

"You doing some kinda Iron Man thing? Crime fighting?"

"Just interested in seeing that the right person dies," I say.

He nods. The barmaid chooses this time to deliver the nachos. The man next to him grabs a hunk and shoves it into his mouth.

I ask, "Did Dooley Brogan and Razor Johnny know each other?"

"Not that we can figure," he says. "Cops asked us that and we told them the same. There's some here who think Dooley just wanted to go back inside, but why, then, not confess?"

I nod. "Indeed."

"Some of us think Dooley got a taste for killing," the leader continues. "Maybe wants to do a few more and then go out with a bang."

"Man ain't right," a gray-haired man says. "Some men ain't right."

The leader takes a slow drink of his beer, never breaking eye contact with me.

Ms. Renfield speaks up again. "Did Dooley interact with any of your fellow Snag Tooth Riders in prison?"

The man nods at a small, wiry biker with frizzy hair. Primitive insignias decorate his face and neck. "Hound there was in Dooley's cell block most of this last year. Tell him, Hound."

Hound sets down his ale with a thunk. "Man kept to himself mostly." His moustache becomes lively as he speaks, food bits catching the light. "Real straight-edge type. Checking out books from the library, kissing butt and all that. No one knew him. Did his time in his own world."

Ms. Renfield fixes her gaze at the wall just beyond his ear. "Anything at all unusual about him doing his time in there?"

Hound thinks about this a moment. "He didn't get many visitors. Didn't seem to have much money. But then in the last few months, that all changed. Guards were coming and getting him pretty much every week. He was flush with commissary money, too. You'd see him giving out candy bars to guys he wanted favors from. Man was broke as a joke before that, so I figured it had to be this visitor juicing his account."

"Candy can be like a currency on the inside," the leader explains to me.

"Do you know who was visiting him?" Ms. Renfield asks.

Hound shrugs. "No clue. Don't see what that has to do with anything, though."

"Wasn't any of us," the leader assures me. "Certainly wasn't Razor Johnny."

Chapter Eight

Alexandru

"So who was visiting him?" Ms. Renfield asks on our way back to her little green car.

I say, "The sister, perhaps?"

She stops, regarding me over the roof. "A busy nurse raising two kids on her own is suddenly paying weekly visits to a prison an hour away and bringing money? I don't see Tilly as a woman with a lot of extra time or money on her hands."

"Certainly not," I say.

"But who else would it be? His lawyer must have been visiting him at some point, but why would his lawyer suddenly be giving him money? That's definitely not how it goes with lawyers."

I smile. "An unknown player has entered the game."

Ms. Renfield's face is illuminated from one side by the streetlights along the river, lending her bold features a certain nobility. "Let's see if Dooley Brogan is still up." She gives me a sly look, pulls out her phone, and begins to speak to it. "Just seeing if you're up... Very urgent question connected to your case."

Her phone chimes a second later.

"He wants to know what our question is." She raises her eyes to mine. "I think not!"

"Agreed, Ms. Renfield."

She text-narrates some more. "Can we stop by quick?"

A few minutes later, we're sitting in plastic chairs out on the small back porch behind Tilly's house. Dooley points to a back window and whispers, "Those are the kids' bedrooms. We have to keep it down."

"Okay," Ms. Renfield whispers.

"I like to sit out here and see the stars. You don't know what it is to not see the stars for fifteen years."

Ms. Renfield and I exchange glances. He does not sound like a man who wants to go back behind bars.

She leans forward. "Who was visiting you so much toward the end?"

Everything in Dooley tightens with surprise, even alarm, but he attempts a confused face. "Who-who was visiting me?"

"Yes," Ms. Renfield says. "We understand you got quite a few visits in the last couple months you were inside. I am asking who that was who was visiting you."

Dooley blinks. "I'm not sure. That must've been my lawyer. We had a lot of visits toward the end when he recognized that there had been a miscarriage of justice."

The deception in him is unmistakable. There is much he is not saying.

"How often was he visiting?" she asks.

"What does it matter?" Dooley is whispering more loudly now, more urgently. "I can't remember. A lot, I would say. He was visiting me a lot."

Ms. Renfield tilts her head. "But you're not sure how much?"

"Not really! It's not as if I tracked it!"

"It's just important that we get all the facts if we are going to help you," Ms. Renfield says. "Can you tell me about these meetings?"

"I thought lawyer visits were kind of confidential," Dooley says with a wary glance in my direction. "But honestly, it was just lawyer stuff."

She says, "He sounds like a pretty good lawyer, working so tirelessly on your behalf all these years."

"Yes." Dooley nods vigorously.

I tire of his lies. "Who else visited you?"

Dooley turns to me, alarmed. "I don't know what a roster of all my visitors has to do with anything. The prosecution withheld key evidence, so of course I would talk to my lawyer a ton. The bottom line is, I didn't do the crime. I didn't kill Benson and surely not Razor Johnny."

I grow hungry, and this man is hiding something. His insistence he didn't kill feels genuine, but he is not telling all. There are a great number of ways to press a man, to get the truth out. I eye Dooley, considering which to employ.

Ms. Renfield stands up. "I just remembered, we have to go."

What now?

She gives me one of her significant looks, which tells me

that her clever mind has come up with something and turns to Dooley. "Thank you so much for clearing this up. We don't mean to seem accusatory. It makes total sense that your lawyer would visit you a ton."

I stand. My little Renfield has thought of something. She puts things together in her own way. She hears "noise in the data," she once told me.

"Thanks for coming by," Dooleys says. "And if you want me to figure out how many times my lawyer visited me, I probably could figure it out if it helps."

"It's probably not important," she says.

"He was lying, frightened, hiding things," I say as Ms. Renfield navigates the car through streets now shrouded in darkness, a great improvement over the cheerful lawns with their geese statuary.

Her eyes flash in the moonlight, a hint of honey threaded through the brown. "Lying about the visits or the whole thing?"

So. My Renfield is going to play coy and conceal her new plan a bit longer. This does not displease me. "Somebody else most certainly visited him, but he does not wish to name that person. His proclamations of innocence do have the ring of truth, interestingly enough."

"But it could be because he's a sociopath who believes his own lies, right?"

"Perhaps. The visits are important, though," I say in a low voice. "I could've gotten it out of him. I could have learned all.

Why did you want to leave so suddenly? What is it that you realized?"

"Two things. One of which is that you were itching to go beast mode on him."

This takes me aback. "How is it that you could know such a thing?"

"You have a tell."

"A tell? I do not."

She smiles mischievously.

"I have existed a century; I would know."

"And I realized that I have another way of getting that information that wouldn't involve waking up the kids or grave bodily harm."

I turn to her there in the darkness. "What is my tell?"

"Oh, you think I'm going to tell you what it is? Hell no."

"I do not jest. You will inform me of my tell this instant."

She turns through the iron gates and into the drive. Gravel crunches beneath us. Oaks arch overhead as the house takes shape in the dark.

"You seem to forget that you are mine to command."

"I'm sorry—is that in the contract? Let me think. No. I don't recall a clause requiring me to disclose non-business information."

"I would choose my next words with great care, Ms. Renfield."

Nervousness pulses through her as she pulls the car to a stop. It is not an easy thing for her, opposing me.

She gets out and strides ahead of me toward the main door. When she reaches the top step, she spins around to face me. "You have a right to command me in matters of your operations and worldly affairs. You do not have a right to my private observations. My emotions. Or...personal whatnot."

I sense a flutter of something interesting at the mention of "whatnot." "What does *whatnot* mean? What is hidden in there, Ms. Renfield?"

"None of your business."

Heat blooms beneath her skin. A faint blush climbs her cheek, and memory strikes—

The wedding killer. The knife at her throat. The way I seized her hand and pressed my lips to it, as if I required direct proof that she was still alive. And it was a struggle to let her go.

I was undone by hunger at the time, of course.

I say, "I do not like a closed book."

She presses her lips together. Her scent shifts. Her skin heats. "Cats do not like closed doors, yet some doors are closed to them and will remain so."

"I find that cats eventually get their way in such matters."

She says, "You should be glad that I can detect when you might turn beastly. It makes me a better partner. It made me a better partner questioning Dooley tonight."

"Is that what you think?"

"Yes. I stopped you before you could reveal that we know he's lying. Here's the thing, Alexandru, there's another way to find out who visited him: I can file a FOIA, a freedom of information act request, and get the prison visit logs. I'm thinking the Department of Rehabilitation and Correction probably has a public records officer I can reach out to. Let's find out who that person is before he figures out that he needs to warn them."

I smile. It always pleases me when she reveals herself to be the battle tactician. "Good. You will file it now, and we will go drag the person out of their bed."

"Well, wait—it's not as if we will get the information instantly. For one thing, it's nighttime and nobody's even in the office. And it's not as if the people are going to arrive in the morning and get right on it. The FOIA is a law that says normal citizens get to know what their government is doing and what their government knows, and the government is forced to comply, but it doesn't mean the government loves to comply. It can be a slow process, generally seven days, sometimes as many as ten business days if they're feeling surly."

"Unacceptable. We will pay them a visit when they are in their office this morning. Clerks who fear for their lives tend to process paperwork with remarkable efficiency. Unless they are shaking too badly. Spilled ink and so forth."

Her pretty lips curl into a smile. "I have a better way, Alexandru. I'll have those reports soon."

I have the utterly irrational urge to pull her to me right then, to crush my lips against hers, to kiss that smile, to taste her, to—

The thought is so outrageous I recoil from myself.

A *Renfield*? To kiss a Renfield? To even imagine it?

The door opens. "Overlord." Gregor stands there, trembling pathetically. She looks over at him and she stiffens. Her jaw tightens. Of course Gregor chooses this moment to put his full wretchedness on display.

But what do I care?

"Please forgive me," Gregor says, trembling like a leaf. "I was attending to your shoes upstairs and did not hear you come in."

"Be quicker next time." I ascend the steps and stop at the threshold and address Ms. Renfield. "You will execute your plan. Best hope the clerks do not dawdle."

"Whatever you say, *overlord*." Ms. Renfield loads the word "overlord" with all the fury her diminutive frame can muster. Her pulse hammers with it.

I proceed to my wing and she proceeds to hers.

Chapter Nine

Harriet

I lie in bed awake. My brain won't stop spinning through everything that happened. Razor Johnny who, yes, was in a motorcycle gang and ran over Jerome's grandmother's flowerbeds, but he didn't deserve to die. The man accepted cookies as his payment for his protection racket after all.

So who killed him?

And then there's Dooley Brogan being so weird and evasive about his prison visitor, but Alexandru says he seems genuine when he says he didn't kill Razor Johnny.

And then there's Jerome, and Sloane, and Granabelle… and of course, Alexandru.

He is such an unbelievable jerk. And he is literally my overlord—forever, if he has his way, and he always gets his way, being that he's a murderous vampire with no moral center. I need to figure out how to get free of this. Some way where he won't, or ideally can't, threaten innocent people as a way of dragging me back.

It's not as if I hate solving mysteries with him. I like it more than I should. I like matching wits with him. And his whole Gothic manor is growing on me in a Stockholm-syndrome kind of way, but a girl likes a bit of autonomy and the ability to exit. Every scenario I run ends with someone getting hurt who isn't me. So for now I stay, and I make myself useful, and I wait for him to show me a crack I can work with.

He was human once. There has to be something left in there.

My mind drifts to the fervent way he grabbed my hand after Bo Richardson almost killed me; he just grabbed it and turned my palm up, and before I could even think to pull away, he pressed his lips there, cool and soft against my skin.

It was...a lot.

I go sit down in my office and wake up my laptop. Before I can think about it, my fingers are moving—the muscle memory of twenty years. NamUs notifications: nothing. Google Alerts: three hits, all irrelevant. Ohio BCI database: no new unidentified remains matching James's profile. The whole ritual takes maybe ninety seconds, and then I close the tabs and push my glasses up, ignoring the hollow feeling.

I didn't really expect to find anything on James, but I keep checking. I will always keep checking.

Someday, somehow, I'll figure out what happened to him. I need him back. I need to see his face again, to hear his laugh. He's out there somewhere; I just need to find the right thread.

And then I get the extremely dark urge, which is happening more and more lately, to make Alexandru tell me where he keeps my father's weird mystical ledgers. The ones that have nothing to do with business and accounting.

I can't shake the sense that those ledgers could help me find

James. I don't know how or why they could help, but there's some knowing there. Some perspective on the fabric of things. Connective material. Invisible noise.

Which is ridiculous on a million woo-woo levels.

I sit up and force myself to do what I actually came here to do—get a jump on filing the FOIA. When that's done, I hop onto my favorite place in all of the internet, the true crime forum, thinking to troll for potential future murderers on the loose for my jackhole of an overlord to drain.

The forum loads with its familiar white text over dark blue background, so very 2010. I'm logged in as Rooster5. The main page shows the usual mix of threads, but one catches my eye immediately, pinned at the top with a red "HOT" tag: "JUST RELEASED: Dawson Trial Transcripts—20 Years Sealed!"

Someone named Justice4Sadie has uploaded everything and is asking if anyone can make sense of the witness timeline.

It has absolutely nothing to do with anything, but I can't help but check it out.

Just to blow off steam.

I scan through the comments and then download the PDF and start skimming. Before I know what I'm doing, I'm copying relevant sections and wrangling timestamps, locations, and witness names into a structured format. I add columns and color coding. I notice a time discrepancy pattern, and I create a visualization involving concentric circles of memory reliability.

I screenshot it all and write a post explaining what I've done and how to interact with the documents I've created.

I hit submit and lean back. At least I nailed one thing.

I refresh the page. My post appears. Both spreadsheets look professional and clear.

A few minutes later, responses start coming in. Glendale129 posts an impressed emoji. TheTorvald says, "Nice geometric analysis."

I refresh again, and there's a new response.

Sherlocksmith.

My stomach tightens. Sherlocksmith has been on the forum for years, and he loves showing up in my threads as a condescending jerk.

This response is true to form, trying to punch holes in my work and make me feel inferior. He drops a link to an article entitled *"Cognitive Psychology of Eyewitness Testimony"* as his final word.

I start to compose a long, ragey post informing him that I'm already very familiar with that article, but then I just shut the laptop. Because what am I doing?

I sit back in my chair. *What I'm doing* is trying anything to get away from the fact of how much I wanted to kiss Alexandru.

I wanted to kiss him. And I think he wanted to kiss me.

He's a monster.

A monster!

Who I wanted to kiss.

I finally move to DEFCON one, my ultimate mind-calming activity: building towers out of quarters.

Sometimes I make stepped pyramids. Sometimes little skylines. Today I'm making a stepped pyramid.

Quarter towers calm me on a level nothing else touches.

I don't build them on my desk, obviously. This is not my first coin-tower rodeo. I had a special table brought in just for quarter towers. Level surface, no wobble. You can't stack quarters on a surface that wobbles.

It's three in the morning when I finish tonight's construction.

Everything lines up.

Everything is where it should be.

Chapter Ten

Harriet

It's a gorgeous morning and there's already a line out the door for Berky's cookies, a.k.a. Berky Bombs. I lock my bike to the decorative streetlamp and walk into the cozy, ramshackle shop with its scents of coffee mixed with scrumptious pastries. Something butterscotch just came out of the oven and I want to eat the air.

I get in line behind some tourists who are having pastry decision difficulties and scan the tables.

Perceval is at his usual post in the back, staring at his laptop, looking all scholarly. I catch sight of my friend Josie's little goth cousin deep in conversation with her goth friends, probably about robotics.

Monique, Berky's Parisian granddaughter and tourist season helper, addresses the next person in line, doing her usual Berky imitation, right down to the way she tilts her head and delivers a bright "bonjour!"

"Harriet!" Berky comes over wiping her hands on her apron. She's got a blue Eiffel tower scarf around her neck today.

"Bonjour. I have them boxing up your order in back. How are things up at *le grand* Kingston Manor?"

"Great! Having my own wing in a mansion is like having my own luxury apartment up there." I find myself saying things like this more and more lately so that people don't think Alexandru and I are a romantic item. "Definitely a nice perk."

She raises an eyebrow. "I suppose." Her words have a slight edge.

"You suppose?"

She purses her lips, staring into the middle distance. "He is from an old family, your Alexandru. You do not have such old families here."

"I guess not," I say, wondering what she's getting at.

"These old families, they do not see people the way we do. These nobles and royals, they can be charming indeed. Until they are not."

I stare at her, dumbfounded. Her analysis is shockingly astute. So astute that I don't know what to say.

"But then, I see that you know." A helper comes out the back with a box.

She takes it from him and sets it on the counter, opening the top to show me the selection of a dozen Berky Bombs I ordered last night. They will be delivered to the Department of Rehabilitation and Correction public records office later this morning.

"You wished to add a note before the boy leaves on his route?"

"I did." I extract an envelope from my purse and tape it to the top. The note inside, handwritten by me, reads:

"Thank you for your hard work processing public records

requests. Civil servants like you make democracy function. With appreciation, Harriet Morgan."

It's not a bribe, exactly. But it's not *not* a bribe.

I have Berky bag up a separate order with a chocolate-filled almond sprinkle Berky Bomb and a selection of macarons. These I deliver myself—to my family's antique store.

"Treats!" I say as I stroll in the gloomy beloved old space.

Granabelle is wearing a linen outfit that gives Hemingway-in-Cuba vibes. She's up front in the window redoing a display that involves lots of vintage hats and scarves and a variety of puppets, including two ventriloquist dummies.

"Nice," I say brightly. "Very lively."

"I'm not so sure." Mom strolls up. "It's puppets and random human clothing items. I feel like the puppets have done something freaky with the people. But yeah, lively."

Granabelle gives an indignant huff. "That's not what the display is, but if people interpret it that way, all the better." She climbs out of the window and brushes herself off. "All publicity is good publicity. Let the crowds gather, that's what I say. Maybe I'll put an axe in there just for fun! Or perhaps that old military sword!"

"You'll do no such thing!" Mom warns.

Granabelle spots the Berky's bags in my hand. "For us?"

"The little one is macarons!" I hand it over and turn to Mom. "And for us..."

Mom plants her hands on her hips and gives me a warning look. "You didn't!"

"Of course I did!" I carry the bag to the counter and go behind and grab one of the plates and put Mom's cookie on it.

Mom comes up and stands next to me, tucking the long side

of her salt-and-pepper bob behind her ear. "Got time for a quick cuppa?"

"Of course! But you know I'm having half of this." I break off a bit while she pours me some coffee. She shows me an order of antique rings that just came in from somewhere in Wisconsin. I grab a polishing cloth, and we polish them together, drinking our coffee and eating our cookie and chatting about the murder.

Everybody that Mom has talked to is stunned that Maverick let Dooley Brogan go.

"It's not like Maverick had anything to hold him on, other than the fact that the guy was killed with a crossbow. I mean, a lot of deer are killed with crossbows, too. Do we think Dooley Brogan did that?"

"That's ridiculous," Mom says. "Hunting a man with a crossbow is known as an MO."

"Look at you, pulling out true crime jargon," I say.

Mom inspects a ring and polishes it a little bit more. "You think I wasn't paying attention all those nights of you watching those true crime shows of yours?"

I grab another ring. "Fair enough."

"So how's Prince Cravat?"

"He's not a prince, and he doesn't wear a cravat," I say. "Other than that, he's fine, and the job's great. I'm automating his accounts payable across six countries—different currencies, different banking systems, different tax-withholding rules. It's like a puzzle, but with money."

Mom gives me a slightly suspicious look. She thinks I'm trying to make it sound better than it is, and she's right. Automations like that aren't super challenging. But I can't exactly tell her the real puzzle that consumes my attention: trying to figure out if Dooley Brogan really did do that murder so that Alexandru can enjoy a heapin' helpin' of his blood.

Though Alexandru's liable to go after Dooley in the end anyways.

"And that butler of his? Gregor? What's that guy up to today?"

I study the side of Mom's face as she polishes a sterling silver ring. "Looking after Kingston Manor keeps him busy," I say, understatement of the year. "He baked some pretty amazing bread last night, though."

"Really! Not everybody can bake a decent loaf of bread," Mom says.

Just then, Granabelle comes up and shows us the photos she took of the macarons. "Laverne DeRue can suck mine," she says.

"No comment," I say. Laverne DeRue is Granabelle's over-seventy influencer rival.

Chapter Eleven

Alexandru

Gregor brings the post from the castle. I take the packet and settle into the chair by the fire.

Most of it is routine. Correspondence from Bruges. A letter from a book dealer in Munich regarding a manuscript I'd inquired about years ago.

I open a letter bearing the seal of the family that has managed my legal affairs through the centuries. The language is careful, as it always is with them. Accounts, property matters, the usual.

Until I get to the last paragraph, set apart from the rest.

It may interest you to know that a mutual friend has made inquiries regarding your new arrangements in America.

I read it again.

Algernon.

Algernon, Duke of Densmere, though everyone calls him Nero. My oldest friend. My most dangerous enemy.

One never sees Nero coming. You see the damage, and then you see him, standing in it, smiling.

His heraldic emblem is the fox. He chose it himself.

There is only one reason Nero would reach out to my solicitors: he wants me to know he is watching. He is aware of my situation. Most of all, he is aware of Ms. Renfield.

"Overlord?" Gregor stands in the doorway. "Is something wrong?"

"Probably nothing." I fold the letter carefully and place it in my breast pocket rather than setting it aside.

Gregor watches me. He knows me too well.

"From the solicitors. Nero is making inquiries regarding my arrangements here in America."

Gregor stiffens. "What does he mean by arrangements? He is asking about the household? About Ms. Renfield?"

"I do not know."

"If I may ask, overlord, what exactly did Nero say? How did he put the inquiry? And did he write it in a letter to the solicitors, or did he see one of the family somewhere?"

"As I said, a line of text," I snap. "*A mutual friend has made inquiries regarding your new arrangements in America.* That is the extent of it. It is hardly surprising that he would reach out. He has been too quiet."

Neither of us moves. The fire crackles. Somewhere in the house, Ms. Renfield's footsteps sound out, steady and oblivious.

Chapter Twelve

Harriet

I roll into InovaSpire at around ten for one of my scheduled consulting days. Back when I resigned my position, I promised I'd come in weekly as long as Serena and the team needed my help. I had my fingers in so many different things—everything from organizing the company to dealing with clients and workflows—that Serena had to hire two people to replace me.

I stop into Serena's office to say a quick hello and grab a lemon drop from the bowl on her desk, and then I head to Varla's office to do "open questions" with her and Malik, which is where they keep a running list of non-urgent questions, and I help them see around the corners a little bit, because I have been around a lot of those corners.

Malik is interested and engaged, but Varla seems frosty—more so than even last week or the week before. She toys with her stylus and barely makes eye contact. I make a mental note to ask Serena about her.

Varla seemed great in the interviews. Is she unhappy with the position?

We order out a working lunch and we're done by three. I walk out of there with Malik and ask him how everybody seems to be adjusting to the change. He tells me it's all going great, and I can't tell if that's his usual optimistic self or what.

I pop into Serena's office on my way out for a debrief. When I ask her how Varla's fitting in, she gets a strange look on her face. "Good. She's doing an A-plus job, but she seemed a little off on Zoom last night."

"So she's not always like that? In your experience?"

"Quite the opposite," Serena says.

"Is it possible that she doesn't like me coming in telling her how to do her work?"

"She knows that's part of her job. I'm going to talk to her."

"No, wait. If her work isn't suffering, I'd rather you don't get involved. It's only been a few weeks, let's give it time." I grab a lemon drop from out of the little bowl on her desk. "Do you think I could use a workstation to check on something extracurricular?"

She grins. "For the hot boss's empire?"

I roll my eyes. "It's a bit of a true crime investigation."

"Your credentials are always good here." She waves her hand. "Nobody's using the southeast terminal."

"Thanks!"

I settle in at the southeast workstation, a.k.a. the guest workstation, which has an amazing view of the Silverton River and the hill country beyond it. I get to work on the dual monitors, and before long I have the network map building itself node by node—red for Dooley Brogan's known connections, blue for Razor Johnny's. I'm hunting for purple. Any overlap at all.

It has to be there!

Their families have both lived in the Silverton Valley or Cleveland area for decades. Something must be in there.

I queue up a geographic clustering algorithm—addresses over time, work layers, school districts, utility records. I'm building a thirty-year social visualization.

Former intern KC appears at the edge of the cubicle, energy drink in hand, hair sticking up like he's been running his fingers through it, though it could be gel.

"Harriet! Didn't expect to see you here." His gaze hits my monitors and he whistles. "Whoa. Dooley Brogan deep dive? Isn't he the Crossbow Killer?"

I plaster on a smile. That is one of the problems with the southeast workstation. It's kind of public.

"Is he, though?" I hit a button. "That first murder was so personal—a business partner he'd been arguing with. But suddenly he gets out of prison and shoots somebody random?"

"You do love patterns," KC says.

I go back to the screen. "I love answers."

"Fair."

KC stays there watching me work. Does he not have something to do?

"You know you can layer timelines, right?" he says, reaching over my shoulder. "May I?"

"Uh, sure."

He hits a few keys, and my flat network suddenly drops into depth—decades stacked like geological layers. "Wrote a plugin last month. Helps you see repeats. Crossings."

I study it. "Not bad. Can we rotate it?"

He leans in. "Alt-drag. And if you want to filter by location type..."

We work together for a bit and suddenly I see purple. "Hmmm. County fair, 2007."

"Both families had booths there," KC says. "Want me to get the vendor maps?"

"I don't want to pull you away from something."

"Don't worry, we got this." He hurries off and returns a few minutes later with a printout. "Their booths were right next to each other! Brogan family was slinging venison jerky and Razor Johnny's mom had a jewelry booth."

"That's pretty long ago, though," I say. "Two families living in the same little cluster of towns, it might be weird for them *not* to intersect."

KC wanders off, and I keep working on the network, digging up maiden names, nicknames, high school sports.

An hour later I sit back, frustrated. Dooley's network glows red. Razor Johnny's is blue. Two islands. Not a single purple node. Except that county fair.

KC is back.

I say, "They didn't go to school together. Didn't work together. Different families, different crowds. Dooley was a mechanic. Razor Johnny running with bikers. They're not even adjacent."

"Did Dooley ever fix Razor Johnny's motorcycle?"

"No. The Snag Tooth Riders fix their own motorcycles. It's one of their primary activities."

"So why would Dooley kill him?" KC asks.

"Maybe he didn't. It is kind of a lot that Dooley would take up crossbow murdering the week he gets out of prison." I'm also thinking how Alexandru didn't sense deception, but obviously I can't say that to KC.

KC folds his arms over his chest. "The plot thickens."

"Can it please not?"

"Hey, you're the data queen. You'll figure it out."

"We'll see. Thanks for the vote of confidence. And I really appreciate your help." I start shutting things down.

"Of course! You've helped me so much. With everything. You're my guru."

I gather my stuff, trying to think how to phrase this next bit. "So, how is everybody fitting together? Like with the new team makeup. Do things feel cohesive?"

"You mean with Malik and Varla?"

"Sure. Any speed bumps?"

KC gets the strange expression. "Malik's great. Varla, she's great, like technically. She just needs a little time to settle in, I think."

"What do you mean?"

KC sucks in a breath. "I don't know. Like you saw her yesterday on that Zoom, she's not usually that quiet. I don't want to say she's *threatened* by you..."

"You don't want to say it? But are you thinking it? That she's threatened by me?"

"Well,obviously, you don't work here anymore, so it wouldn't really make sense, would it?"

"It definitely wouldn't make sense. Maybe I should talk to her."

KC frowns. "It's just been what, a month and a half? If you want my opinion, let it sort itself out."

My best friend, Josie, is already in our favorite booth at Tres Hermanas, the steakhouse her family has owned for generations. I give her a hug and slide in across from her.

She waves at the two champagne cocktails sitting there. "I took the liberty."

"Much obliged," I say. "So, you have three urgent things for the cone zone?"

That's what she had texted earlier as I was setting off from the InovaSpire offices.

Cone zone has been our name for this booth since middle school. What is said at the booth shall never leave.

"Three things…sort of. In a sec—"

I follow the direction of Josie's gaze to see her mother, walking across the dining room floor toward us. We rise for hugs. Her mom slides in next to her and we chitchat, and like everybody, her mother wants to know how it's going up at Kingston Manor. I'm the one local who's been let into the strange and exotic palace on the mountain, and people need details!

I describe my wing and my new job and she leaves slightly unsatisfied.

"You need to get Alexandru to have an open house party or something," Josie says. "Otherwise you're going to be the lightning rod for this town's curiosity forever."

"An open house. It boggles the mind."

"At least let the press in. Let somebody do an interior décor feature on it or something."

"Dude, you've been there. You saw that bizarre chandelier of weaponry. And the weird serpent stairway railing? That place is not exactly *Architectural Digest* ready. More like *Architectural Spanish Inquisition*."

She stirs her drink with a little swizzle stick. "Well, your prince is an eccentric."

I snort. "Not mine and not a prince. It's just some crusty heritage name. It's not as if he has a kingdom."

"But he has a castle."

"White Castle has a castle. So does that putt-putt place off Highway J." I take a swig.

"Somebody's salty about their hot boss."

I don't even know what to say about that. Our waitress delivers us an artichoke ramekin, a warm basket of bread, and a plate of crabcakes with their house-made hollandaise.

I ask her if she's heard anything on the crossbow investigation. Josie is on the city council, and she often gets news before everybody else. "Could that be one of the three things you need to tell me?" I ask hopefully.

Josie's used to my interest in local crime by now. She thinks it's all about my passion for justice and understanding patterns. Better than the truth: managing my employer's monstrous appetites. Though I do hate lying to her.

She rips apart a hunk of bread. "Thing one: I can tell you that the police are looking hard at Dooley Brogan, but they don't have enough to hold him, much as they want to. Thing two is a piece of gossip I have that comes from ol' Uncle Sam and Aunt Pilar." She tips her head in the direction of Hardware Sam's. "There were no prints on the weapon, and it's the kind that could be bought from any big box sporting goods store, so the crossbow itself will be hard to trace, but they seem to think the bolt is traceable, so Maverick and his team are going all around to sporting goods stores, like literally traveling the region. Nothing's turned up so far, but they're pretty hot on it, per Sam's hardware store text chain."

"Your uncle is on a text chain with other hardware stores?"

"It's the bro retail gossip network. I wouldn't be surprised if Sam and Pilar find out where the bolt came from before the cops do."

This is definitely interesting. It's too late to pay a visit to the hardware store tonight, but it might be something for Alexandru and me to do tomorrow.

"And the third item?"

Josie glances at the dining room. Business is brisk with tourist season on the upswing, and this place gets consistently good reviews on the travel sites. "The third thing is more of an event."

"What's that supposed to mean?"

"It's an event that will occur in five to ten minutes."

I frown. "A polka band?"

"Take the last crabcake and sit tight." Josie catches me up on her little boy, but she keeps glancing at the entrance.

Suddenly, there's a hush in the dining room. I look up and spot them: Dooley Brogan, his sister, Tilly, and Tilly's kids are shown to a table near ours.

"This is the event?" I whisper.

Josie puts on her fake innocent face, which is pretty much the opposite of innocent. "Whatever could you mean?"

"Somebody peeked at the reservation book," I say.

Josie grins. "A little bird told me they were coming in

tonight," she whispers. That little bird being her mother, no doubt. "I thought you might want a chance to talk to him."

"Well, Alexandru and I actually have talked to him."

"Wow! You two are really getting serious about this mysteries thing!"

I shrug.

Nobody is looking at the Brogans, but everybody is aware of them.

I catch Tilly's eye and wave. She waves back and then Dooley sees me and smiles and waves.

"What were your impressions?" she asks.

"He's a bit of a doofus, but not a fool, and only a fool would go on the kind of public walk that he went on, visiting all these shops, and then do a murder where he's obviously at the scene of the crime using a weapon he's already associated with. I've heard the theory that maybe he just wants to be back inside but then why not confess?"

"There's not a lot of rhyme or reason to some people."

"What do you know about the prosecutor who withheld that fingerprint evidence during Dooley's first trial?" I ask.

"Yeah. That guy. He was up for reelection. Ashwood wanted somebody caught, and Dooley was convenient. I'm not saying Dooley was innocent, but I am saying that partial print deserved to see the inside of a courtroom."

"Will there be a retrial?"

"No way," she says.

Our cheesecake dessert arrives, and I fill her in on the drama at InovaSpire, including Varla's strange frostiness to me, and my very unhelpful evidence that Razor Johnny's family and the Brogan family had side-by-side booths at a county fair in 2007.

Steaks have appeared at the Brogan family table. Tilly is smiling. The kids are laughing. Dooley savors a bite with a look on his face that is just rapturous.

He's a man enjoying his new life. I try not to think about how short that new life might be if I don't figure a few things out.

Chapter Thirteen

Alexandru

The drive to Lindenfield, another suburb of Cleveland, takes just under an hour. Razor Johnny's mother manages a grocery store named Giant Eagle there.

Giant Eagle sits in a "strip mall" between a drugstore and place devoted entirely to the decoration of women's nails, if Ms. Renfield is to be believed.

Constant beeps emanate from contraptions up front, and the whole place hums with unseen machinery. There are a startling number of babies in here as well, judging from the wailing sounds. All in all, decidedly hellish.

Ms. Renfield pauses near a checkout stand, straightening her jacket.

"What are we waiting for?" I ask impatiently.

"I'm getting up my nerve," she says.

"Razor Johnny's mother agreed to speak with us, did she not?" It was Ms. Renfield's idea to ask her if Johnny had enemies, and to determine whether the state fair booth detail is significant.

"Still." Ms. Renfield approaches a young woman in a green apron and inquires after Mrs. Kennison. We are directed to a door marked "Employees Only." We find Razor Johnny's mother in a small office cluttered with papers. She is a stout woman in her sixties, steel-gray hair pulled back, glasses perched on her head. Her green shirt bears the store's eagle insignia.

"You're the folks who called about Johnny."

"Thank you for seeing us," Ms. Renfield says. "We're so, so sorry for your loss."

Johnny's mother gestures wearily to two plastic chairs. "Sit if you want. I've got ten minutes before I'm back out on the floor."

We sit.

Ms. Renfield folds her hands in her lap. "We're looking into your son's death. Privately. Not connected to the police."

"I figured as much. You don't look like cops." Her gaze slides to me. "Do you... have a podcast or something? Is that what this is?"

"We're interested in seeing this solved," Ms. Renfield says.

She's staring at my gloves. "Are you a movie star from England or something?"

"Just a concerned neighbor from Ashwood," Ms. Renfield says. "Can you think of anyone who might have wanted to hurt your son? Anyone who had a grudge against him?"

"I'll tell you what I told the cops: Johnny never talked about any enemies or people wanting to hurt him. Johnny wasn't the kind of man people wanted to hurt, I can promise you that." She rubs the bridge of her nose. "I know how people saw him what with the motorcycle gang and all. But he wasn't like that. He just wanted so badly to be cool. Fighting and all that. To have girls look at him and think he was somebody."

"Did he ever mention Dooley Brogan?" Ms. Renfield asks.

"Never heard of him until it was all over the news. Do you think he did it? The police let him go."

"We're going to find out," I assure her.

"Okay. Well... I don't know what help I can be. Johnny worked at an auto parts warehouse. He came by for dinner every month or so. Loved my meatloaf. I'd cook extra to send home with him." She looks down, and I fear she might cry, but she collects herself bravely. "Lord knows he made mistakes, but he always had a kind word and..." She heaves a sigh.

Ms. Renfield looks genuinely sympathetic. "I'm so sorry. He was too young."

The mother nods.

Ms. Renfield leans forward. "This might seem like an odd question, but do you remember having a booth at the county fair back in 2007?"

The woman blinks. "The county fair?"

"Your family and the Brogan family both had booths there. Right next to each other."

"The *county fair*? In 2007?"

"It's probably nothing," Ms. Renfield says.

"Well, I used to make earrings, and I'd do fairs now and then. Feathers and beads and all that. You're telling me the Brogans had a booth by me? It doesn't stick out as anything I recall..."

"So you don't remember meeting the Brogans during the fair? Or any weirdness with them?"

"I wasn't aware I ever even met a Brogan, but if you say we were at the fair..." She looks bewildered.

"Likely just random," Ms. Renfield says. We thank her for her time and make our way back through the fluorescent labyrinth. I pull my hat down as the electronic doors admit us to the dreadfully sunny parking lot.

We get into the car, but Ms. Renfield does not start the engine. "That was a whole lot of nothing."

"Indeed."

"So Dooley Brogan randomly killed that poor guy or somebody else is trying to frame him."

I'm barely listening. The mother's words keep circling back to me. *He just wanted so badly to be cool. Fighting and all that. To have girls look at him and think he was somebody.*

The thought surfaces before I can stop it: the training yard behind the castle, the smell of dust and horses. The cool weight of a sword in my hand and the warm sun on my cheeks.

And Elisabeta watching from the gallery above, dark hair loose over her shoulders. How hard I fought when she watched. Showing off. Desperate for her regard.

I feel Ms. Renfield watching me. "You all right? You got quiet."

"This investigation becomes tedious."

"We'll figure it out. Let's see if Hardware Sam knows anything new when they open tomorrow." She starts the car and we pull out of the parking lot, leaving the Giant Eagle behind.

Village men sit on chairs outside Hardware Sam's the next morning, paper coffee cups in hand, speaking in low voices. Ms. Renfield greets them brightly; even so, they are wary as we pass.

The store smells of sawdust and metal inside. A peasant pretends to be examining a package of lightbulbs but is in fact staring at me over the top of it. Truly. Even kittens know better than to gaze upon predators.

I greet Hardware Sam, a lanky man of perhaps seventy with leathery skin—a farmer once, by the look of him. Or perhaps he once drove a supply wagon.

Ms. Renfield grins at him. "I hear the police have been reaching out to every sporting goods store in the western hemisphere to find out who purchased that bolt that killed Razor Johnny."

Sam rolls his eyes. "Good luck with that. No murderer worth his salt's gonna buy something like that with anything but cash, and he'll go out of the region to do it. Or better yet, order it online."

"Oh, right," Ms. Renfield says. "You could order those things from anywhere in the world."

Pilar gazes adoringly at her mate. "Sam and the guys have been laughing about that."

"I think our boys in blue enjoy a little road trip around Ohio on a nice May afternoon, that's what I think," Sam says.

Bored now, I stroll around the store. The axe handles are of decent quality. The chains are sturdy. One could do worse for supplies, should certain needs arise.

Hardware Sam comes up next to me. "So who do you have doing your handyman stuff up there at Kingston Manor, if you don't mind my asking?"

"I don't mind in the least," I say. "My underling, Gregor, attends to the building."

"Underling." Sam laughs uncomfortably. "Well, if you ever need a specialist of any sort, I'd be happy to give you reliable referrals—electricians, plumbers, all licensed and bonded."

"Gregor sees to such matters. There is very little he cannot master." I pick up an octagonal metal item and turn it in the light. "He once repaired a collapsed wine cellar while three of his ribs were still knitting themselves back together."

Sam blinks, as if he cannot discern my meaning. "Okay. That's...impressive. But some of these older buildings have tricky wiring. Electricity's no joke. Your man could get quite a shock if he doesn't know what he's doing. Knocked flat on his back or worse."

I put back the octagonal item. "Could such a shock kill him?"

Sam frowns. "Not usually, but it's possible."

I wave my hand. "Gregor will be fine. He has an excellent constitution. He once fell from a battlement and was walking again within the week. More like dragging himself around, actually, but it did not seem to hamper him."

Sam's pulse kicks up—a bright spike of alarm—and then he begins to laugh. "Okay, okay, I get it. Message received. Your man's got it under control through thick and thin."

Pilar emerges from a nearby door marked "staff" with a tray of pastries. "Hot cross minis?"

Ms. Renfield is suddenly by my side. "We're saving ourselves for lunch."

"Your loss." Pilar ferries her tray out to the front, where the men sit talking. Ms. Renfield once told me that Pilar brings those pastries out at unpredictable intervals, just often enough to keep the townsfolk lingering, the gossip flowing. Clever woman. It is the same principle as a slop trough.

"So, did you hear anything else interesting?" Ms. Renfield asks.

Sam touches the side of his nose. "The police have an unusually open channel with the Snag Tooth Riders. They're promising to share any findings with those folks, trying to get a jump on extracurricular vigilantism, if you know what I mean."

"The police do not look kindly on that," Ms. Renfield says.

"There's something else..." Sam hesitates, serious now. "I talked to my mother on Sunday. She says she remembered something new. I don't know if it's anything. It might not be. You know her."

Everything in Ms. Renfield suddenly and quite mysteriously changes. Her pulse pounds furiously. Grief and dread roll off of her in waves.

"Is this about the Crossbow Killer?" I ask.

Hardware Sam and Ms. Renfield exchange glances. There is much they are not saying.

"Just a cold case." Ms. Renfield lies. "A thing from a long time ago."

"Hey." Sam snaps his fingers and turns to me. "Have you given any more thought to joining in on the men's poker game?"

I straighten. This peasant would try to distract me? "I would prefer to hear about this cold case."

"It's not important," Ms. Renfield insists.

I do not like this one bit. I turn to Hardware Sam. "This would be the poker game attended by Maverick Cooper and Derek Van Pelt the teacher?"

Sam smiles. "Them and a revolving cast of guys. Very low stakes. Get me your contact info and I'll send you the details. We'd love to have you."

"I look forward to it."

"What is this cold case that troubles you so?" I demand as we head back down the walkway.

"You know me," Ms. Renfield says. "Always trying to find people for my overlord to drain."

"You are hiding something."

She unlocks her car. "I think your vampire senses are on overdrive."

I get in and turn to her, letting a bit of ice creep into my voice. "I am not one of your village friends to be managed and deflected."

"Oh, don't worry, I'm well aware of that," she says.

"I await an explanation."

"Guess you'll be awaiting awhile." With that, she simply starts the car.

I know that tone. She will brook no further argument. I am thwarted. Genuinely, thoroughly thwarted, a sensation I have not experienced since before the Mongols burned the Carpathian Valley.

Thwarted by a human who should, by all rights, be kneeling at my feet.

It is intolerable.

I would have thrown her father into a dungeon for such impertinence. Three days in the darkness counting grains of rice tended to correct his behavior. I should consign her to the same fate.

The idea sits ill with me.

She would not break anyway.

I gaze out at the maddeningly quaint homes we pass on the way up to Bluff Road. The stupid geese with their mocking eyes. No Renfield has ever infuriated me so.

But then, that is not true.

The vision comes to me unbidden—Elisabeta draped in rubies and silk, looking down at me, eyes flashing in the torchlight.

"Tread carefully, little Renfield."

Ms. Renfield goes straight to her office, and I retire to my library.

The book I am reading, an account of equestrian practices in the 1700s, does not hold my attention in the least. I cast it aside and look for another, but I cannot banish the frustration this Renfield causes me.

I finally settle into my chair with a book of maps. I set to studying the lines, losing myself in memories of long past battles and hunts.

Gregor scuttles in to tend the fire. I watch him labor, a pathetic figure in front of the grand green marble surround. The admittedly magnificent stonework is one of the finest original architectural features in this old house. The marble had been plastered over some decades ago; the workers who toiled to restore this home informed me that this is what saved it from being vandalized by the hordes of squatters and marauding teenagers who dwelt here during its decrepitude.

Gregor pokes at the logs, attempting to arrange them in a pleasing way, hair clasped at the nape of his neck as it has been since he turned up at my door all those years ago.

I sit back and tune into the sounds of the mansion, mapping the slight groan of roof beams settling in the midmorning sun. A squirrel traversing the roof. The scratch of a beetle in the wainscoting. The *ticktock* of the foyer clock and the faint whir of the mechanical motion behind its casing. Wind stirs the trees along the bluff and the town beyond gives off a distinct hum.

And then:

Crunch.

Crunch.

Crunch-crunch-crunch.

Crunching. Cutting through it all.

Harriet.

Eating Bugles.

Crunch. Crunch. Tap tap. This is the sound of her working away in the south wing.

"Anything else you wish, overlord?" Gregor asks expectantly.

Annoyance spikes through me. These two underlings of mine truly are infuriating.

"Those Bugle corn chips of hers are an infernal breakfast food," I say. "I will not have my Renfield dying of scurvy or some such thing. You bring her an apple."

"Shall I inform her that you have instructed her to eat it?"

"No. You will carve the apple into a pleasing shape and then set it upon her desk. An untouched apple she might ignore, but an apple cut up specifically for her in a pleasing shape... She will not ignore that."

"Yes, overlord."

"You will hand-roll the pasta. Bring out your eyeglass and fashion each piece into a hawk—the hawk upon the crest of House Miramonte."

"Yes, overlord," Gregor says.

"You will once again mill grains from which you will bake bread, and you will hand-churn the butter, this time without making a dramatic show of it to Ms. Renfield, are we clear?"

"I have but eight hours. I am not sure I can accomplish these things, overlord. The pasta fashioning alone..."

"Am I to understand that you would rather languish in the cistern?"

"I will get right to work." With that, Gregor backs out of the room.

My enemy and once friend, Algernon a.k.a. Nero, would kill them both without a second thought. But then, Nero has no moral fiber whatsoever. No sense of propriety.

Chapter Fourteen

Harriet

I'm setting up some automations for Alexandru's minor holdings in Yugoslavia, but I'm not being very efficient. I just can't stop thinking of Sam's mother, Alma, possibly remembering something new about that day that James was taken.

Alma worked as a teacher at James's school. She told police she'd been walking home—she'd gotten just a block away from the school—when she passed a well-dressed man she didn't recognize. A tourist who didn't belong. Her report was dismissed. It was nearly full tourist season, and half the people in town didn't belong. Privately, I think it was also dismissed because she was sixty-five.

But I always thought Alma saw something real.

People think it's strange that I'd cling to such a vague detail. But Alma grew up in Ashwood, same as me. When you grow up in a tourist town, you develop a sense for who fits and who doesn't. It's not something you can articulate; it's something you know in your bones.

I had my own version of it: a black car I noticed that day that wasn't a tourist's car and wasn't a townie's car. I couldn't have said why. It just wasn't.

I grab a handful of Bugles.

It's probably nothing. Alma Washington has had flashes of memory before that amounted to nothing. One time she thought he wore dark blue shoes. I asked her if she thought they were tennis shoes or blue boots or some kind of loafer, but she wasn't sure.

Sometimes I think she just likes to connect with me about it. It was an intense time for both of us, me because it was my fault James was taken, and she saw that strange man, and nobody thought it was anything.

Was the man she spotted the culprit?

I told myself so many stories about what happened in the years after James disappeared. He was always wandering off, of course. I would imagine he'd joined the circus or a cowboy ranch. He could've wandered off and been picked up by somebody desperate for a child of their own to love. He could've hit his head and gotten amnesia.

What could Alma have remembered now? Maybe I shouldn't go, but I always do. And I always bring her an antique spoon for her collection when I visit, and she makes us cranberry tea.

I click into our antique store's email account to see what's been delivered lately in order to get a sense of what old spoons we might have on hand, and I note with some consternation that Mom and Granabelle aren't doing a very good job with inventory.

Right then, Gregor comes in with a plate with three coils on it, like strange little Slinkys. He tremblingly sets the plate on my desk.

"What are these?"

"They are apple slices, milady."

I pick up one of them and it expands. "How'd you do it?"

"It is a spiral fashioned of apple."

"Really?" I look up. "That's amazing. Is this a hobby of yours?"

"A hobby?!"

"Yeah, a hobby. Something that you enjoy doing?"

Gregor blinks. "It's for you to eat."

"This is so cool though. Are you sure it's not your secret hobby?"

"It is not!" he protests, weirdly alarmed.

"No, it's cool. It's good to have a hobby. Look, come here." I lead him over to the table by the window, where my coin tower complex sits. "This is my secret little hobby—stacking up quarters and making them into towers and buildings and things. It probably seems stupid, but it calms my mind so much, you have no idea."

"What do you do with these...towers?" he asks.

"Nothing. It just calms me in a deep way to make them, and to look at them. It calms me and it centers me and it's also pleasurable. I'm just showing you because a hobby can be as stupid as that. We should think of a hobby for you to do!"

He seems fixated on the little stacks that I've started. "What do you do when you run out of coins? Do you knock them down and start over?"

"No way! I would never knock these down. I don't even like thinking about it. They're like my anchor, you know?"

He nods.

I'm pleased he's asking questions. Questions show interest. "A hobby doesn't have to be really obvious, like Alexandru doesn't even have to know. You could hunt for four-leaf clovers in the grass and when you find one, we could press it into a book. A hobby can be as simple as that."

"It would not be for me to have a hobby."

"Why not?"

"It is not for me."

"How can it not be for you. Who says? Is that what Alexandru says?"

Gregor shakes his head vigorously. "It is simply not the way of things with me."

I pick up a spiral. "But look how creative you are. This could be your hobby! Carving apples into cool shapes like this?"

"That is for you to eat."

"Alexandru didn't tell you to carve them like this, did he?"

"This carving is of my own design."

"Newsflash: you could go to the state fair with these. You'd probably win a prize."

"These are for you to eat. Nothing more."

"How am I supposed to eat it when it's so beautiful?!"

Gregor seems alarmed at this point. "Perhaps a bit of cinnamon shaken onto them? Would that make them more pleasing?"

"I can't eat them *because* they are so pleasing! They're too beautiful! Wait—I have to take a picture!" I whip out my phone and take a few pictures.

This seems to upset Gregor even more. He walks out of the

room, returning a minute later with some sort of a small mallet and smashes each of the spirals.

"What are you doing?"

He sets down a spoon. "A snack. Nothing more." He turns on his heel and stalks from the room.

"I'm eating them right now!" I call after him, because obviously that's important to him. "Delicious!"

I feel like a jerk. I want to help him, not upset him, but it seems like that's all I do.

I take a spoonful of smashed apple spiral and update some spreadsheets.

The day is a whirlwind of little fires to put out. When I next look up, it's three in the afternoon. I have a conference call with Tokyo scheduled for 4 p.m.; the perfect amount of time to zip down to the store.

I stroll behind the counter. "Somebody's been neglecting inventory."

"An antique store has no need for keeping inventory," Granabelle says. "It's not as if we can re-order a taxidermy weasel from the 1950s when Dawson sells." She shifts her gaze to Dawson, who's been collecting dust behind the counter since before I was born.

"But you could re-order more weird mid-century conversation items of a certain price point. That's how I always did it."

Mom strolls up, tapping her head. "The inventory is here. To what do we owe this honor? Don't tell me you're here just to lecture us."

"Just out doing errands and things."

Granabelle adjusts her cap, a 1970s newsboy number, very Annie Hall. "Any sleuthing updates?"

I catch them up on what we've learned. It turns out that they already know about Hardware Sam's retail text chain. I mention the two families having booths near each other at a long-ago state fair.

Mom snorts. "That's thin."

"Maybe they sabotaged each other's booths," Granabelle suggests.

"I think she would've remembered that." I pull out my phone. "Check out what Gregor did this morning. He carved an apple into little spirals."

Mom takes the phone. "Wow. He did this by hand?"

"He does everything by hand. It's a thing with Alexandru, which, it's a bit excessive, honestly."

Granabelle examines the photo over her shoulder. "Very impressive."

"Sometimes he hand-churns butter."

"Why the hell would he do that?" Mom barks.

"I know. I told Alexandru it's so screwed up to have him do that when they can buy it at Gable's, but..." I shake my head.

"That man really gets a lot done," Mom says. "You know he was over the other day to clean the windows and repair the leaky shower."

"Wait, what? He was?"

"Alexandru sent him. You didn't know?"

"Not at all."

"Did you know about the steps back there?"

I frown. "The death trap steps?"

"Not anymore."

I follow Mom through the store toward the back. I live in fear of somebody falling on them—either Granabelle or Mom or a customer, who would definitely sue the store. Sure enough, there's a beautiful new set of steps leading down to the alley— with a safety railing and everything.

"These must have cost a mint."

"They had a mixer truck," Granabelle puts in. "An entire mixer truck for our back steps."

"You think Alexandru sent the truck?"

"I know he did. Gregor was overseeing the whole thing. I thought you were in on it."

I'm thinking suddenly of the household repair list I made one night in the study after dinner. Alexandru and I had been sitting by the fire, and he'd asked what was bedeviling me. Those were the words he used. I told him it was antique store stuff. Had he caught sight of the list with his hawk-like vision?

"Well...weird." I don't love the dissonance of Alexandru doing nice things.

"I think it's thoughtful," Mom says.

"I need to pay him back."

"From where I'm sitting, you've made him a pretty penny compared to what your train-jumping freak of a father managed for him," Mom says.

Mom is very un-sentimental about my father, who she met exactly once on a train speeding through the Carpathian Mountains in Eastern Europe. She was twenty-two and back-packing through Europe, and he was...well she claims that he was hot. They played cards, drank whiskey, and banged, and then he jumped out of the train. The speeding train.

"I updated the systems. Anybody would've done it." We talk some more store business. On the way out, I grab a cute linen tablecloth for my side table, and I rummage through the spoon box and find a 1910 spoon commemorating the statehood of Tennessee to give to Hardware Sam's mom, Alma, when I visit. I stuff them both in my bag and make a note of it in the borrows and barters area of our sales book.

"What's the spoon for?" Mom asks.

I cringe; I was hoping she wouldn't notice. "Just some stuff I'm grabbing." I pull out the tablecloth. "This is for my little table on the wall opposite the fireplace."

"And the spoon? You're not going over to Alma's again, are you?"

I straighten. "I can't visit an old friend?"

"She's not your old friend; she's a lonely old woman who's discovered that having 'information' gets people to visit. Don't let her do this to you, Harriet."

"She's not doing anything to me."

"She's saying she remembers something more, isn't she? Maybe there's a freckle on his hand now. Maybe there was a plane in the sky at the time she passed him on the sidewalk."

"All data is worth having," I say.

"Not if it's hogwash."

Mom blames Alma for "getting my head all spun around" on James, as though Alma's the one who made me think what happened to him is something other than the Cuyahoga Killer taking him.

As though Alma's responsible for my unshakeable belief that James is still alive.

The Cuyahoga Killer confessed to burying his victims "in

the wild" before he himself died. Mom and Granabelle and pretty much everybody else thinks James is one of those victims dead in the wild.

I won't believe that. I can't.

I don't fault her for feeling upset that I won't accept his being dead. I can't pretend to know anything about the torment she's been through with it all.

But I know he's alive. I know it with everything in me.

I get out of there, but not before Mom invites Alexandru and Gregor and me to dinner on Thursday. I make a mental note to figure out how to never have that happen, because I can't think of a worse dinner party.

I leave a message on the way back to Kingston Manor for Alma to call me. I tell her I have a little something for her.

As I drive up to Kingston Manor, I catch myself thinking how having all those things fixed at the shop was almost...decent of him. Which is a dangerous thought to have about someone like Alexandru.

Realistically, I should be looking for ways to kill him—he sees people as livestock, after all.

Then again, is being mad at a vampire for killing the same as being mad at a cat for catching a mouse? And when you look at it logically, *the only-murderers-drained* policy is making people safer.

Though he did force me to be his assistant and to work for him—and to live in his mansion. And he does seem to make a cottage industry out of mistreating Renfields, but he has become better in other ways, like he isn't making Gregor call him master anymore. And I'm pretty sure he heard me when I told him how I don't like it when Gregor labors over these elaborate dinners.

If I charted his behavior over the past few months, there'd be an actual upwards trendline. A small one. Barely visible to the naked eye. But it would be there.

I asked more of him and he came through.

And now I keep circling back to the thing I haven't told him —James. It is a central feature of my life, losing my brother the way I did. I think about it all the time, even obsess about it.

My fingers find the key around my neck.

I wouldn't exactly say that he deserves to know but letting him in about that is a gesture of trust, I'm telling him that I believe he's capable of some humanity.

A little voice in my head reminds me that he's not human.

I stop in front of the mansion and stare at the steps, remembering how it felt to stand there with him, how much fun we were having, and my heart suddenly swooping with the strange, giddy sense that we fit in some weird way.

The way he went still, eyes dark, fixed on me like I was something he wanted to devour.

And how badly I wanted to let him.

My face goes hot. I grip the wheel. Get ahold of myself.

Chapter Fifteen

Alexandru

Ms. Renfield is not one to dress for dinner. She wears what she always wears: her knit jacket—brown tonight—over slim pants and brown boots. Her raven hair is clipped back, exposing the pale column of her throat, and her lips are painted the usual bright red, a color that draws the eye, though I refuse to let mine linger. She wears the long gold chain bearing the mysterious key she pretends is merely decorative, but I can tell that it is more.

Aside from the red-painted lips, her presentation is practical, as befitting a Renfield. Right for her in a way that I cannot describe. Even the little clips that hold her hair.

She is very much exactly as she should be. Nothing to improve upon, nothing to adjust. Not that it matters. One is simply gratified when one's subordinate presents herself adequately.

She takes her place to the right of where I sit at the head of the table. Gregor has set out cheese and crackers and Bugles. He pours her a glass of beer.

"Not too much! This is a working dinner," she says.

Unlike her cowering predecessors, Ms. Renfield enjoys working dinners. Probably because she is the first to have anything worth presenting.

She proudly shows me the "PowerPoint" of all that she's been up to. Something about automations in Yugoslavia. She makes much ado of the increasing balance in my various bank accounts, which is, admittedly, impressive.

We discuss the mystery and next steps. She is still struggling to find a connection between Dooley and Razor Johnny.

She places a slice of cheese upon a cracker. "We need those prison visit logs to come through."

"How much longer must we wait?" I demand.

"It's only been a couple of days. Trust me. This is the fastest way of obtaining them. Without bloodshed, at least." She chews thoughtfully.

"I believe that is my line," I say.

Her eyes sparkle. Then, "So, I need to tell you something."

I study her face, sensing the gravity behind her words.

She will tell me her secret. At last.

"What is it?" I inquire casually.

Just then, Gregor comes in with the meal, interrupting us. It is so very like him to choose this moment to intrude.

"Thank you!" Ms. Renfield takes a theatrical whiff of the food he spoons onto her plate. "Smells delish!"

"Thank you, milady."

I give him an icy look. He startles and backs out of the room.

Ms. Renfield furrows her brow. "Are these little bats?"

"No, they are hawks."

"It would be better if it was bats," she says. "I've heard vampires can turn into bats."

"We most certainly do not. I believe I have informed you—"

Her pretty lips twist into a playful rosebud. Ah. So she teases me.

She stares at her bowl. "Where did you get little pasta things shaped like hawks? I didn't know that pasta came in shapes like that. Is it a Romanian thing?"

"The hawk is the sigil of the house of Dracul."

She blinks into her spoon. "Dude, you have custom pasta? Wait...the hawks look almost... hand-made." Her gaze flings up. "Don't tell me that Gregor spent his entire afternoon carving these tiny hawks!"

"Who else would have done it?"

"That's not even the question! This must have taken him forever!" It is here her gaze falls to the butter. "Did you make him churn butter again?"

"It is the way of this house. He is lucky that I did not put him in the cistern after his dramatics the last time he churned."

"I seriously can't believe you."

"I tire of your pathetic morals. Perhaps I should put you in the cistern."

Ms. Renfield stands. "Perhaps I would prefer the cistern to your company." With that, she stomps off.

I remain in my seat, stewing.

Thoughts of putting Renfields in cisterns have always brought satisfaction in the past. The Renfields owe me a debt that cannot be repaid in a single lifetime—indeed, cannot be repaid in ten lifetimes—and it is right and correct that they should suffer—all of them. Forever.

And yet, when I picture Ms. Renfield huddled down there in the darkness, pulling her sweater jacket tightly around herself against the cold and batting spiders from her hair, something in me revolts.

Ms. Renfield orders "to-go" food the next day—a pungent dish of broccoli and chicken with hot garlic sauce, delivered by a young person who reeks of fear and fascination—and retreats to her wing for the remainder of the day.

Hiding.

With her odorous chicken. As if I do not notice.

What secret was she going to tell me? It is truly infuriating.

The following day she informs me through Gregor that she has determined a slate of properties must be sold quickly before they depreciate.

Through Gregor. As though he is an appropriate intermediary between a Renfield and her overlord.

I demand that she produce the spreadsheet I know she has created to support this decision, and that she present it to me immediately.

She brings the sheet to the great hall, lips fixed in a frown. She weighs it down with four candlesticks, setting them down with rather more force than necessary. And yet, as she walks me through her reasoning, each conclusion building upon the last, her irritation seems to lift. She does so love to display her data.

I request clarifications. The administrative minutiae of former Renfields never held my attention, but this Renfield has a way of making things interesting. When I have heard enough, I roll the sheet and hand it to her. She snatches it from my hand, amber eyes bright in the firelight.

"And the visitor logs?" I ask. "The crossbow bolt? What news is there on my next meal?" I settle back in my chair, voice sharp, now. "The hour grows late, little Renfield."

"I feel sure the visitor logs will come soon," she says, and goes on to inform me that hapless Officer Maverick Cooper and his bungling underlings have still not identified the origin of the bolt that killed the man; this she learned from her Granabelle, who learned it from Hardware Sam.

"This progress is not impressive." I remind her that I will soon take my meal of convicted murderer Dooley Brogan, since he did at least one murder.

"Well, he might not have done any murders!"

"He was tried by a jury of fellow peasants."

A thrum of outrage swells in her chest. "But there were problems that made the trial unfair. Also, they are known as peers, not peasants."

"As you wish." I move to the fire, savoring the contours of her emotions and the way the scent of her blood intermingles with the burning oak. "If there are any other developments in the case, you will inform me at once."

The following afternoon, she orders a "rice bowl" from the "Bowls 4U" down on River Road, and it is delivered by the same young man, less fearful now. This meal was especially confounding being that no bowl was included in the delivery, according to Gregor.

I am attending to some correspondence the next morning when I hear the exclamation from her office.

"Come to mama!"

I set down my pen, intrigued. My Renfield has borne no children and indeed no other human has entered the mansion.

Footsteps come my way. She bursts into the library holding her electronic ledger aloft like the head of a slain warrior. "The prison logs!"

"Where?" I demand.

"In here!"

"That is your electronic ledger."

"They were emailed to me," she says. "It's not like they keep them on paper."

I grumble. "And what do these so-called logs say?"

"I thought we could look at them together!"

I narrow my eyes. She could simply have opened them and informed me of the answer.

I do not know why she has not done so, but I find I am glad for it.

"Come. Make haste, Renfield."

She smiles and takes the seat next to me and points to a line of nonsense words. "That's the email address of Evergreen Correctional," she says. "That's where Dooley Brogan served time. Subject line: FOIA number 5430449VLS requested logs." I can feel her gaze upon the side of my face.

"Are you waiting for something?" I demand.

"Yes! For you to savor how fast these came, and how unbelievably effective it was to send their office those cookies from Berky's."

She wishes me to smile. To take pleasure in her pride. "You had no way of knowing how long it would have taken them to send those logs had you *not* sent those pastries," I point out.

"It's usually seven to ten days and this was only five! Pastry diplomacy beats intimidation every time."

I make a sound of disgust.

With a flourish, Ms. Renfield taps the screen and slides her finger up, doing her "scrolling" and there it is, a sort of grid that seems to be composed of dates, names, duration of visit, and some other random numbers.

"What the..." she mumbles. "This can't be right."

I lean in. "Jerome Goodwin. Was that the man in the shiny purple undergarments? Who we spoke with the day of the murder? Your friend from the high school newspaper?"

"Yeah. He visited eight times in the last few months, and there are as many phone calls."

"An interesting development," I say. "I seem to remember informing you that he was fearful. Hiding something. And what was it that you said in reply?"

She snorts softly, refusing to look at me.

"I believe you said my vampire senses were working overtime."

"Whatever you say, Bitey McBiteface." She makes notes on the tablet with her fake pencil.

Never have I encountered a human so determined to vex me—nor one I found it so difficult to silence. Well, never would be incorrect.

I will not think of that.

She strolls to the fireplace. "I don't understand. Why would he be calling and visiting Dooley so often? And even weirder, why would Dooley not tell us. We didn't ask Jerome point-blank about the prison visits, but we asked Dooley. And he *hid* it."

I sit back and cross my legs. "Perhaps your Jerome Goodwin is not what he seems."

Ms. Renfield frowns. "I don't like this. Jerome is an old friend."

"Old friends can be among the most dangerous of liars."

She turns to me, interest sharpening. "Do you have an old friend who's a dangerous liar?"

"I do. Needless to say, he's not my friend anymore."

"Sounds like quite a story!"

"Oh, it is." I rise from my chair and go to stand next to her, feeling pleased at this shift in her mood. "Where can we find this Jerome? Do you know?"

"I've got his address somewhere. I think he lives up by the music conservatory." She ponders a bit, examining the fire.

I wait, enjoying our companionable silence.

I turn to her, gazing down at her. Right then, she looks up at me, and for a moment neither of us speaks.

The firelight catches the curve of her throat, and I find myself marking the steady pulse there, resisting the impulse to trace that path upward, from pulse to her parted lips. I can feel that rise in her—the quickening pulse, the warmth blooming beneath her skin. I would not kiss such a one. The notion is preposterous.

And yet I do not step back.

She blinks, seems to snap out of it. "Okay, well, should we see if we can catch Jerome home? Better sooner than later, I guess."

"Agreed."

She grabs her electronic ledger and hurries out of the room. I follow her down the curved stairway on into the great foyer.

Gregor is waiting there for me. He hands me my gloves and a day walking hat.

"Thank you, Gregor," Ms. Renfield says on my behalf, and proceeds out the door.

Gregor watches her leave, scowling.

I give him a hard look and he lowers his gaze.

Chapter Sixteen

Alexandru

"This is a really cute area," Ms. Renfield says as we stroll down a street overlooking the river. She points to three vine-covered stone buildings. "The Ashwood musical conservatory is in those buildings. Lots of students and artsy types live and work in these old buildings all around here."

The buildings are older and statelier than the quaint shops down by the river, the "downtown."

What *is* bedeviling about this place is the music assaulting me from all angles. Violins sawing away to my left, a saxophone braying to my right, and what sounds like an electronic clavichord from a window above.

I've had centuries of practice filtering out human noise, but this is overmuch even for me. "The cacophony."

"Look! Your house." Ms. Renfield points east.

And there it is. Kingston Manor, perched on the ridge not a half mile distant, its spire rising up like a dark finger against the sky.

We set down the sidewalk towards Jerome's building.

"Is Jerome some manner of artsy type?"

"Journalism is kind of artsy-adjacent. His Substack really is excellent. I'm thinking that's why he was visiting Dooley all those times—he was working on some sort of story."

"Why would Dooley lie about it?"

"I'm sure there's an explanation." Ms. Renfield stops in front of an old brick building with rows of windows marking its three stories. Nervousness radiates from her. A little bit of dread. She is loath to question her high school friend.

"Well?" I ask impatiently.

"I just hate showing up unannounced like this. I don't want him to put us off, and it's not like we can do this in text. I want you to be able to get a read on him."

"That I will do," I say to her.

She turns to me with a pleading look. "Just don't antagonize him. Let me run this question-and-answer session."

I shrug wearily. "I will allow it. For now."

She takes a breath and pushes a button mounted next to the door. A corresponding buzz sounds from one of the second-floor windows. There is movement. An indistinct figure appears in front of gossamer curtains, there and gone.

We wait.

She tries again. "What if he's not home?"

"He's home. He just looked at us from the window."

"You saw him in a window?"

"He came to see who was calling."

"How do you know which apartment he lives in?"

"I heard the buzzer. Second window to the far right."

"Come on, Jerome, just answer," Ms. Renfield says under her breath.

"He is at the window again," I inform her. "Wave at him as though you see him."

"I feel like such a jerk." But she waves at him nevertheless. A moment later there's a crackling sound from the buttons console. A voice: "Hello?"

"Hey, Jerome," Ms. Renfield says. "It's Harriet! So sorry to drop by so weirdly without texting, but Alexandru and I were in the neighborhood, and we have a really important quick question for you."

"Ummm, can't it wait? I've got a million things happening right now."

"Just a quick sec? It's kind of important!" she says brightly.

"I mean, okay, If it's quick."

A buzzer sounds, and Harriet pulls open the heavy door. We climb a short flight of stairs with treads covered in faded patterned carpet. An old chandelier hangs overhead, and numbered doors line the second-floor hallway.

"I am expending so much social capital," Ms. Renfield says.

"Social capital?"

She lowers her voice. "It's like, how much leeway you have to push your friends. How much they'll roll with it."

We reach the door marked 207.

She spins around and whispers, "Remember: I'm doing the talking."

Behind her the door is flung open, and there is Jerome, looking haggard. His short dark hair is not formed in the uniform shape that it was when we first met him, he carries the faint salt of recent exertion.

"Hey, uh—what's up?" he asks, fairly vibrating with tension.

"Thanks for seeing us," Ms. Renfield says. "You remember Alexandru."

I extract a calling card from the gold case. "Miramonte."

Jerome stares down at the card and up at me. I enjoy the moment of outrage pulsing through Ms. Renfield.

Ms. Renfield says, "I know you're busy, but we've been looking into this whole Razor Johnny killing just because... well, reasons."

Guilt and fear pour off of Jerome. "What does that have to do with me? I didn't see anything that day."

"Right, but as you know, Dooley Brogan is a lead suspect, and I had taken the liberty of requesting some of the prison visitor logs. You know me, always there with the FOIA stuff, and it turns out that you had visited him a bunch of times and you had also had a number of phone calls with him."

His fear spikes. "Th-the visitor logs?"

"Well, yeah, and I thought maybe you might know something that could potentially cast some light on the whole situation since you were talking with him." She smiles, seeming to want to put him at ease, Lord knows why. Certainly not for the purposes of an effective interrogation.

Jerome tries for a smile. "So you two are conducting an investigation of some kind?"

"Yes," Ms. Renfield begins, forgetting that she is not the subject of this interrogation. "You know me—"

I break in. "Why did you visit him so many times?"

"Um... Alexandru..." Ms. Renfield says.

"It is what we wish to know," I point out.

Fear tightens its grip on Jerome. "Okay, okay, but I don't have much time." He gestures us into a small, spartan apartment. Papers and laptops litter a table; a threadbare couch sits against one wall. He closes the door behind us. "Look, here's the situation—just between us—I've got a book deal—"

"What? Jerome!" Ms. Renfield hugs him. "Oh my gosh, that's amazing!"

"Well... thank you. It's about prison life, like tales from the inside and how people adjust psychologically. The social groups. I signed an NDA with my publisher, and Dooley signed one, too, so... you can't tell anybody, Harriet. I don't want to screw up this deal."

Ms. Renfield gives me a triumphant look. "An NDA is a non-disclosure agreement. It means that you're not supposed to tell anybody about the book." She turns back to Jerome. "The police are going to find out about your visits sooner or later. They'll take a look at those logs soon if they haven't already."

"So... they're that sure it's Dooley?"

"I don't know. Dooley has no alibi and it is his MO. You're a reporter. You know how this works."

Jerome sinks onto his couch and puts his face in his hands. "This is such a mess."

"Why is it a mess? You signed an NDA. I'm sure there are exceptions to that sort of thing, like police making you tell. Surely your publisher would understand."

"I know, I know," Jerome says morosely. "The idea he could do such a thing. It's shocking, is all."

I detect something sharper. His heart rate has climbed, and his cortisol levels are spiking. This man is panicking.

The wail of police sirens rises in the distance, mingling

with the instruments. The two of them don't seem to notice. These humans have such paltry senses; it never ceases to amaze me.

"Jerome," I say. "Did Dooley Brogan know Razor Johnny?"

Jerome looks up. "I don't know. I don't think he did."

"Have you spoken with Dooley recently?" Ms. Renfield asks.

"Not since all this..." Jerome waves a vague hand. "I can't imagine...I just...hate that it would be Dooley Brogan."

"You've formed a bond," Ms. Renfield puts in on his behalf.

"I suppose."

Ms. Renfield gives him a sympathetic look.

Does she not see what is happening? Jerome is hiding something. Feeling guilty about something, and it is connected to Dooley Brogan.

"Dooley Brogan was just my second subject," Jerome says. "If you look, you'll see that I paid a similar number of visits to a guy named Mason Hamlin."

"And you were giving Dooley money for his commissary?" she asks.

"You're really thorough," Jerome says. "I shouldn't be surprised, I guess."

A twinge of guilt rolls off Ms. Renfield now. There is a familiar flavor to it... it comes to me that she's thinking about the high school newspaper incident again. "You know me. Triple-checking everything."

"No—I didn't mean to say it like that," Jerome says. "I wasn't talking about the swim team scoop. You were doing your best back then. You made the best call you could."

"No, I was wrong. We didn't need that extra week of

checking things," Ms. Renfield says. "Sloane has a right to be mad."

"But holding a grudge sixteen years later? It's not like you were maliciously trying to squash her story."

They discuss Sloane a bit more—Sloane, the peasant who runs the fancy paper shop. Ms. Renfield's "frenemy."

Jerome is feeling more comfortable now that he has moved the conversation off of Dooley Brogan.

Which only serves to put his previous panic and guilt into stark relief.

Chapter Seventeen

Harriet

"Seriously? With the calling cards?"

"That male is hiding something."

"Yes, he is. A book deal that he's not supposed to talk about."

"It's something more."

"Are you mad I hugged him or something?"

"No, though it might've been best if you hadn't supplied him with answers to the questions you asked."

I stop at the car door and turn to him. "What is that supposed to mean?"

"The man is a friend, and you have a bias that does not allow you to see him clearly. When you were asking him about his feelings regarding Dooley Brogan, you broke into his explanation, offering that he had formed a bond with the man. You presented a reason for his emotions. I wanted to hear his reason, not the one you supplied."

"I guess I offered it up, but..."

"And then you allowed him to switch the subject to the

high school newspaper and Sloane. You have such an emotional charge about it that you could not see that he was doing it. You were not observing him objectively in any way."

"I can be nice to a person and still retain my objectivity."

"Can you?"

I get in. "Don't you remember what I told you about being nice to people? How it makes them cooperate more? Because you can't hang them from their toes in this country?"

Alexandru buckles his seat belt. Not because he needs to care about safety, but he hates that little beep, thank goodness. "Jerome is awash in guilt, fear, paranoia and panic. Mark my words, he's hiding something."

"Oh, he's a suspect now?"

Alexandru shrugs. "He did have a so-called 'beef' with the murder victim. That's more than you can say of Dooley Brogan."

"We've already discussed this, Alexandru. Journalists fight with words. He's not going to go killing a person because they rode a motorcycle over his grandmother's flower bed years ago. And then framing an innocent man for it?"

Alexandru stares out at the river, or maybe the rolling hills and patches of farmland beyond it. It's early evening, and the sun is low, casting long shadows across the landscape.

"Flashing blue lights."

"Where?"

"The center of town. Gazebo Park."

"Gazebo Park's not visible from here."

"The treetops are. Can you not see? There were sirens before. I believe a police incident took place in town. And that incident continues."

"I hope it's not a fire or something!"

"Or another murder."

"Are the lights near my family's store?"

"They are not."

I nod, relieved.

Alexandru and Gregor and I were just over there for dinner. Granabelle was in 1940s garb. Mom was annoyed that Alexandru was on his strange European intermittent fasting diet, and bewildered at Gregor's gruel-only diet, but all in all, it went okay.

Gazebo Park sits at the center of town, the jewel of Ashwood with its expanse of green grass and trees and groups of benches and picnic areas. A bluff rises up behind it, forming a sort of overlook over it all.

It's quite pretty, except for the bright yellow crime scene tape stretched from the Victorian gazebo to a wrought-iron bench to a large oak tree.

A giant triangle. A crime scene.

We get out and wander over to stand by some kids I don't recognize.

There's a group of officials at the far end of the taped-off crime scene. When the crowd shifts, I get a view of a body covered by a white sheet. And that sheet is tented.

Another crossbow murder.

"No," I whisper.

The body is loaded onto a stretcher and brought to a nearby van.

"Do we know who that is?" I ask the strangers around me.

What I get is that it was a man. Thirty-ish years old. Brown hair.

I look around for somebody I know so I can ask them what happened. I lock eyes with Maverick Cooper.

"Please promise not to antagonize Maverick," I say.

"I have no interest in antagonizing the hapless," he says.

"What? I'm a hapless human and you antagonize me all the time."

"You are made of different stuff, Ms. Renfield."

"Not my name," I say as Maverick lifts the crime tape and strolls on over to us, chomping his gum, with an expression something between a smile and a look of suspicion.

"How's it going, Maverick," I say. "You remember Alexandru."

"The *prince*. How could I forget?" He says the word prince like it's in quotation marks.

"Maverick," Alexandru says, also quotation-marks-sounding.

"So what happened?" I ask.

Maverick doesn't answer right away because apparently we've gone directly to the pissing-match portion of the interaction which involves Maverick staring at Alexandru while chomping his gum loudly, and Alexandru looking ever so faintly amused.

Alexandru thinks Maverick's still hung up on me. And Maverick dislikes Alexandru due to Alexandru's general arrogance, and I sometimes wonder if he maybe intuits Alexandru's disregard for human laws and let's just say all sense of morality. Cops have Spidey senses, too.

"So…" I try again.

"What happened is police business," Maverick says finally.

"Who was that?"

"And that would be police business," Maverick says. "Understood?"

"Is it somebody I know?"

Maverick squints into the middle distance. "I understand you two paid a visit to Dooley Brogan the other day. What was that all about?"

"We wished to assess his guilt or innocence in the crime," Alexandru says unhelpfully.

"Is that for you to do?" Maverick asks him.

"It is if I wish it," Alexandru says.

"That would be where you're wrong," Maverick says. "In America, the police investigate the crimes, and it is up to the judicial system to determine guilt or innocence. There is no place in that equation for a Euro prince."

Alexandru smiles at Maverick. "I have always found equations to be rather flexible things. One simply needs to introduce the right variable."

"Come on, Maverick," I say. "There's no rule against citizens caring about their community."

"Until it rises to the level of obstruction of justice," Maverick says. "I'm warning you, stay out of this investigation."

"I can't believe you won't tell us something that everybody up and down Commerce Street probably already knows."

Maverick turns and heads back to the scene.

"Like he won't even tell us what happened?"

Alexandru's voice goes icy. "There are those who, once they have power over another, cannot resist grinding it in.

Taking all that they can." His lip curls. "Eventually, that debt comes due."

I look up at him, surprised by the intensity of his words.

He's not talking about Maverick anymore. I don't think he's talking about Maverick, anyway.

"We need to find out what's going on." I gaze up the street a ways and catch sight of Josie's mom, Rita, watering the flowers in the flower boxes that separate the sidewalk from the restaurant's brightly decorated outdoor patio.

I drag Alexandru over to have a little chat with Rita. The place is half filled with tourists having an early dinner.

"Harriet! Prince Miramonte! Are you coming to dine?"

"No, we were just wondering what happened over there."

Rita claps a fist to her chest. "You haven't heard? It was another murder. Another crossbow murder."

"No!" I say. "What happened?"

Rita gazes darkly in the direction of the park. "It was Milo Cirillo. Do you know him?"

"I feel like I've heard of him."

"He came to town maybe a year ago. Lives down on some of those river condos. Works for the *Great Lakes Dispatch*."

"A journalist," Alexandru observes.

"Fern from the Golden Stag was the one who discovered the body. She was down there on a vape break and you could hear the scream to Creighton. Maverick and the boys got here right away." Rita looks around as if to confirm nobody is listening, and then she lowers her voice. "Fern says she saw Dooley Brogan in the bushes nearby. Hiding."

Ms. Renfield's eyes widen. "Seriously? She's sure?"

"That's what she said. She sees the body, calls 911. There

were tourists around, and one of them tried CPR. And then something catches Fern's eye up beyond the gazebo and she's ninety percent sure it's Dooley Brogan. She said he made out of there like a bat out of hell."

"Hiding in the bushes. Highly suspicious," Alexandru observes.

Rita sighs. "It's just so shocking. Dooley Brogan of all people. I couldn't believe it the first time around. He'd always seemed a decent sort."

"You knew him, Rita?"

"I took my van to him all the time. And my little Vespa. He was fair in what he charged. Kind to everybody. Did great work. Never made sense that he'd go and shoot a man with a crossbow, but you never know what's in a man's heart, I suppose."

Some customers come to the host stand and Rita excuses herself.

I turn to Alexandru. "Sounds like we should go have a cocktail at the Golden Stag."

Chapter Eighteen

Harriet

Whereas the Tres Hermanas steakhouse is bright, retro, and casually elegant, the Golden Stag is a darkish supper club with dusty chandeliers, vinyl booths, and historic photos of old-timey Ashwood on the walls, and about fifty percent of those pictures show men in hats and suspenders trying to push vehicles through the muck along River Road.

The place is doing a pretty good business for happy hour, though.

We request a table in Fern's section and are led past the long, heavily mirrored bar area where Sloane and local photographer Valerie Johnson seem to be having drinks and into the dining room where we're seated at a nice table against the wall.

"Grrreat. Look who's up at the bar."

"Ah, it is Sloane, your stationary shop frenemy," Alexandru observes.

"Shop frenemy and reason everybody thinks you're a prince. So ridiculous."

"It is not so ridiculous. Yes, it is an archaic title that has fallen out of use, but it makes sense that people would call me thus being that my kind is superior in every way, and your kind is there to feed me and, in your case, serve me."

"Groan. So wrong."

"I suppose it is wrong in that a prince serves under a king. I bow to nobody."

"Do you recognize the woman with her?" I ask, deciding not to indulge him further. "Valerie with the bright red glasses?"

"Of course. The photographer from Bo Richardson Photography."

Alexandru met them both last month when we were investigating the wedding murders. Bo Richardson turned out to be the culprit. He "mysteriously disappeared" a.k.a. was drained by Alexandru.

"Well, Valerie runs the show now. It's Valerie Johnson Photography now. I didn't know they were friends."

Sloane gives a little finger wave.

"Please, no, don't come over," I whisper into my menu.

"Maybe they have information to impart. Who is it that is always saying all data is valuable?"

"Shut the bitey hole," I say.

When next I look up, I see Sloane and Valerie wandering over. The two of them are dressed in vintage 1960s cocktail dresses. My gaze flips over to the tip jar on the piano in the corner. Riiight. It's piano bar night, where patrons are allowed to sing an oldie of their choice, usually something really old, like Frank Sinatra.

Sloane loves anything not of this century.

Alexandru stands and brings out his gold case, extracting two calling cards, one for Sloane and one for Valerie.

"Wonderful!" Sloane says. "This is how it's done! Look, Valerie!"

"Isn't there supposed to be contact information?"

"It's a calling card. You hand it over when calling on somebody."

"Oh," Valerie says, still confused. "And what does *princeps* mean?"

"Don't ask," I say.

"It means a first among equals," Alexandru says.

Valerie looks slightly baffled. It occurs to me that she's a bit drunk.

Sloane says, "I know why you're here. You want to talk to Fern. They're doing amateur sleuth hour," she explains to Valerie.

"You should try to figure out where Bo Richardson went," Valerie says. "That's the real mystery."

"To me, the real mystery is who's been doing these crossbow murders," I say.

"That's not much of a mystery," Sloane says. "But we know our Harriet likes to be extra sure of things."

Alexandru fixes Sloane with a hard look. "I have known generals who lost wars for want of Ms. Renfield's care for details. Certainty is not a weakness, Sloane."

Sloane blinks at him. I'm not sure what to say in the face of this unexpected smackdown. "Um...are you guys here for piano sing-along night?"

"Yes, we are," Valerie says.

Sloane narrows her eyes. "Will we be graced with a song from Alexandru tonight?"

"We shall see," Alexandru says mysteriously.

Fern comes up to the table just then, and the two of them titter back to the bar. Fern has retro teased hair and colorful earrings. "Harriet! I was just out to lunch with Granabelle this afternoon. And this must be the prince!"

Alexandru stands and takes Fern's hand. You'd think she'd just been introduced to the pope. Thankfully, he does not produce another one of his weird calling cards.

"Fern, how are you doing?" I say. "I hear you discovered that body in Gazebo Park. Horrible!"

"Yeah, it was pretty scary. I'm having a vape and admiring the tulips and suddenly there's a foot sticking out from under a bench. I knew without even looking that it was a dead body, but nothing prepares you for actually seeing it."

"I hear it was a crossbow," I say.

"Yup. Shot in the back like Razor Johnny. And the minute I screamed, I saw Dooley Brogan dart behind some bushes and hightail it up the hill to the overlook."

Alexandru gives her a grave look. "That is indeed suspicious."

"Did it seem like he'd been lying there a while?" I ask. "Like was there blood in the grass around him?"

Fern frowns. "I guess."

"Do you know if the police picked Dooley up?"

Fern says, "I heard them say it over their radio that they got him at his sister's house. And it sounds like they brought him in. I overheard another of them saying they'll probably be holding him as long as they can. Whatever that is, they need to make it longer."

"I think the maximum they can hold him is twenty-four hours, though they can stretch it to forty-eight, but they usually don't. Anything over twenty-four hours can be a little bit of a legal gray zone."

"If they know it's the guy, they should be able to hold him indefinitely," Fern says. "And look at this place! It's half full. It should be all the way full on a nice May evening like this. Anyway, what can I get you?"

I order us two draft sour cherry ciders and a basket of onion rings. Fern sticks her pen into her hair and promises to be right back.

"Sour cherry cider? That is a child's drink," Alexandru says.

"Their ciders are really good here," I say. "I'm drinking for two now."

Somebody at the next table scowls.

"Because I always end up drinking his! Good grief!" I lower my voice. "And I don't want to hear anything about how much more efficient our investigation would be if we could just walk in here and bluntly ask questions. I'm going to answer that complaint preemptively. We can't. Effective investigating is about relationships."

The pianist has started up and suddenly there is this guy singing "My Way." I'm surprised to note that the guy singing is Fire Chief Knox. He looks so different in a suit and bowtie, and he's not a bad singer.

Fern delivers our ciders.

I grab my tablet and google the victim, Milo. "Dooley

Brogan went to jail fifteen years ago, and Milo came to town a year ago from Cleveland. How would they know each other?"

Alexandru slides his finger around the condensation on the outside of the glass. "It seems likely that Jerome would know this new victim, considering that they're both journalists."

"Yes, they are journalists, but they are working in very different realms. The Great Lakes Gazette or whatever it's called covers Michigan, Ohio and Western Pennsylvania. It's way more of a crime and statehouse sort of thing, whereas Jerome's Substack is hyper-local on Silverton Valley. Milo came up in Cleveland. It's not like Cleveland is that far away."

I'm thinking here about doing a little deep research. I could pop into InovaSpire and check out their connections—with Dooley Brogan and with each other.

I ponder this for a while until I notice that Alexandru's eyes have fallen to my lips, and I realize I've been tapping my stylus against them. "What?"

"Nothing." He turns his attention to the piano player and the new singer.

It's here I notice there's a big lipstick mark on my white stylus. I grab a napkin and wipe the red lipstick smears off of it. Is that what Alexandru was staring at? God, does it remind him of blood?

"I think I should pop into the office," I say. "Researching the connections could yield some helpful data."

"I will accompany you," Alexandru says.

"No need. There are always people working late in that building."

"But I have never seen your former office."

"You've never been interested in seeing the office before."

"But now I am."

I'm a little suspicious. Alexandru always has dubious motives for things. "Okay, but no calling me 'your underling' or talking about draconian punishment methods. Especially when you meet Serena. She's been a mentor and a role model to me, and somebody I absolutely admire."

Alexandru's gaze sharpens.

"Okay?" I say. "I mean it. You have to act cool."

"When do I not act cool?"

"No comment." I send a quick text to Serena to let her know I might be stopping by.

She gets right back. She and some of the team are still there finishing up some testing with the West Coast.

It's after 8 p.m. by the time we're riding up the elevator.

"It's going to be boring," I warn.

"I have lived long," he says. "I am no stranger to stillness."

"Like a house plant?"

"Not like a house plant, Ms. Renfield."

His deep voice sends a shiver through me. In the close air of the elevator, I'm suddenly very aware of the sharp line of his jaw, that drift of dark hair over his brow.

No, he's definitely not like a house plant.

Or a vampire.

He feels like a man, and that strangely compelling energy of his fills every square inch of this elevator.

Casually as you please, he begins to tug off his day-walking gloves, one finger at a time. My mouth goes dry, watching him. The leather loosens over his knuckles, his long fingers.

And then I raise my gaze to his.

Our eyes lock.

Is he doing the glove thing on purpose? Toying with me? He can sense heartbeats, cortisol, who knows what else. Every bit of heat inside me, laid bare.

And then the doors open to the top floor.

"Here we are." My voice sounds strange to me. I bolt out and head through the InovaSpire office, which is beautiful at night, all tastefully lit exposed brick walls and the giant photos Serena took on her travels. We pass reception and then the break room where a row of pizza boxes is set out. We continue on through to the main area with its huge windows and sweeping views of the starry night sky over the Silverton River Valley.

"This is my old office," I say as we pass a corner office.

A voice. "Can I help you?"

I spin around. Varla stands in the doorway. "Sorry! Didn't mean to disturb you. I was just showing Alexandru my old stomping ground."

"Okayyyy." Varla doesn't seem to like the idea of us even looking at her door.

"Serena knows we're coming. I just have to hop on the southeast workstation for a bit. Is everyone in conference room two?"

"Yup," Varla says tightly. She retreats back into her office, closing the door.

"That's one of the people who replaced me," I mumble

under my breath, leading Alexandru down the hall to the far side of the space. "Not my fan."

"Certainly not," Alexandru agrees.

I poke my head into conference room two. I spot Serena and Malik up at the whiteboard speaking in low tones. Some of my other former coworkers are hunched over laptops at the conference table and the couch. The huge screen at the far end shows the Sacramento team, also heads down.

"Hey, guys," I say in a loud whisper. "Just wanted to let you know I'm on site."

"Harriet!" Serena caps her marker and comes over to us, eyes on Alexandru. "Come on in and say hi. This must be Alexandru."

"Yes," I say nervously. "This is Alexandru. My new boss."

"The man who stole the best thing that ever happened to my company," Serena says, offering her hand for a handshake. "I hope you know how lucky you are."

"Serena!" I exclaim, nervous about the praise and also about whatever weird thing Alexandru might say back to her. "I've watched you make your own luck for years."

Alexandru shakes her hand with his usual aplomb. "The value that she has brought cannot be overstated. She sees what others cannot. She has a nearly mystical connection with the data."

Serena smiles. "Indeed she does."

"The prince of Kingston Manor." Malik comes up to meet Alexandru, followed by KC, who says, "There's nobody who can do what Harriet does. Though I'm giving it a go."

A few other people come to be introduced. Varla strolls in

with a sheaf of papers and proceeds to ignore us as she hands them out.

I glance over at the whiteboard. "Is everything under control here? Let me know if…"

"We have it well under control," Varla says. "We got it."

Serena gives her a strange look, as does KC.

I thank Serena for letting me pop in and we get out of there.

I breathe a sigh of relief when I'm finally in the driver's seat at the southeast workstation. "So you met the office. I think that went well."

Alexandru leans on one of the large wooden beams that separates the massive windows overlooking the river. His eyes gleam in the moonlight. "It hardly went well," he says casually. "Serena is an excellent actress, but she does not trust me whatsoever. She is a panther in the grass, biding her time until she can take you back or, so she thinks. Varla feels extremely threatened by you—she wishes you would leave and never come back. KC is obsessed with you in a way I find I do not like. But the rest of them seemed genuine enough."

I twist around in my chair. "You think Serena doesn't like you?"

"She does not trust our situation. She does not understand why you are working for me."

"Yeah, well, it doesn't make sense unless you know the truth, and it's not like we can tell her that."

"I don't care if you tell her," Alexandru says.

I roll my eyes and turn back to the workstation, tapping a few buttons. "Yeah, so Serena: I've taken my hereditary place as a Renfield at the side of a centuries-old vampire, and I would've said no to his job offer, but sadly, he'll go on a killing spree of my neighbors and friends if I don't manage things over there, so what's a girl to do?" I tap a few more buttons extra hard.

Alexandru watches me, still as a mountain. Does he even feel bad that he made me leave my awesome job?

I build my analysis methodically, scouring every nook and cranny of public and private databases, social media sites, and everything in between, looking for any kind of overlap between Dooley Brogan and Milo Cirillo. The data begins to populate across my screens in cascading networks. Red for Dooley. Blue for Milo. I'm looking for purple.

"You really think Varla feels threatened by me?" I ask.

"No doubt about it. I sense fear from her, along with a territorial aggression."

I look up at him. "Aggression is a pretty strong word."

"Yet it is precisely the correct one."

"I feel like she's just a little frosty."

"More heat than frost, Renfield."

I scribble a few ideas for my next query on a bit of scratch paper. "And I don't think KC is obsessed with me, FYI. He was an intern, and then when I left, he got promoted to junior analyst. He's smart and ambitious and he likes to show off his skills to me. I bet you anything he's gonna come by and tell me something to tweak."

"It is more than showing off. It is obsession. Pointed at you."

"You think every man is obsessed with me. Maverick and now KC? And last week you said the UPS guy—"

"Take heed, Renfield," Alexandru says in a warning voice.

"Well, luckily you're here to protect me."

The data has finished populating. There's nothing. No intersections whatsoever.

"Two men, both killed with a crossbow. What links them?"

"Death by crossbow links them. Being in the same vicinity with Dooley Brogan links them. Why do you resist concluding it is Dooley Brogan?"

"Asked and answered. I'm gonna try to see if there is anything between Milo and Razor Johnny. Maybe they have something in common."

"More on the crossbow case?" I look up to see KC ambling over, soda in hand. "There's still pizza out there if you want some."

"We ate," I say, tapping a few buttons. "But thank you. How's it going in there?"

"Winding down. A few integration issues on the West Coast. Are you here because of that killing downtown?"

"You know it," I say. "Just looking at connections."

"You know, I actually built a link analysis tool for some historical network mapping for Topco Logistics. Want to try it? Might speed things up."

"I'm halfway in on this one," I say. "But thanks. It sounds cool."

I am highly aware of Alexandru focusing on KC—that odd stillness he gets when he's cataloging someone.

KC says, "If you tell me your parameters, I could run alongside and you wouldn't lose time over there."

"I don't want you to have to waste your time duplicating our efforts."

"Fair," KC says. "No, that's fair. Fair fair fair."

My results pop up slowly. Excruciatingly slowly. It's a lot of data.

I turn to KC. "So...do people in the office talk like I'm going to come back to my old job here?"

He looks surprised. "Are you coming back to your old job here?"

"She is not," Alexandru says in a low voice.

I snort. "For the benefits package at Alexandru's place, I'd have to be half crazy to leave. But I was just wondering if maybe Varla thinks it."

KC's eyebrows shoot up practically to his hairline. "That might explain a few things."

"Like what?" I ask.

"She's just an odd duck."

"In what way?" Alexandru asks.

KC furrows his brow, as if he's struggling to formulate a way to describe Varla's odd-duckness, or maybe how to be nice about it. One of the techs comes to bring him back to the conference room, and he mumbles his goodbyes.

"He was not happy that you rejected his way," Alexandru observes.

"What?" I ask.

"His offer of help. He did not like that you rejected it."

"I didn't reject it."

"He felt it as a rejection."

"I'm starting to see the downside of reading everybody's emotions. Like everybody has emotions about things!" Purple on the screen. "Look! A hit!"

The first hit is nothing—parking tickets from the same waterfront festival, thousands of people.

And then something even more interesting: a name. Jerome Goodwin.

"What is it?" Alexandru asks.

"This is odd." I tap a few keys and pull up the details.

"Milo wrote a piece for the Great Lakes Dispatch. Look at this comment.

Alexandru leans in and reads: "'This story was more interesting the first time, when *Silverton Uncovered* covered it days ago. Why not cite that journalist? Either do your own work or cite who you're stealing from.' This from Horatio57@yahoo.com."

"*Silverton Uncovered* is Jerome's Substack."

"Jerome thought Milo stole his work."

"Exactly. And here's Jerome as Horatio57 commenting on a couple other stories that Milo seems to have lifted from his Substack."

"Interesting."

"A legit journalist would say 'as reported in *Silverton Uncovered*,' at the very least. Troubling," I say, transferring the key findings to my tablet. "but it's not something to kill over."

Alexandru says, "We do not know when Milo was killed, but the body was discovered while we were speaking with Jerome. Though Jerome did seem significantly distressed when we appeared at his door."

"Everybody's distressed when they get a visitor out of nowhere. It's a weird thing to do."

"Perhaps his distress had nothing to do with unexpected visitors at the door."

"Jerome going around killing for things like this? I just can't see it."

"You trust too easily, Ms. Renfield."

Chapter Nineteen

Alexandru

I pause in the doorway of the kitchen while Ms. Renfield tears into a bright red and yellow bag of her "Bugle" treats like a starving peasant.

She has changed into her so-called yoga pants and T-shirt, utterly inappropriate for the way the fabric showcases the line of her thigh. Strangely fetching. The thighs of one who is stubborn. Tenacious. One imagines a lover such as her would give as good as she gets, that she would make demands with those soft thighs of hers that conceal so much strength.

I snap my attention to Gregor, who is hovering with a bowl. "For your Bugles, milady."

"Thank you, but I'm good with the bag," Ms. Renfield pops a Bugle into her mouth and crunches loudly.

"A bowl is more festive, milady."

"Seriously, I'm good."

He opens his mouth to protest further. I catch his eye and he scuttles away with the bowl clutched to his chest.

"I just can't believe Jerome would kill for a couple of stolen stories. It's so not him. Also, don't forget Dooley was there in the vicinity. Hiding in the bushes."

"So now that your friend has cause to kill both of the victims, you are more willing to entertain the idea of Dooley committing the murders?"

"I'm willing to entertain the idea of the murderer committing the murders," Ms. Renfield says, eyes glued to her electronic ledger.

"Perhaps Jerome is killing his enemies and ensuring that Dooley Brogan takes the blame for it."

This gives Ms. Renfield some pause. She studies a Bugle and then bites off the tip, crunching thoughtfully with her little front teeth. "I guess that makes *some* sense, but not if you know Jerome. He's not that kind of guy." She pops the rest into her mouth and chews.

"Perhaps Jerome is killing two birds with one stone. Putting a murderer back behind bars while taking care of his enemies."

I can feel the contours of Ms. Renfield's interest sharpen. My theory makes a good deal of sense to her, much as she dislikes it.

"So you think he killed Milo down at the park and then doubled back up to his apartment in time to answer the door?"

"He did have the salt of exertion on him," I say.

Ms. Renfield looks skeptical. "What we need to do is get a sense of Jerome's whereabouts during both murders." She takes two Bugles now and stuffs them both in her mouth. "I'm telling you, though. He's not a killer."

She's so sentimental about their high-school attachment. I say, "Let us pay a visit to Jerome right now."

"It's eleven at night! He could be sleeping."

"It is a simple matter to rouse him. I find that a person startled fresh from sleep easier to read, and altogether more pliable."

"If only we knew the exact time of Milo's death. It's possible he was killed while we were talking to Jerome."

"The time of Milo's death?" I close my eyes, remembering the scent of the body as they carried it past. The blood had begun to thicken. None of the sweetness of fresh blood. The body itself—it held some warmth, but not much. "Ninety minutes before we arrived there."

"Excuse me?"

"When did we arrive at the scene?"

She looks at her phone. "Around 3:55."

"The time of death would be 2:35."

"How can you possibly know that?"

I shrug. "The same way you might know whether milk has gone sour."

"Wow." She looks surprised and impressed. "That is a massively helpful skill."

An odd warmth spreads through my chest, not that her opinion matters. It is only right she recognize my superiority.

Berky's Patisserie is bright and bustling the next morning, full of pastry smells and cheerful music and daylight streaming through the windows.

Hellish, in other words.

I adjust my hat and gloves to ensure full skin coverage.

The female behind the counter gives us a wave. "Bonjour!"

Ms. Renfield gives her a big, bright smile. "Bonjour, Monique!"

Monique continues helping another customer who is taking an unseemly amount of time deciding on the type of cookie they wish to consume.

In a low voice, I say, "I do not see why treats are necessary. Jerome will not welcome us either way. The pastries are simply gilding the gallows."

"Dude, we are nowhere near the gallows part. We're still at the friends part, and I want him to understand that."

"Your friend is hiding things. Guilt and fear churn inside him. He had motive and opportunity for both murders, but yes. Perhaps it is all quite innocent."

Ms. Renfield forms her pretty lips into a frown, eyes narrowed behind her glasses.

I raise a brow.

She huffs around and examines the pastries. It is eventually our turn, and she orders a selection of croissants.

We are just about to get out of there when none other than Ms. Renfield's mother, Lorna, comes in the door. "Look who the cat dragged out," she says.

"Hey, Mom!" Ms. Renfield hugs her mother.

"Lorna," I say, tipping my head.

"Again with the three-piece suit. Are you expecting to be painted in oils, or is this just how you dress for a trip to the bakery?"

"This is indeed how I dress for every occasion," I say. "And I would be extremely surprised if there were any decent portraiture artists in this town."

Lorna smiles. "Touché. Oh, and thank you again for

sending that crew over for the back stairs. And Gregor as well. You really didn't have to."

"Of course I had to. I can't have my underling distracted by accidents and mishaps at the store. We have much work to do."

Lorna gets a strange look on her face. "That's some bullcrap reasoning, but the stairs are solid, so I'll take it." She nods at the bag. "Are those for Gregor?"

"No," Ms. Renfield says. "Gregor is *not* a big foodie. He is the opposite of a foodie."

"I've noticed that," Lorna says. "What's up with you Karsovians and your strange diets?"

Ever the efficient underling, Ms. Renfield changes the subject to the murder of Milo Cirillo, asking if her mother has heard anything through the retail grapevine.

"I hear they're holding Dooley down at the station, and as far as I can tell, it sounds like it was him," Lorna says.

"Maybe," Ms. Renfield says.

"Skulking around in the bushes feels pretty high on the 'I'm guilty' spectrum of behaviors," Lorna says.

Ms. Renfield sighs. "I wish we could ask him a few questions."

"I'm sure ol' Maverick would be thrilled to hear that," Lorna says, and then she brings up some matter of the store.

I ignore them, my attention suddenly snagged on the world beyond the bakery window.

The street looks the same as it always does. And yet something out there makes me still. A presence I haven't felt in decades. It's gone before I can place it. I turn back to Ms. Renfield.

"We must go."

Jerome does not answer when we buzz.

"Is he there?" she asks.

"Oh yes. He is very much there." I focus my senses on his windows on the second floor. "His heart rate is extraordinarily high. He knows that we are here and I have no doubt that he wishes us to leave. But when he finds we have pastries, I'm sure all that will change."

"Very funny." Ms. Renfield taps on her phone and speaks into it. "Jerome, I'm down at the door. I really, really need to talk to you. It's absolutely critical." When no response comes forth, she speaks into the phone once again. "I know you're there. Please, just a minute of your time. We have pastries!"

After some long silence, a voice comes out of the box. "Harriet? Sorry, I had my headphones on. What's so urgent? This really isn't a good time."

"I'm sorry. I know it's kind of bothersome to just show up, but it's important." She turns to me, cringing prettily.

"You can't just say what this is about?"

"It's important."

"Can you come back later? I'm on a deadline."

Ms. Renfield sighs. "What time?"

"This afternoon? Just text me."

Much to my shock, she turns and heads back to the car.

"You would consent to such a delay? You are too nice."

"He wasn't going to invite us in and we're not busting his door down."

"Jerome is a ball of intense and fearful curiosity. So many secrets. Guilt."

Instead of getting into her car, she leans back against it, gazing out into the distance. "Is it weird just to feel all that?" She turns to me. "I mean, do you feel something from everybody in that building?"

"Indeed I do."

"Wow." She pulls a croissant from the bag and takes a bite, chewing thoughtfully. "Isn't it bothersome?"

"You can see the river in front of you and the rooftops of downtown Ashwood and farmland beyond. So many trees. The boats, the little people, the sky. Is it bothersome to you?"

"So you're able to focus when you need to."

"Unless they are quite close and intense, like at that bridal expo last month. That was something of a kaleidoscope. The many musical instruments the other day, that was very bothersome."

"Is it less today?"

"Very much so."

"Do you think he's watching us?"

I gaze up at his window. "Yes."

"Well...don't look!"

"Our interest in him is no secret."

"I get that he's hiding things, but he's not like this criminal mastermind type."

"Most criminal masterminds do not seem to be the type. It is part of the mastermind skillset to project innocence."

Her phone makes a sound just then and she takes a look. "It's Mom! They let Dooley out of jail."

This is interesting news, indeed. "The twenty-four hours isn't even up," I observe.

"Granabelle's gossip grapevine for the win!"

Chapter Twenty

Harriet

Dooley ushers us to the dining room table. There's a bowl of pink cereal swimming in milk. He sits down in front of it.

"It was kind of you to bring baked goods. I've got this cereal, but Tilly and the kids will sure be happy to see those."

I set the bag on the buffet, and Alexandru and I sit across from Dooley and his cereal.

He digs in. "Did you know that there are twice as many cereals at Gable's Grocery from when I went inside?"

"I guess fifteen years is a long time," I say.

"You're telling me. And to answer your question I know you're gonna ask, no, I didn't kill that Milo guy. I know it looks bad, like everyone says I was waiting around for somebody to discover the body, but the truth is, I was sitting in the grass in the shade of the gazebo playing Tetris when I heard Fern screaming. I went over there to see if somebody was in trouble or something, but the minute I saw that body lying there, let's just say I noped out pretty fast." He takes another bite. "Not the best decision."

"Did they establish an alibi for you? Is that why they let you out so fast?" I ask.

"Nineteen hours and twenty-three minutes. I wouldn't call that fast exactly."

Alexandru crosses his legs, observing Dooley carefully. What is he picking up? Dooley seems so guileless, but then I keep thinking about Alexandru's mastermind's toolbox thing.

"Legally, they could've held you a bit longer," I say.

"My lawyer threatened to sue the department for harassment, and I suppose they took it pretty seriously. He's really been stepping up lately."

"We learned something interesting the other day," Alexandru begins. "We learned that you've been lying to us."

Dooley stares at Alexandru in alarm. "Excuse me?"

I want to rush in and smooth over the situation, soften the edges of the question, but I fight the urge. Alexandru was right; I do have a hard time hanging back and letting people answer for themselves.

Alexandru's voice is low and resonant. "I believe you heard what I said. You. Lying. To us."

Dooley looks over at me, and I feel super uncomfortable now. "Or...leaving something pretty big out."

"Like what do you mean?" Dooley asks.

"We know that Jerome Goodwin was visiting you a lot in prison," I say.

"Did Jerome tell you that?" Dooley asks.

"Why didn't you tell us?" I press, feeling proud of myself for not answering Dooley's question. I think old me would've explained exactly how we got that information, but we're the ones asking the questions here.

"I didn't tell you because it's supposed to be a secret. He's working on a book project—did he tell you that?"

"And that is all?" Alexandru says.

Dooley's expression falters. "What more could there be?"

"The rest of what you're not telling us," Alexandru says.

Dooley casts a desperate glance in my direction.

I try to look sympathetic. "Well...if there *is* something..."

"There is something," Alexandru says casually.

Is he picking something up? He must be.

"Did Jerome say there was something else?" Dooley asks.

Alexandru fixes him with a raptor-like gaze. "The subject is you, and what you're not telling us."

"I don't have to tell you anything." Dooley drops his spoon back into his cereal with a decisive clink. "You don't get to question me. I'm done with having you in my house." He points at the door.

I stand, because what else do you do when someone tells you to leave their house?

Alexandru stays seated, calm as can be. "Better us than the police."

Dooley looks wildly back and forth between Alexandru and me. "What's that supposed to mean?"

Alexandru takes this moment to tug his gloves off, one finger at a time. Slow. Deliberate. He knows something. Dooley watches each finger like Alexandru might be pulling the pin on a grenade.

"I've said all I'm going to say." Dooley's voice has thinned. "You're not the police."

"Lucky for you, that," Alexandru says, starting on the other hand. "Does this secret you're keeping have something to do with why you're killing Jerome's enemies?"

Dooley's eyes round with shock. "I'm not killing anybody! Jerome's *enemies?*"

Alexandru waits. I know what he's doing, letting the silence be excruciating. Well, it is excruciating!

"I'm not killing Jerome's enemies. Why would I do that?"

"You tell me," Alexandru says.

Something flashes behind Dooley's eyes just then. Even I can see it—thoughts connecting. Something coming together, maybe.

He mumbles a profanity under his breath.

What does it mean? Is he starting to suspect Jerome is framing him for the murders of Jerome's enemies? Is that what's going on? Which...I can't imagine it.

"Yes?" Alexandru says.

Dooley turns to me, expression wild. "You have to understand I'm not killing anyone! You have to believe me! I was just walking around during the time people were killed. Both times, just rambling around. And where would I even get a crossbow? With what money?"

"That all makes sense," I say.

"Jerome visiting me, it's not important. It was just that book of his—period! And I didn't tell you because he made me promise not to tell anyone. It's something with his book company."

Alexandru's dark eyes glitter. "What else?"

"What!" Dooley exclaims.

"What else are you hiding?"

"What could I be hiding?!"

Alexandru waits. He's being so harsh, but I suppose that's nothing compared to having someone's fangs sink into your neck and drain all the blood from your body like two horrible little straws. Compared to that, he's practically showering Dooley with gifts.

Dooley is overwrought at this point.

Alexandru places one of his gloves on top of the other glove, lining them up exactly. His fingers really are long and elegant. Mesmerizingly so. Does he know it? Of course he knows.

OMG. Is this gloves thing for Dooley or for me?

"Fine! Okay!" Dooley says. "You know that technicality I got out on? The prosecutor had hidden some evidence that would have helped me. I don't really understand it, but Jerome is the one that figured it out. He was researching something random about my case for his book, and he noticed a gap in the files or something like that."

"Jerome found the technicality?" I say.

"Yes. He alerted my lawyer and my lawyer got on it, but Jerome's the reason I got out."

"I don't understand—why the secrecy?" I ask.

Dooley sighs and looks up at the ceiling. "Well, my lawyer was pretty embarrassed that he screwed up like that. He told me if Jerome and I just act like he found the loophole, he'd give me free lawyering. Getting me out, and so forth. And considering all of this crossbow killing, that deal is really working out and I don't want to lose it. There is no way we could afford him."

I narrow my eyes. He doesn't sound like a very good lawyer, but it's Dooley's decision.

Alexandru lowers his voice. "You are grateful to Jerome."

"Well, yeah! I'd still be in prison if it weren't for Jerome." He straightens right then. "But that doesn't mean I'm going around killing his enemies!"

Alexandru eyes him like prey.

"What?! Look. I'm asking you not to tell anybody about the lawyer thing. I'm putting my sister through so much already. We don't have the money—"

There is commotion at the door. Dooley's sister Tilly comes in with her two children, face bright and smiling. "Welcome!" She grins, gesturing at Dooley. "Isn't this great news?"

"So awesome!" I point at the pastries. "We have to go, but we left a parting gift. Some croissants."

"That is so thoughtful!" she says.

"Very thoughtful," Dooley says, following us out. He gives me a look and mouths the word, *please,* meaning, *please don't tell anyone about the lawyer and loophole thing.*

I give him a nod. I'm really, really hoping there's no world where we have to tell. Because I'm guessing Tilly will be bearing the brunt of those costs.

"That was intense," I say on the way back home.

"I found it rather diverting," Alexandru says.

"Don't you feel at all guilty about pressing him and hounding him like that?"

"I find guilt a rather useless emotion."

I snort. "Says the guy who would happily drain a small child and that child's puppy."

"I would not drain a small child. Too much work just for a fraction of a meal. And a puppy? Repugnant."

No comment.

"Did you get a vibe on his truthfulness?"

"He seemed genuine."

"So he might be innocent."

"Or a sociopath," Alexandru says.

Gregor is nowhere when we get back home. Alexandru doesn't seem surprised.

"Do you think it's possible that Dooley is killing Jerome's enemies as a thank-you gift for getting him out of jail?" I ask.

"Dooley is indeed grateful for his freedom. But it is secured either way. He wouldn't need such an extreme gesture of thanks."

"Well, people do like to express their gratitude."

"You humans are so very sentimental."

"I don't know, can you really call it sentimental when it's like, 'thanks, let me show my gratitude by doing grisly murders'?"

"You found those murders grisly?"

"All murders are grisly," I say.

"Huh," he says simply in his *totally disagree* tone. "I find it far more plausible that Jerome found the loophole and realized that it had value. He struck a deal with Dooley—he would help get him released from prison in exchange for Dooley eliminating two of Jerome's enemies."

I stare down at the polished marble floor with its intricate inlays. "I guess it makes more sense than murder as a thank-you gesture."

"Indeed. And if I am right, it was probably Jerome who had

the idea to keep who found the loophole quiet. To allow the lawyer to take the credit."

"But what about all that guilt you sensed with Jerome? Why get somebody to do murders for you and then feel all guilty about it?"

"It would not be the first time that a human does something atrocious and then regrets it."

I shake my head. "Jerome. It's so hard to imagine."

"We'll get it out of him this afternoon—if you'll allow it," he adds darkly.

Chapter Twenty-One

Alexandru

We are just passing Gazebo Park when flashing red and blue lights appear behind us.

"What the heck?" Harriet pulls the car to the side of the road. "It's Maverick."

This, of course, is no surprise. The male pines for Ms. Renfield. I do not like it.

"Let me handle this," she says.

Officer Maverick Cooper saunters up to her side. "You two wanna exit the car?"

"Not particularly," I say.

"Alexandru, please," Ms. Renfield whispers beseechingly. "*Pleeeease.* I'm begging you. Be cool. Let's just get out and chat."

It is unlike me to comply with the petty demands of an unworthy male such as Maverick Cooper, but I find myself putting on my hat against the afternoon sun and walking around the car to take my place next to Ms. Renfield. I position myself just slightly forward of her. Close enough that Maverick's gaze must include me whether he wishes it or not.

As usual, Officer Maverick Cooper is chomping on gum like a cow chewing the cud.

I fold my arms across my chest. "I hope you have a good reason for interfering with Ms. Renfield's operation of her automobile. You know as well as I do that she operates an automobile well within the parameters of safety and legality."

"Is that so?"

"It is."

"Great!" Ms. Renfield puts in. "We've all established that I'm an awesome driver. What is this about?"

Maverick turns to her. "Imagine my surprise when I heard that you asked for the prison logs and interviewed not only Fern but Jerome Goodwin." He chews harder. "I would hate to arrest you for obstruction of an investigation."

"She requested the logs on my behalf," I say.

"And why would that be?"

"A bit of bedtime reading."

Maverick's jaw tightens. "I'll remind you: we're in America here. We'll jail a prince as readily as we'll jail a Peeping Tom."

"Exemplary," I say.

"Do you have an actual charge for us, Maverick?" Ms. Renfield asks.

"That would be obstruction if you're withholding evidence that might be material in this case. Right here's your opportunity to come clean with any information you might have."

I look over at Ms. Renfield, wondering if she sees the situation as clearly as I do. Maverick requested the logs as well. He and his fellow officers have interviewed Jerome and learned that we are a step ahead of them—by a day at least.

They probably found out about the secret book contract, too, but it's unlikely they found out that Jerome was the one to find the loophole.

"If you must know, it seems that Jerome is writing a book on prison life," I say.

A sprig of surprise from Ms. Renfield. Why would I reveal anything?

"Yes, we've heard all about the book," Maverick says. "What else? You have a theory."

"Me?" she says.

"Yeah, you," Maverick says.

So he has nothing. Just flashing lights and the poorly veiled threats.

"A motorcycle gang member and a journalist," he says, scrutinizing her face. "Let's have it."

He's infatuated with her, so he would likely be able to interpret the look she wears now: eyes bright with private pleasure, a hint of smile she's trying to suppress, head turned slightly so she regards you more from one eye than the other. It's a look with a little bit of mischief in it. It's a look that says she does not say all she knows.

I lean back against the car, confident Ms. Renfield can handle it.

"Well?" Maverick says.

"I'm wondering if Dooley even did the first crime," she says.

Maverick's gum-chewing slows. "That's not a theory, that's a hunch."

"Her theory is implied," I say. "If Dooley did not commit the first murder, somebody else did."

"Still seems like a hunch to me. Anything else?"

Ms. Renfield shrugs. She and I exchange looks.

He'll be getting nothing else.

"This is your last warning. Stay out of my investigation."

Jerome Goodwin stands in his doorway. The shadows beneath his eyes have deepened; his heart races quick and desperate. Most interesting is the guilt coming off him in waves. He's been ignoring Ms. Renfield's texts, so we stopped by.

"How did you get into the building?" he demands.

"We need to speak with you," I say.

"You can't just come to my door like this."

"Jerome, please." The gentleness of Ms. Renfield's tone seems to calm him or at least remind him they were once friends.

With a sigh he relents. He steps aside and lets us in.

Papers lie scattered across the desk, and a pizza box on the floor reeks of old cheese and meat. The curtains are drawn, sealing out the daylight. That I approve of.

"So what is this about?"

"We spoke with Dooley Brogan," I say.

"And?"

Ms. Renfield watches Jerome with a mixture of hope and dread. "Dooley says you're the reason he got out of prison."

Jerome folds his arms in front of him, looking confused.

"Well…I kind of can't believe he told you that, being that he wanted it to stay secret so his good-for-nothing lawyer could take credit and…honestly, this is why you're here? No offense, but I'm on like ten deadlines—"

"Jerome," Ms. Renfield says softly. "Razor Johnny harassed your grandmother. Milo was stealing your work. Both your enemies. What's going on?"

He blinks. The silence stretches tight, then he lets out a long hiss of a breath. "Well, yes. That hadn't escaped my notice."

"And?" she asks again.

He sinks onto the arm of his sofa. "I don't know. I don't know."

"Tell us," I say.

He looks up at me. "What's going on is I'm freaking out. Yeah, my enemies are dying. By crossbow. Dooley says it wasn't him. Well, I don't know who else it could be."

"But you found the loophole, the technicality that got him freed?" she asks.

"I found it going through his files, doing background. This really obvious sequential gap in the fingerprint files. I couldn't believe nobody else had seen it, and I felt obligated to tell him and suggest he inform his lawyer. I thought—" He breaks off, pressing the heels of his hands against his eyes. "I thought I was doing a good thing. It was pretty obvious prosecutorial misconduct. He deserves to know, don't you think?"

"Of course he does," Ms. Renfield says.

"He was released," I prod.

"Yes." The word comes out like a confession. "And

suddenly Razor Johnny turns up dead. And I thought, or more like hoped to high heaven that it was a coincidence. But then Milo..." He shakes his head. "I've been terrified that Dooley is killing them to repay me. Like some kind of twisted gesture. But at the same time, well, you've met Dooley. This is the guy going around shooting people with a crossbow? I don't know what I'm supposed to think. And maybe I should've gone to the cops by now, I don't know..."

"I would be freaked out, too," Ms. Renfield says softly.

"I swear to you, I never asked for this. I never even hinted at it." His pulse races. So much fear and guilt.

"Okay," Ms. Renfield says.

"The police were here, and I told them about the book, but I didn't say anything about finding the missing parts of the fingerprint files. I didn't think Dooley would go blabbing it. He's getting free legal service from the crap lawyer if we pretend the lawyer noticed it. The guy deserves free legal service, considering, but now it all just looks suspicious, as if I wanted Dooley to do it, or at least I liked being the beneficiary of his murder spree. And what if Dooley says I directed him? Like a *quid pro quo*? He could say that."

Ms. Renfield sucks in a breath. "Right."

"But how did Dooley even know about Milo stealing my stories?"

I lean in, interested, now. "You did not complain to Dooley about Milo?"

"No! Why would I? Our interviews were about prison life. And my feud with Milo was not at all public; I don't want to be the griping journalist. I told maybe three people. And I did confront him about it at Berky's one day, but to any outsider, that would've looked like one journalist reminding another about ethics and professional courtesy."

"Was that the last time you saw Milo?" I ask.

Jerome widens his eyes. "Yes!"

I give him a hard look. "Dead or alive?"

"Alexandru!" Ms. Renfield scolds.

"It's a simple clarification."

"Wait." Jerome looks puzzled, suddenly. "How did *you two* find out about Milo and me?"

Ms. Renfield shrugs. "You know me. Digger of data."

"Yeah, right. Of course you'd find it." He lets out a breath. "What am I gonna do?"

Ms. Renfield sets a hand on his shoulder. "We'll figure this out. You're not alone."

"What if he did it as a thank-you, and the murders are on me, now?"

"The only person responsible for those murders is the one wielding the crossbow." She hands him her electronic ledger. "How about you write down the names of those three people who knew you were angry with Milo. It might be helpful to figure out how that information traveled."

With trembling hands, he starts typing in names. "I'm not sure if I'm getting everybody. I've been feeling so turned around. Do you think I should tell the police about my suspicions?"

"No," I say.

"What? No, don't listen to him. You should!" Ms. Renfield says.

"So...okay," he says, confused. "Are you guys going to tell the police?"

"Certainly not," I say. "We would do no such thing."

"A hundred percent not telling them," Ms. Renfield says. "That's up to you. Maverick is interested in solving this crime the right way. If you didn't do it, he'll get to the bottom of things."

I withhold comment.

Gratitude radiates from Jerome. "Thank you. Thank you so much. But I don't get it. You're investigating for fun?"

"Kinda," Ms. Renfield says.

I give him a reassuring smile. "Incidentally, do you have an alibi for the time of Milo's murder?"

"W-what?" Jerome says. "Me?"

Ms. Renfield shoots me a dark look. "He's asking because of course the police will ask."

Not why I'm asking.

"Oh, man." Jerome blinks. "I don't know... Do they have a time of death for Milo?"

"Two-thirty-five," I inform him.

"Wow, that's specific. Okay... I think I was here taking a nap."

I raise my brows. *Interesting.*

"What?" he says, staring at me.

"Can anybody corroborate that?" Ms. Renfield asks.

Jerome is positively pale at this point. "Who can corroborate a nap or being home alone?"

"We need to go." Ms. Renfield closes her hand around my arm and all but drags me out of there.

"Dude," she says in a low voice as we move down the hall. "In what world is he a suspect?"

"This one," I say simply. "I haven't sensed that much guilt in a man since Roy the Red left his brother to hang in his stead."

"Jerome feels guilty because he thinks he caused a murderer to get out of jail, and that murderer killed two people."

"Perhaps."

"Perhaps?!" She whirls to face me in the small lobby. Her cheeks are flushed with indignation, quite becoming on her.

I say, "He has no alibi, he has motive, and I couldn't help but notice that he did not answer my question about the last time he saw Milo dead or alive."

"It sounds like he saw him last at Berky's," she says.

"That's when he saw him last *alive*."

"He would've had to see him alive to kill him."

"Not if he shot him in the back."

"That doesn't even make sense. I can't even. And what's up with you telling him not to go to the police? He absolutely has to, or he'll just look guilty."

"But what if he *is* guilty and the police decide to keep him?" I lean closer, letting my voice drop. "You forget our objective here, Ms. Renfield. We are finding a meal for me, and I must remind you: dinnertime approaches."

"We still have eight days and he's not the murderer."

"Your certainty shows me you are not seeing clearly."

"You are not draining Jerome."

"Even if he ordered the killings? Even if he did the killing himself?"

"Let's find the real culprit, how about that?" This she says in her very end-of-conversation way.

And I am more than fine to have that serve as the end of the conversation, though later that night as I listen to her huff around in her quarters, I have a strange, unsettled feeling about the whole thing.

As if I need to smooth things over with a Renfield.

Chapter Twenty-Two

Harriet

The following afternoon, I'm reorganizing my library shelves, re-sorting by publication date within subject when my phone buzzes with a news alert: **BREAKING: Man killed outside Hawthorne Hills Apartments.**

Hawthorne Hills is a senior apartment complex in Creighton. I scan the article. What catches my eye immediately: the weapon was a crossbow.

I pull up social media and there's an avalanche of information.

The victim is Nick Lernov, a retired history teacher. No suspect was found, but they did recover the weapon: a crossbow identical to the ones used in the previous two murders.

Mr. Lernov had last been seen stepping outside at around 1:00 p.m.. A groundskeeper found his body.

I piece together more from the comments on the article. He'd taught at Creighton for twenty-two years. Students describe him as demanding but fair, the kind of teacher who'd stay after school to help anyone who asked. He'd coached the Quiz Bowl team for two decades.

And of course, there is speculation: *Has to be Dooley Brogan. Three crossbow murders? Come on.*

I set up some news alerts and go up to the library to find Alexandru.

I pause at the door. He's in his usual chair by the fire, absorbed in one of his antique atlases. I think this one is the Ottoman cartographer one. He just stares at the maps for a really long time.

Granabelle sometimes reminisces about old Ashwood with her friends. They'll remind each other of the deli that used to be on River Road, or how Sloane's stationery shop was once a malt shop where she and Grandpa had their first date. Things like that.

Is that what Alexandru does with his maps?

I want to ask him. But he's been such a jerk about Jerome, dismissing my judgment like I'm some naive idiot. I don't want him thinking I'm interested in what he's doing or his opinion or anything.

Even though some pathetic part of me still wants him to trust me. To see me as a partner, not just an easily replaced servant from a family he mortally hates for reasons he won't explain.

"Another murder?" He doesn't look up from his atlas.

"How do you know?"

He turns a page. "Your heartbeat quickens when you are on the chase." Dark eyes lift, assessing me with predatory focus. "You are hot on the chase, Ms. Renfield."

I stroll in, casual as you please, and lean against the cool marble side of the hearth. The firelight glints in his unruly dark hair. An errant strand falls over his brow, softening the sharp angles of his face. He looks like a human man. Of the annoyingly attractive kind.

"Tell me," he commands.

And I do. Despite everything, I enjoy telling him, enjoy his sharp questions, the way his mind works through the puzzle, even though he treats it all like an armchair game.

"You will research this teacher as you have done the others," he commands. "You will discover what connection he has to Jerome and to Dooley."

"Obviously I was going to do that."

"Go, then. Do not dawdle."

"Yeah, I'm going. And I don't dawdle," I say hotly.

He picks up his book, a clear dismissal.

I turn and leave, gritting my teeth.

I head out to InovaSpire without inviting him. I pull out every tool at my disposal—cross-referencing databases, social media deep dives, financial records. I even use one of KC's experimental graph visualization apps that maps degrees of separation.

There is absolutely no connection between Dooley and Mr.

Lernov, and no connection between Jerome and Mr. Lernov, either. They lived in neighboring towns, but that's it.

The three names on Jerome's list yield three deeply awkward phone calls and precisely nothing useful. I stop by Hardware Sam's and neither he nor Pilar have heard anything. I text Josie. She hasn't heard any city council gossip.

I head back home and flop into the chair next to Alexandru's by the fire. "Nothing."

Alexandru closes his book. "No connections at all?"

"I looked high, low, and sideways. Maverick is keeping things weirdly quiet, too. Maybe they're chasing down alibis. Maybe they're as baffled as we are. Why this teacher?"

"Misdirection, perhaps?"

I consider this. "Like if Dooley's doing these killings to thank Jerome, maybe this is how he protects him? Kill someone random to break the pattern and prove it's not about Jerome's enemies?"

"Exactly. Or Jerome is directing this, he told Dooley to kill someone unconnected to get him off the hook."

"How am I not surprised you'd say that?"

"Because you know I am an excellent tactician."

"That's it," I say.

"Or perhaps Jerome is doing all the killing himself and framing Dooley. Perhaps he freed Dooley specifically to use him as a scapegoat. Who better to blame than an ex-convict with the same MO?"

"And then kill a random person as misdirection?"

Alexandru smiles. "The plot thickens."

"Truly random murders are actually the hardest to solve because there's no logical thread connecting victim to killer.

But they're also the rarest; most killers have *some* reason, even if it's a twisted one. True random violence is usually impulsive; not methodical. But this killer is methodical." I pull up my spreadsheet and stare at the grid of names and dates and circumstances. "What am I not seeing?"

"Whatever it is, you will discern it eventually."

I appreciate his faith in my abilities more than I want to admit, but the spreadsheet feels so inadequate. Like I'm trying to solve a 3D puzzle on a piece of paper.

Variables swim before my eyes. Timeline, motive, opportunity, connections.

And that's when the ledgers surface in my mind again. My father's ancient black books filled with symbols that weren't math and weren't language or anything I could name, except that some part of me understood them anyway. I'd ordered them shipped back to Karsovia. Alexandru had overruled me. They're somewhere in this house, and when I'm stuck like this, I can feel them like a low hum through the walls. *We know. Come look.*

"Can I ask you something? When my father first came to work for you, was he into it?"

Alexandru closes his book. "I thought you never wanted to hear about your father."

"The things you told me about my father were a bit disturbing, but they were all when he had been serving you for forever. You never talk about my father when he first came. When he was a more normal person. What was he like? You said he was a London-born lawyer?"

"Indeed he was. He was eager to serve me. He saw it as an interesting challenge, and a puzzle. He liked the international aspect of my business. I believe he was bored in London, working mostly on petty real estate cases. Like you, he thought his parents' books were in utter disarray."

"So he was good with just dropping everything and coming to live in your castle for an indeterminant amount of time?"

"I suppose he saw it as temporary at first."

"So he tried to leave after a while."

"You all try to leave."

I spent a lot of time demonizing my deadbeat father, but now I feel this wave of compassion for him. He was probably a decent person when he first arrived.

"And you wouldn't let him leave. And you punished him and you broke his mind."

"I grow weary of your moralizing."

"I grow weary of your medieval-horror-show personality."

"You would not say that if you knew what your line is truly like."

"Why don't you enlighten me. What is my line truly like?"

"You do not want to know," he says.

"I think you do not want to tell me."

"Not particularly."

"Usually people get to find out what their crime was before they're punished for it."

He turns a page. Is he seriously reading right now?

"And what's up with the ledgers?"

He looks up. The firelight catches the copper in his hair. "You track and manage my business with them."

"You know I'm not talking about the accounts ledgers. The mystical ones. What did my father do with them? Did he talk about them to you?"

"He asked about them a good deal, just as you are asking."

"And?"

Alexandru ponders a long time, perhaps weighing what to tell me. "The ledgers are bound to the Renfield bloodline."

"Like it's a Renfield practice to write strange mystical symbols in ledgers and be weirdly drawn to them?"

"I do not pretend to know how to read them. The ledgers cannot be destroyed. Or more, they can be destroyed, but once destroyed, a Renfield will instantly set about recreating them, like termites rebuilding their termite hills over and over. The scribbled symbols are a quirk of your family left over from the days when you practiced the dark arts."

If there was a thought bubble above my head at this point, it would be filled with exclamation marks.

"Sooo.... those ledgers are dark arts things? A hobby of the Renfields?"

He inclines his head.

"Who tried to destroy them?"

"It's not important who."

"It's important to me."

He shrugs.

The dark arts?

The mystical ledgers don't feel like spellbooks or anything like that. It's more like they track and describe things in dimensions a regular spreadsheet can't reach. But beyond that, I can only grasp the edges.

"Does that whole dark arts thing have something to do with why you're so angry at us Renfields?"

"The Renfields are despicable for so many reasons. Reasons

that predate your father, your grandfather, and a dozen generations before them."

"That's not an answer."

"No," he agrees. "It is not." This he says with a finality that I have come to know. I will get no more from him tonight.

My head is spinning with all this new information, though.

I return to my more mundane spreadsheets with names, crimes, connections, circumstances. Sometimes the answer is in the noise between the data points.

But I keep going back to our conversation. And those other ledgers.

I catch myself wondering where Alexandru keeps them. Whether they're in the east wing vault, or his private study, or what. And what exactly can they do? Can they help me see more? Could they help me better solve this mystery?

Could they help me find James?

Chapter Twenty-Three

Harriet

I stop by the antique store on my lunch break the next day, hoping for the latest buzz on the killing, but mostly I'm hoping for a sanity break from Chez Dracul.

Do I get it? Not so much.

Granabelle's wearing something that looks very Betsy Ross —not a good look for her, to be honest—and she's placed herself in the middle of the early American era display; her phone is mounted on a tripod nearby.

Her curmudgeonly handyman "friend," Denny Cole, stands by, arms folded across his chest.

A man kneels beside her; when I get a better view, I see that it's Gregor, seeming to fix an overturned chair.

He's removed his long dark green coat—which I've never seen him do. I spot it hung neatly over a display case. In his shirtsleeves, the severe military cut of his clothing is more pronounced. He's applying something to the chair's joints with a small brush, his movements confident.

A double boiler sits on a hot plate beside him, the smell of something earthy and faintly live-stock-ish rising from it.

I go up next to Denny. "What's going on?"

"That's hide glue," he says. "My grandfather used to make it just like that. You can't buy it anymore, not the real stuff."

Granabelle is suddenly talking to the camera about her special guest demonstrating the lost arts. "And, ladies, yes, he *is* single."

Gregor simply continues his work.

"Tell them how he's heating it," Denny calls out. "Has to be the right temperature. Too hot and it breaks down. Too cold and it won't flow. Most people don't have the patience for it anymore."

Granabelle wags her finger at the camera. "Don't worry, darlings, I'm not pivoting to home improvement. Though I *could* watch this all day."

"Yeah, real riveting." Mom comes up next to me. "A man making his own glue. What will they think of next?"

"Lorna, hush," Granabelle says, adjusting her bonnet. "My followers are going to eat this up. 'Antique Restoration: The Old Way.' I'm thinking a whole series."

"That'll bring in the customers."

Gregor reaches into a small cloth roll beside him and produces a wooden peg.

"Just in case you're wondering," Mom says to me in a low voice, "Gregor made that peg."

If Gregor heard, he doesn't show it. He holds the peg up to the light to examine it, then he fits it into one of the chair's joints.

"He's not using any metal fasteners at all," Denny marvels.

"You know, the original craftsmen who made these chairs in 1910? They would've done it exactly like this."

Mom makes a disgusted noise, her coral-painted lips pressed together in a thin line of something that isn't quite disapproval.

"The bones are good," Gregor says quietly, not looking up. "But this work..." He makes a small sound of disapproval. "The apprentice who made these pegs did not wait for the wood to cure."

Granabelle claps. "Where is that apprentice? Off with his head!"

Denny says, "A hundred years ago, and Gregor can still tell the quality. Man knows his stuff."

"The wood remembers," Gregor says. He taps a peg into place with a wooden mallet, the sound soft and hollow.

"He's been at this for an hour," Mom says under her breath. "He was up there fixing the roof, and your grandmother invited him to 'consult' on that chair we couldn't sell because it wobbled, and now suddenly it's a whole production." She snorts. "*Fashioning his own pegs.* Next, he'll be out back fashioning wooden teeth for people."

I take another look at her as it sinks in that she is wearing lipstick. Since when does Mom wear lipstick? But I don't say anything, because Mom would be weird about something like that.

Instead, I ask her about Nick Lernov's killing. "Have you heard anything new? Are they looking at Dooley for it?"

"I was wondering about that myself. Who knows? Things are pretty quiet."

"Careful," Granabelle calls out, zooming in on Gregor's hands. "Careful, careful—oh, that's beautiful."

Gregor glances up briefly, and for just a moment, something almost like satisfaction flickers across his weathered face. Then it's gone, buried again under his usual grim expression.

Mom doesn't take her eyes from him. "He is the strangest man I have ever met, and I say that as someone who met your father."

"Yeah," I say noncommittally. I have lots of thoughts about my father right now, but not a lot I can share with Mom.

Mom sniffs. "Better keep him out of the hammer-and-nails section of Hardware Sam's or he's liable to have a full-on heart attack. Is it possible this is how they do things in Karsovia?"

"The most modern thing they had in that castle was a 1940s rotary phone there, no lie," I say.

I leave out that Alexandru once seriously proposed tying scrolls to the throats of carrier pigeons as a superior alternative to email. He also threw a perfectly good Jitterbug phone into the fire because it made a sound he didn't like.

"Has he been here fixing stuff all day?" I ask.

"Yes. I thought you knew."

"The boss sent him again?"

"He did," Mom says. "And all kidding aside, there is a reason they invented the nail. I mean is this the level of workmanship Prince Cravat demands?"

"Yeah, they have a weird relationship."

Mom looks at me. "Gregor here calls him overlord. What's up with that?"

"Uh...Inside joke. Sort of."

"I'm not sold on that boss of yours, Harriet. He took advantage of your mentally enfeebled father. I don't feature it."

"Apparently dear old Dad wasn't mentally enfeebled when he first began working for Alexandru. Or even when you met him on that train that night."

"You're saying the prince kept your father on out of pity?"

"Who knows?" I say. "Anyway, off to do some reconciling." I grab the ledger books and head to the back nook where we do the accounts. The nook is barely bigger than a closet. There's a little desk with a banker's lamp with a green glass shade and an ancient adding machine Mom refuses to throw away. I settle into the creaky chair, open the ledger, and take a deep, centering breath.

Numbers. Columns. Debits and credits that will, eventually, balance.

Exactly what I need.

I sort last week's receipts. The familiar rhythm of book-keeping for the shop settles something in my chest. By the time I've worked through the week's transactions and confirmed that yes, the drawer was six dollars over on Tuesday, my shoulders have dropped from my ears and my breathing has slowed.

I sit there and enjoy the moment. Things may be careening out of control with Alexandru and the mystery, but at least I have this nailed down—no dark arts needed.

When I go back out, I find that poor Mom has gotten conscripted into ye ol' Early American streaming event. I decline the opportunity to don a wig and be "hot Martha Washington" and head across to Hardware Sam's.

The Hardware Sam grapevine does not disappoint. There's big news: Dooley has an ironclad alibi.

"You're sure?" I say to Pilar. She's holding the ladder for Sam, who's busy putting up a summer sale banner.

"It turns out that Dooley was up in Cleveland applying for a job in one of the mechanics shops there. Big shiny corporate place with security footage and everything. He was literally on film thirty miles away during the entire window when the murder would've taken place."

"So it's impossible that he could've done it," I muse. "Do they have any other suspects?"

"Our network's big, but it's not that big," Pilar says. "I don't think there have been any arrests, though."

"Nothing that we've heard," Sam says.

I go straight to my office when I get home, not wanting to tell Alexandru about Dooley's alibi for the new murder. He'll definitely think Jerome did it now.

I hate that he'll think it. I hate that Jerome looks so guilty now. Most of all, I hate that small, treacherous part of my brain that's whispering: *what if he's right?*

If Jerome could do this—Jerome, who cared about ethics and kindness back at the high school newspaper, who was one of the few people who understood why I held up that story even when he disagreed—then what does that say about anyone?

Does everybody have darkness lurking in their hearts?

Alexandru fills my doorway, one shoulder against the frame, hair slightly tousled, perfectly at home in his gorgeous cashmere suit. I think he arranges himself in these poses without knowing he's doing it, the way spiders don't know their webs are beautiful.

I focus back down on my laptop. "Thanks for sending Gregor to the antique store again. You really don't have to."

"It keeps him occupied."

"I'll say. He's using weirdly old-fashioned methods, as in pegs that he *carves* and glue he makes himself. Does he not know modern techniques?"

"Of course he knows them."

"Then why—"

"I prefer the old ways."

"But it takes three times as long."

Alexandru's shoulder lifts in an elegant shrug. "A man needs purpose."

I look up. "Are you punishing his family as well? Or is it just Gregor himself?"

"It is not what you think." He pushes off from the doorframe and moves into my office, but not toward me. Instead, he traces one finger along the spines of my bookshelf, taking inventory of my territory. A predator circling. When he finally stops, it's behind my chair, and I have to choose whether to turn and acknowledge him or pretend I don't feel the weight of his presence.

I stay put.

"Now, then," he says, lips near my ear. "Tell me what you have learned."

"How do you know I've learned anything?"

A pause. When he speaks again, his voice is closer than I expected, low and thoughtful. "Your pulse is elevated. Your skin has flushed with heat."

Another pause. What now? Is he tasting the air?

"You have found something. I can always tell. The hunt suits you, Renfield. You become...vivid."

Something flutters in my chest. I like the vivid thing. I do feel kind of vivid. "You think that's going to make me tell you?"

"You will tell me one way or another."

"Oh, is that so?"

His hands settle on the armrests of my chair, and slowly— so slowly—he rotates me to face him. Now we're at eye level, his face close to mine, and I can't roll away. He's not being threatening; he's simply there, gazing into my eyes.

And somehow, it's impossible to breathe.

"It is so. The puzzle is everything to you. You cannot stand an unclosed loop."

"Fine." The word comes out breathier than I intended. I clear my throat. "Dooley didn't do this last murder. He has an alibi."

Alexandru doesn't move. Doesn't blink. "Well, well, well."

"And I know what you're about to say, so don't bother."

"What am I about to say, little Renfield?"

"That Jerome for sure did it."

"Not *for sure,* but I would admit it as more of a possibility. Wouldn't you?"

I grit my teeth. My heart is beating like mad, and I know he can hear it. I know he can feel everything, being this close.

"Your loyalty does you credit," Alexandru says. "But you are no fool. You see what he might be. You simply hope otherwise."

"He's a good person."

He nods.

But even good people have it in them to kill. He's said it before, and I know it's true.

How many people have tried to kill him in the past? What is it like to be an object of terror?

Right then, it hits me: I miss the feeling of being allies. I miss working through clues with him. And that strange sense of triumph when we make a leap.

He continues to study me with those dark eyes.

"If I didn't know any better, I'd think you were trying to do some kind of whammy on me."

The corner of his mouth ticks up. "If only."

"Okay, fine," I hear myself saying. "I'll admit it could be Jerome. Obviously, it could be him. But you have to admit it might *not* be him."

The sharp planes of his face soften. "I will admit that."

The air between us seems to thicken. Neither of us moves.

His gaze drops to my mouth. Just for a moment. Just long enough for my breath to catch, for me to become aware of the exact distance between us. Just long enough for my pulse to spike... and I don't care if he knows.

The sound of weird old chimes breaks the spell.

Alexandru straightens. "Expecting someone?"

"No."

"Nor am I. Gregor is not here. You will have to get that."

Oh-kay, I think. *Back to overlord-and-underling mode.*

Probably for the best.

I get up and pass by him, careful not to brush against him, and head down the hall past the fire-hazard-lighting-and-gruesome-art display.

I pull open the creaky door, and I'm face to face with Jerome, laptop clutched under his arm. "I need your help," he says. "They're framing me."

Chapter Twenty-Four

Alexandru

I linger at the far side of the foyer, the better to evaluate the notes of guilt and terror rolling off of Jerome.

Ms. Renfield pulls him in and shuts the door. "What happened, Jerome?"

"I've been paranoid, okay? Obviously, somebody was framing Dooley, but I heard that he couldn't've done that last murder and, well, as you know, Milo and Razor Johnny were my enemies of sorts. So I wondered, is somebody framing me? I downloaded one of those recovery programs—the kind that finds deleted files? I wanted to make sure there was nothing on my computer." He tightens his grip on his laptop and lowers his voice. "I found searches, Harriet. *Deleted* searches. Stuff like 'Avoiding traffic cameras.' 'Crossbow bolt trajectory.' 'How to shadow a person without being noticed.' They'd been buried in my deleted browser history to make it look like I searched for them and then tried to cover my tracks."

"Jerome—"

"I didn't do those searches, Harriet. I'm telling you I didn't.

But they're sitting right there in my deleted files, and if the police wanted to, they could find them, and it'll look like I'm a murderer who tried to frame Dooley and then hide the evidence."

Ms. Renfield adjusts her glasses, going into her thoughtful mode. "You're thinking somebody planted that search history."

"I'm not just thinking it! I know they did. Don't you believe me?"

Ms. Renfield hesitates, unsure. For all of my complaints about her bias, it really is a credit to her that she is keeping her mind open.

Jerome, however, does not like it. "Harriet! This is me! We worked together for how many years on the school paper? You *know* me. And okay, yes, I helped get Dooley out of jail and didn't tell you. And I didn't tell you about the book—that's on me, too. But you know I'm not a killer. I don't have it in me. Somebody's framing me just like they framed Dooley."

"Okay, let me think."

I can feel him wanting to protest, to badger her into saying he's not the killer, but he seems to reconsider. "No, I get it. You want to think about it and follow the data, that's your thing, and I respect that. But I feel like, there has to be some trail, right? You know computers. You could take a look and see that it was planted." He holds out the silver laptop to her.

She takes it, genuinely unsure what to do. "I'm not sure that I have the capacity to examine this properly."

"But InovaSpire would, right?"

She sucks in a breath. She doesn't like this idea.

It's here Jerome notices the curved stairway with its carved serpents coiling up the balustrade, their scales rendered in dark wood so detailed they seem to ripple in the dim light. "Are those... snakes? Biting people's feet?"

"Don't ask," she says.

"Indeed they are," I say, emerging from the shadows. "The design depicts 'Night of the Coils,' a Karsovian folk tale where God finally abandons the earth and serpents rise to reclaim it, devouring mankind from the feet upward so that people might watch their own consumption." I gesture toward the sitting room. "Shall we?"

Jerome stands rooted in his place.

"Yes, a truly charming tale," Ms. Renfield says. "Let's go to my office. I have thoughts." She turns on her heel and leads the way back to her office.

I gesture for Jerome to proceed, and I follow. The torchlight throws shadows across the walls of the short hallways.

We follow her to her markedly brighter office. Ms. Renfield sets the laptop on her desk. She motions for Jerome to take the chair in the corner, but she herself does not sit. She plants her fists on her hips, regarding the machine like a foe.

I linger in the doorway, enjoying her in this mode: short of stature, but so oddly mighty.

She asks him for his password.

He gets up and comes around to her side of the desk and types it in. Fear and hope wash through him as he waits to see what she'll do next.

It is imprudent to allow one's primary suspect to deliver evidence to one's own doorstep, but I must admit things have become more interesting.

"Where are the weird files?" she asks. "Can you show me without moving things around too much?"

He bends over and does a little typing. Again, he stands aside.

Ms. Renfield leans in and studies the screen. "I would give them maybe a B-plus on duplicating your search language."

"What do you mean?"

Ms. Renfield points at something. "Look at your search history. You search noun-first. 'Budget deficit school board 2024.' 'Crime statistics Silverton County quarterly.' These supposedly imposter ones are modifier-first. 'Untraceable anonymous payment methods cash transaction.' 'Covert residential monitoring surveillance equipment.'"

Jerome's eyes widen. "Yeah! You're right! If it was me, I'd say, surveillance equipment residential monitoring covert. So do you believe me?"

"Well, maybe you knew I would notice it."

Jerome scrubs a hand through his hair. "Right. I get it."

The flavor of Jerome's emotions has shifted. The guilt has thinned; perhaps it was always about Dooley, about having inspired those murders. What remains is fear. The raw, animal kind. He believes he is being hunted. But then, a hunter who has become the hunted would feel much the same. Ms. Renfield glances up at me. I shrug.

"Look," Ms. Renfield says. "I'm going with your theory for now, okay? I'm going with the idea that somebody is framing you. Assuming we're right, then that person believes the police will get access to this laptop at some point."

"Do you think we should take an axe to it?"

"You think like quarry," I say, disgusted.

"Excuse me?" Jerome gusts out.

Ms. Renfield shoots me a look. "All he means is, if somebody's setting a trap, we have to turn the spotlight on that person. We have to play offense, not defense."

"Hunt the hunter," I add.

Ms. Renfield gazes at me, the gold in her eyes catching the light. "Hunt the *stuffing* out of them."

I find myself smiling at her. "This is all so wonderfully interesting. Almost like a puzzle constructed by some unseen hand. A nesting doll of sorts. You open one to find another inside, and another, and another."

"It's not that interesting to me," Jerome says.

Ms. Renfield turns to him. "The police are going to get a warrant for this laptop. That's inevitable. But before they do, I can copy the hard drive."

"Copy it?" Jerome straightens. "Like, make a backup?"

"More like a forensic image. Everything on the drive— deleted files, metadata, all of it. If someone hacked into your system to plant evidence, they left traces. The how and the where of the intrusion. Unfortunately, I don't have the tools to analyze it. Not really."

"But InovaSpire..." Jerome asks.

"Probably, but I don't want to involve them in anything that might look like obstruction of justice. Anyway, I've got something better. Less local." She pulls out her phone.

I watch her thumbs move quickly across the screen. A slight furrow appears between her brows. It truly is pleasurable to watch her work.

"My half-sister Irina lives in Vienna," she says, not looking up. "She's a forensic specialist who sometimes works with my other half-sister, who's in Interpol."

"I didn't know you had half-sisters," Jerome says.

"I do. And a half-brother in Vienna. Recent development." Ms. Renfield catches my gaze. "Alexandru here knows them, don't you, Alexandru?"

"I do indeed."

"Alexandru hosted us when we were in Karsovia for our father's funeral. Such hospitality as you've never seen."

My cunning Renfield. "Renfields deserve nothing less."

She twists her red lips in a half smile.

She's alluding to the fact that I once planned to kill those siblings of hers. Who could blame me? But Ms. Renfield used her wits to save their worthless lives.

Irina's existence is handy enough now, I suppose.

Ms. Renfield's phone buzzes. She types some more. "Good. Irina says she can analyze it remotely if I send her a proper forensic image." More typing. "She's sending instructions. There's a specific way to do it so that we capture everything, not just the visible files."

"And she can find who did this?" Jerome asks.

"Let's hope!"

The work goes quickly, and not twenty minutes later we're standing at the front door.

Ms. Renfield sets a hand on Jerome's arm. "What you need to do now is go home and sit tight."

"I don't know how I can possibly do that."

"You can, and you will," I say to him.

"The last thing you want to do is look guilty," Ms. Renfield explains.

"It's a little late for that! Somebody's already doing it for me! And they're doing a pretty good job of it."

"But you have us on your side, don't you?" Ms. Renfield

glances at me and I give Jerome a tight smile. "And you have the truth on your side," she adds. "Nobody wants to put away an innocent man. Nobody wants that; certainly not the police."

"But I also was instrumental in getting a murderer released from jail. They can't love that."

It takes about three more rounds of tedious assurances to get the man out the door, laptop in hand. We watch him drive away.

"He is going to run," I say.

Ms. Renfield looks up at me, shocked. "No way. We asked him to sit tight. He knows we're on his side."

"His mind is not clear."

"Did he seem sincere to you when he was talking about his horror of finding those searches on his machine?"

"He would not be the first murderer to be horrified by his own actions or his own stupidity."

"But you sensed that he was sincere in his horror. I think that's what you're saying."

"I did. And I'm sensing that you still very much want him to be innocent. That is not a disposition of a good detective."

"I can be rooting for somebody and still keep accurate score."

I am in my library reading by the firelight the following morning, enjoying the sound of the rain pelting the slate roof, anticipating a great thunderstorm to come, when Gregor appears at the door.

"Overlord. Do you require anything?"

"No."

He hovers, as is his tedious way.

From below comes the sound of movement—footsteps, the jingle of keys. Ms. Renfield.

"Go and see where she is off to."

Gregor's footsteps descend the curving staircase. "The overlord wishes to know where you are going."

"You may tell the overlord that it's none of his business."

"He would request it, milady."

"I would deny the request."

As usual, I must do everything myself. I descend the stairs to find her donning her rain hat. Her defiance sounded convincing, but something beneath it feels wrong. I cannot name it. I simply know.

"Where are you going?"

"Out." She does not turn. "To see an old friend."

"You are lying."

Now she turns, those gold-flecked eyes flashing with defiance. "I'm not lying. I'm just not elaborating."

"You are distressed."

"I think your Spidey senses need a tune-up, because everything's fine."

"It is the dark feeling that you get when we pass the ice cream shop." I step closer. "What is the matter?"

For a moment I think she might tell me—I can feel the explanation gathering. But then something changes. "I can't do this with you. It's personal—nothing to do with the case, nothing to do with my work here. Or with you."

"You are my Renfield; your distress has everything to do with me. You will tell me and you will tell me now."

"Not happening."

"I will not abide this situation!"

"Abide you will." She pulls open the door.

"Ms. Renfield!"

"Not my name! Don't wait up, overlord." With that she goes, a tiny warlord in a sweater jacket, rushing through the rain to her car.

I stand in the doorway, watching her taillights disappear down the drive.

I slam the door and whirl around to face Gregor. "She would refuse my request for this information?"

"You did not request, you demanded."

"As is my right. I am her overlord."

"Indeed you are," Gregor says insufferably.

It is infuriating.

"Is she not aware what I can do?" I turn, climbing back up the stairs to my library, though no serene reading will be taking place now; this is how vexed I am. "If something bedevils Ms. Renfield, she is to inform me of that thing, and I will solve it—so that she may resume her service to me at her fullest capacities."

I stride into the library, Gregor at my heels.

I point to his corner and he goes. I do not want to see his sad face nor hear his drivel. I throw myself down in my chair, unsure what to do, so extreme is my vexaciousness.

"What?" I demand, feeling the words crowd within Gregor.

"Perhaps it is something you cannot solve."

"Such as what?"

"You cannot solve guilt."

I ponder this. It is indeed guilt that I feel associated with the ice cream shop. Extreme guilt.

But how can it be?

"She is a paragon of virtue, toiling to save the worthless lives of peasants. So conscientious and charitable. If she feels guilty, it is because she dropped a paper clip or failed to compliment a villager's shoes."

"Perhaps she acts virtuous *because* of her guilt, overlord."

I turned my gaze to where he stands, sallow eyes barely visible in the gloom. If anybody should know about guilt, it would be Gregor. "You have further thoughts. You will reveal them to me."

"Perhaps she is afraid."

"Ms. Renfield? Afraid of me? Why would she be afraid of me? I have never so much as thrown her one day in the dungeon."

"Perhaps it is not you she is afraid of. Perhaps she is afraid of what she carries. Afraid to reveal it."

This makes no sense.

How is it, of all the servants in the world I end up with these two? A trembling coward and the most obstinate Renfield in history.

I take out my book, opening to some page, I care not which. My eyes trace the familiar lines of Constantinople's walls, but my thoughts drift back to Ms. Renfield. That dread. And yes, the guilt. I have tasted such feelings in others. Never has it nettled me so.

I look up, annoyed. "What else?"

"You should ask her nicely."

"An overlord does not beg."

"Perhaps you would go to her as something other than her overlord. Perhaps then she will yield."

"Go to her as something other than her overlord? She is a Renfield. I am her overlord. It cannot and will not be other than that. Not ever."

Gregor says nothing, but he vibrates with opinions.

I stand, causing the book to fall to the stone floor, a few of its ancient pages detaching from the binding. "Go! You will count the stones in the north wall. I believe you miscounted last time."

Chapter Twenty-Five

Harriet

Mrs. Alma Washington uses a small silver tongs to extract a sugar cube from the painted little bowl at the center of our doily-laden table. "One cube?"

"Yes, please." I lean in to inspect the tiny frosting design on one side of the sugar cube. "Is that a bunny?"

Alma's smile widens and she drops it into my oolong tea, extracts a cube for herself, and holds it up for me to see. "Yellow flowers! My lucky day." She drops her cube into her tea.

This is a ritual that we have gone through for years.

The antique Tennessee spoon I brought for her collection sits on the table between us. That's another part of the ritual. She was pretty excited about getting Tennessee; she now has forty-one states.

Alma lives in a three-story brick senior apartment on the north end of Ashwood, just a few streets up from Tilly and Dooley's place.

We sip our tea and I ask her about her granddaughter. She takes out her tablet and shows me some of the latest shots from Instagram. The girl's ballet career is booming. "Such a sweet family. You did good, Alma."

"They are my treasures." Alma tells me about a picnic the extended family took and then afterward they all went to the Muddy Pint. "That scoundrel Kip Kidderson was there eyeing our girl, and I told him in no uncertain terms to steer clear of her." She has some choice words for Kip with "his playboy hair."

She goes on to ask about Granabelle, and I give her the latest updates.

Alma Washington was the one and only witness to the strange man wandering around downtown Ashwood near the school the day James disappeared. She described him as a "well-dressed tourist wearing a brown coat who looked like he didn't belong."

The police didn't put much stock in Alma's observation because tourist season was moving into full swing; of course there would be tourists, and tourists by their nature do not belong, and some are well dressed.

The police paid a lot more attention to a local girl who reported seeing a man resembling the Cuyahoga Killer on the river walk around that time, right down to the denim overalls with the hole in the left knee.

But here's the thing: I went to school with that girl. She was a few grades younger, and she told a lot of tall tales, one memorable one involving the Jonas Brothers staying at the Silverton Inn, which led to kids camping out there for days. And the Cuyahoga Killer was our ultimate bogeyman at the time; the iconic picture of him with his denim overalls and bushy gray beard was burned into our minds.

He hung himself in his kitchen wearing those overalls.

Alma disappears into the kitchen and brings out a plate with an almond chocolate Berky Bomb cut into four quarters. I once told her that kind is my favorite, and I get the feeling that she buys them by the half dozen and freezes them, bringing one out to thaw when we're going to have a visit.

What Mom said about her—that she pretends to remember new things about the day James was taken as a way to get me to visit—may be true. Sometimes she recalls insignificant details, like the part of his hair (but not the color), or she wants to stress that his jacket was a rich brown rather than an ash brown.

It's okay. Alma and I share a bond. We both saw something that day that didn't feel right. We're the only two people to question the official story of what happened to James.

I eat a bit of the cookie and get to it. "So Sam said you thought you might've remembered something new about the strange tourist."

She places one of the quarter cookies on her own little plate. "It's not so much that I remembered something new, but rather I thought of something new…or not so much thought. I'm not certain how to characterize it."

I give her a smile. "Let me know what it is and maybe we can characterize it together."

"I was down at Gazebo Park with some of the girls from the building. We were watching the tourists, and it came to me that, even though I described him as a tourist who didn't belong, tourists belong here, don't they?"

"I'm not sure what you're getting at. You thought he was a tourist."

"Yes." She grabs my hand. "I said he was a tourist who didn't belong here, but I think deep down. I knew that he wasn't a tourist. He wasn't a tourist *and* he did not belong...ohhhh, I don't know if I'm explaining this."

"No. You're doing great. I believe that you perceived something off. A well-dressed man who did not belong in that scene."

"I'm starting to think he wasn't a tourist. Or from the town."

"Really?"

Alma nods.

"Do you think it was the way he was dressed? Or his demeanor?"

Alma repositions her cookie quarter to the center of the small, flowered plate. Her description of the man always was more impression than details. She couldn't remember his height or his hair or skin color or whether he wore glasses or a hat or anything. He was nicely dressed. His jacket was brown.

She continues to fuss with her cookie. "I'm not sure. Watching those tourists the other day, that is what came to me. I should not have called him a tourist at all."

"Well, that is extremely helpful," I say, even though it really isn't.

"I swear, I don't know what this town is coming to. First your brother, and then those horrible wedding murders, and now Dooley Brogan shooting the place up with a crossbow?"

"The police don't think it's him anymore," I say. "He was in Cleveland during the most recent murder."

She waves a dismissive hand in the direction of the police station. "The police aren't telling us everything they know."

"Why do you say that?"

"Because they were keeping a watch on Dooley and Tilly's house before the first murder even happened and then tried to pretend it wasn't them who were watching the house!"

"Wait, what? What's this?"

"Well, you know that Francine and I do our morning constitutional down Kempton to Greentree. Well, we started noticing a car parked on the street outside Dooley's sister's house with a man inside. We thought it was strange, but then the crossbow murders started and they put yet another man outside the house. Two cars watching that house. But when I asked Officer Maverick about it, he said they only had one car watching the house, and that was only after the crossbow murders started. I ask you, what is he hiding?"

"You and Francine saw a man in a car outside of Tilly Brogan's house before the murders started?"

"We certainly did, and what that says to us is that they knew something was going to happen before it happened."

"And Maverick says it wasn't the police?"

"They were very sneaky about it," Alma says. "They used a car that is not their usual car."

"What did the car look like?"

"A small car. Very commonplace. Dark gray."

"And the person inside?"

"A man—I think. Could be a woman. They wore a ball cap."

"But you are quite sure they were a police officer."

"Who else would sit out there?" Alma asks. "What's more, there was no license plate."

This gets my attention. "No license plate? On either end of the car?"

"Well, we only saw the back."

I'm wondering if it could've been the killer, getting to know Dooley's routine.

I question her a bit more, but that's all she's got.

I make a mental note to find out what color car Jerome has, and then we go back to normal chat. I show her pictures of my new digs.

It's not easy to make these visits, to go back to that memory of how I failed my little brother, my best friend. But I think it's important to keep the memory alive and to keep talking with her about it, because maybe she'll find something significant in that memory of hers. There's always a chance.

Maybe she'll give me a new clue to follow. One more thing to put on my spreadsheet about James's disappearance. A way to find him.

I know he's alive—I know it in my bones.

I miss him every day. And I will never stop trying to find him.

I take the long way back, stopping into the store to say hi to Mom and Granabelle and to make sure things are running smoothly.

Granabelle is organizing the glass drawer pull display, wearing a 1950s safari outfit with a metal military hat that has pieces of brush taped to the top of it. I give her a kiss. "Who are you supposed to be?"

"I'm a resident of Ashwood, hoping to blend into the scenery so that I'm not next!"

"They wouldn't go after you," I say. "You have nothing to do with any of it."

"None of the other victims had anything to do with any of it as far as I can tell," Granabelle says, and she's not wrong.

What am I not seeing? And how many more people will die before I see it?

I point out that the attacks happened outside in public spaces. "It might be a good idea to limit your trips around town until they're caught."

"That's my thought. Except when I'm doing lives at the various murder scenes."

"Excuse me? You're doing what?"

"I'm doing livestreams at the murder sites. People love them."

"Granabelle, no!"

She shrugs. "The public has a right to know."

"A right to know what weird outfit you're wearing while parading at various murder scenes? Not in the Bill of Rights."

"So much for lying low, huh," Mom says coming up beside me.

"Until we figure out why they're targeting the people they're targeting, wandering around town could be dangerous."

Mom says, "Hardware Sam says they're doing a manhunt for the guy right now. That kid you went to school with—Jerome."

"What? They're doing a manhunt for Jerome?"

"If they don't already have him," she says. "You should talk to Sam and Pilar. They're all up on it."

I kiss them both and head across the street to Hardware Sam's.

"Hey, you!" Pilar says as I walk in. "Did you hear about Jerome?"

"Mom just told me. What happened?"

"I don't think they've got him yet, but if you wanna know the most up-to-date information, you should get home. Sam says he's headed to Kingston Manor this very instant."

I break seven traffic laws getting back to Kingston Manor.

There's a squad car out in front when I arrive. The one time I actually need Ashwood's finest to move slowly, they decide efficiency is an A-1 priority.

Voices reach me the moment I'm through the door—Maverick's flat Midwestern interrogation tone, Alexandru's aristocratic rumble. I take the stairs two steps at a time up to the dining hall.

Maverick and Officer Wright are seated on the side of the stupidly long dining table, looking uncomfortable beneath the iron chandelier. Alexandru occupies the head of the table, a king granting audience.

Maverick's got his cop notepad out. Officer Wright is staring up at the pugilistic chandelier. He's got questions.

Alexandru's lip quirks. "Ms. Renfield, how fortuitous. Officers Cooper and Wright were just inquiring about our recent visitor."

"Ah!" I paste on a smile that hopefully reads as *cooperative citizen* rather than *person hiding something*. "Hi, Maverick. Officer Wright."

Maverick gives me a quick nod, never breaking the chomp-tastic rhythm of his ever-present gum. Wright tears his attention from the chandelier. "Ma'am."

Gregor stands in a shadowy corner like a naughty yet eerie schoolboy.

Okay, I tell myself. Be chill. Everything's chill.

I grab a chair and bring it to the corner of the table between Alexandru and Maverick. It's a weird thing to do, but we are a ways past weird now.

Maverick says, "We were just discussing Jerome Good-win. His GPS puts him on the premises yesterday for about forty-five minutes, but Alexandru here seems fuzzy on the details. He's telling me..." Here Maverick looks down at his notebook. "I do not keep a guest book for persons of no conse-quence." He eyes Alexandru. "That's really what you want to go with?"

"Jerome was here for me." There's no point lying; Maverick will find out eventually. "He was scared. He thought someone hacked his computer and that they were trying to frame him."

"Really." Maverick's gum-chewing slows. "Frame him for what?"

"Obviously the crossbow murders. He said they planted searches, making it look like he was doing them and then deleting them."

"And you believed him?"

"It's Jerome!" Maverick knows him as well as I do.

"That's not an answer," Maverick says.

"Ms. Renfield is a very loyal human," Alexandru puts in somewhat unhelpfully.

Maverick eyes me. "Yes, so loyal that she didn't think to contact the police."

"Excuse me?" I say. "I'm sorry, I seem to recall the other day when I floated the theory that maybe Dooley didn't commit the original murder, you didn't want to hear it."

A muscle twitches in Maverick's jaw. "I believe I told you to stay out of the investigation."

"He's an old friend who wanted my help."

Maverick contemplates this a bit. "And were you able to determine whether he was hacked?"

"I'll tell you what I told him," I say. "I don't have those kinds of resources here. It's not as if I work at InovaSpire anymore."

Maverick considers this. "Did you get a look at his computer?"

"Yes, but I couldn't tell if he was hacked or not. I wasn't exactly on the technical side of InovaSpire. I was more about the overall organization of things. And then he took his computer and left." I leave out the part where I made a copy of his hard drive for Irina. It's not an outright lie, though it is a lie of omission.

"Hmm." Maverick gazes at a stained-glass window. "Any idea where he might've gone off to? Who might be helping him?"

"He was scared and he left. I don't know where he went and I haven't been in contact with him since."

Maverick's jaw tightens. "So he came with his computer,

telling you he was worried he'd been hacked, and you took a look at it and sent him back off on his merry way."

"That's about it," I say.

Maverick turns to me. There's something in his eyes that might be concern. "This is an active murder investigation, Harriet. If you're hiding something—"

"I'm not."

"—or if *he* is—" He jerks his chin toward Alexandru. "—I will find out."

"I have no doubt," Alexandru says pleasantly. "You seem a most diligent investigator."

"If you hear anything, and I mean anything, I'm telling you right now to contact me. Understand?"

"Sounds good," I say.

Maverick stands and jerks his head at Officer Wright, who scrambles up from the table.

Gregor takes this opportunity to materialize weirdly from the shadowy corner.

Maverick snaps his pad closed. "We're good. We'll see ourselves out."

Officer Wright hesitates. "Mav."

"What?"

Wright gestures up at the chandelier. "Does a fella need a permit for some of that?"

"Some of what?" Maverick turns his gaze up at the chandelier and his gum-chomping slows, which I suppose means that he has discerned that the giant weird, twisted iron chandelier is in fact studded with swords, maces, axes, and guns. The whole thing bristles with weaponry. "Now what in the Sam Hill is that?"

"It's a chandelier," Alexandru says, sounding more English than usual.

"Is it, now?" Maverick says, sounding very cop-like.

Officer Wright says, "I feel like some of those firearms could be functional. Isn't that a Colt Python? And look—an M14."

"That M14 was used by a peasant in the Carpathian Mountains to try to end my life. Unsuccessfully, as it turned out. The sculptor Emil Van Horn incorporated it into this chandelier he created for me, alongside a host of other weapons, all of them used—"

"Used in all kinds of battles!" I interrupt before Alexandru can complete his explanation—that all of those weapons were once used to try to kill him through the years. "It's quite expressive, don't you think? A very evocative commentary on the futility of conflict!"

Maverick stares at it. "Are you into the fighting arts, Prince Miramonte?"

"I did a bit of sword work in my time. Jousting. A spot of archery. The occasional battle-axe."

Maverick eyes him. "You a fan of the Rennaissance Festival, then?"

"Oh, he is, very much so!" I say. "And the great battles of history, and he decided that all the horrible weaponry should be fused into a work of art instead of used for war. I think it's amazing!"

"Real homey," Maverick says.

Alexandru waves. "See them out, Gregor."

Gregor leaves with the men, and I sink into one of the chairs—one of two positioned near the hearth, mercifully far from the main table and its overhead armory. "That went well."

"I thought so." Alexandru settles into the chair across from mine.

"He'll be back," I say. "With more questions."

Something shifts in his eyes—something old and amused and not entirely human. "I have dealt with more formidable investigators than Officer Maverick Cooper."

I don't doubt it. Alexandru has centuries of practice evading authorities of all kinds. "I thought you did a really good job of not antagonizing him. More or less."

"Thank you."

Five days until the absolute limit of his hunger. He has to be feeling it, but he's hiding it well. "How is your hunger level?"

He says, "We should have kept Jerome in the dungeon. If and when Irina gets back to you about the computer being hacked, that would've been convenient."

"I honestly can't imagine he even knows how to operate a crossbow."

Alexandru sighs.

I hold up a hand. "I know, I know. Everybody can be a murderer. Humans are despicable little creatures."

"Not all of them."

"Oh my God, has hell frozen over?"

Alexandru studies me with an unfamiliar expression. The usual Italian-menswear-model menace is absent. He looks... disquieted.

"Something on your mind?" I ask.

"Your errand to town. Did it settle anything?"

"I seem to recall telling you that whole subject is off the table."

"This distress of yours. The ice cream shop. I need to know."

"Why?"

"Because I find your suffering—" His jaw tightens, like he's swallowing something distasteful. "I do not wish it."

That stops me.

"This from the man who thinks an example of outstanding service from my father is using his dying breath to crawl uphill in agony to finish a delivery for you?"

"Your father's suffering was merely pathetic. It did not..." Something flickers across his face. "It did not *reach* me as yours does."

Oh.

Suddenly I'm thinking about the intensity with which he kissed my palm last month. The rawness in his voice when he vowed that the man who hurt me must die. I'd told myself it was ownership. Control. Something transactional.

This feels different.

"Alexandru, have you come down with a case of empathy?"

"Hardly," he growls.

But I think he's lying. And I think this is new territory for him.

"Look, it's not really about the ice cream shop. Or, in a way, it is." I take a breath. I find that I want to tell him. I want him to know. "I have a little brother. His name is James, and he's four years younger than me."

"A brother?"

"Not a Renfield, obviously. Different father—some loser

boyfriend of my mom's I barely remember. But James was amazing. He was the light of my life. I loved him so much. Mom did too, and Granabelle..."

Alexandru's tone sounds dangerous. "What happened?"

The whole story tumbles out of me—how I would pick James up at the grade school on my way home from middle school and we'd walk home together. But one afternoon I saw a boy I had a crush on go into the ice cream shop across the street, and I told James to wait and play some more while I went to say hello.

Alexandru sits perfectly still, watching me.

"In normal times it wouldn't have been such a terrible sin," I say, "but the Cuyahoga Killer was active in the area, snatching little boys all over eastern Ohio. I knew about it, and I still left him there so I could talk to a boy. I left him there even though I saw a strange car parked nearby. It was shiny and black and boxy, and something about it seemed odd to me."

"And still you went," he says softly.

"And that was the last time I saw James." My voice catches, but I push through. "He vanished. Eight years old. It was horrible. Everyone thought he'd been taken by the Cuyahoga Killer, of course. There were search parties sent out, combing high and low for days. Even this place, back when it was still a ruin." I look around Alexandru's living room, remembering it gutted and crumbling, volunteers calling James's name through empty windows. "I was so scared for him, and it was all my fault."

Alexandru doesn't interrupt. Doesn't offer platitudes. Some quality in his stillness makes it easy to keep talking.

I tell him about the grimness that settled over our family. How Mom couldn't function for years afterwards. The way

Granabelle became a little untethered, putting this weird bright face on everything. How I stayed at Josie's house a lot. How I blamed myself for all of it.

"You were a little girl," Alexandru says. "You were twelve."

"Old enough to know better. We were all completely paranoid about the Cuyahoga Killer. How could I have done such a thing? But at the same time, I don't think it was the Cuyahoga Killer who took him—if anyone even took him. The Cuyahoga Killer was a rural type with a big beard, and he was wearing overalls with a rip in the knee, and he drove a white van. But there was something about that black car I saw that day. It was gone when I came out of the ice cream shop and discovered James missing, and something in my gut said he'd been taken away in it. A shiny black car. Everyone said it was probably just a tourist."

I pause, gathering the threads. Alexandru waits. It strikes me that I've never told anyone the whole thing like this—not in one piece, not without being argued with.

"Hardware Sam's mother, Alma Washington—she was a teacher at the grade school back then, a year before she retired. She walked home every day, and she said she passed a man—a tourist wearing a brown jacket who looked like he didn't belong. No other details." I toy with the key around my neck. "People ignored it because a lot of the tourists who come here are well dressed, and it was jacket weather that day. But I've always thought it was something."

"Is that why you went to see her today? To talk about this tourist who did not belong?"

"Yes. She thought maybe he wasn't a tourist at all. Because tourists do belong here." I let out a breath. "Mom thinks Alma just reaches out to me because she's lonely. But I trust her intuition. And honestly, I don't think it's exactly intuition. I think she saw something that wasn't right about that man—something she couldn't articulate. Same with me and the car. I saw something off—I know I did."

Alexandru's dark eyes hold mine. "You are a Renfield. You see below the surface. If your instinct says the black car was off, then the black car was off."

His belief shouldn't mean this much. But nobody—not Mom, not Josie, not Maverick—has ever just said *yes, you saw what you saw.*

"But...the whole town thinks it's a delusion. Like it's a way for my mind to relieve itself of the guilt, by me telling myself he might still be alive."

Alexandru growls deep in his throat. "They think that because they do not understand you."

"I feel sure he's still alive."

"Did they ever find this Cuyahoga Killer?"

"Yes, but not before he hanged himself—wearing those overalls, just like in all the pictures. They dug up his property and found five skeletons in the yard. Boys from all over Pennsylvania and Ohio." I swallow hard. "But none of them were James. There were ten missing boys in total, and the theory is that the guy had another burial ground somewhere that they've never been able to find. And he probably does, but James isn't in there. He can't be. I know in my heart he's still alive."

Alexandru doesn't tell me I'm in denial. Doesn't suggest therapy or acceptance or moving on. He simply inclines his head, as if my certainty is good enough for him.

"I imagine you are working on this mystery as well. I presume you have a spreadsheet."

"That and more. But there's not much in it. It's as if someone plucked him out of the world without leaving a mark."

We sit there for a while, not speaking. The fire settles. The rain keeps on. And for the first time in twenty years, the weight of it feels like something I'm not carrying alone.

Chapter Twenty-Six

Alexandru

A child of twelve. A momentary lapse. And she carried it all these years, a stone in her chest. "Your brother, James, would be twenty-eight now."

"Yeah, and people point it out like, why wouldn't he reach out? As a fully grown adult, he'd be able to make his way home. But there's some reason he hasn't."

"If anybody can find him, you can."

She whispers a soft *thank you.*

I study her in the firelight, hands folded in her lap. Her pulse has steadied. The grief is there, but beneath it runs a steely strain of resolve.

"But there is one thing I do not understand. Why keep it from me?"

She gazes into the fire, and I think she will not answer, but then she does. "I've lived here my whole life with everyone defining me by that one moment. They think I'm damaged. Like my talent at spreadsheets and organizational things is this coping mechanism." She looks at me. "I didn't want you to see me that way too."

"What you carry is not damage."

"Thank you." Her voice is quiet. "For believing in me. It means a lot."

It means a lot.

Something uncomfortable shifts inside me. I have been feared, obeyed, desired, despised over the centuries. I have been begged for mercy and cursed with dying breaths. I know what to do with all of these things.

I do not know what to do with gratitude. I cannot abide it.

Truly, this Renfield will not cease to vex me.

The distance between my chair and hers has grown too small.

I rise. "I shall leave you to your rest."

I retreat to the dungeon—what Ms. Renfield insists on calling "the cistern." It lies below the old house, accessible through a heavy oak door. The basement itself is unremarkable, but the cistern is something else entirely. A well dug deep into the bedrock, twelve feet down and ten feet across, its walls lined with old brick gone dark with centuries of damp. The original builders intended it to hold water.

It is well-suited to hold other things.

Should we ever need to hold two murderers at once, for example, this is where the second would wait.

Gregor has done excellent work scrubbing the place clean. The old stains are gone, the floor swept, the chains oiled and ready. I descend the ladder and stand in the darkness.

A human would be blind here, groping at walls. But I see

perfectly—every ridge in the brick, every groove in the mortar, the faint gleam of the iron rings set into the walls.

I breathe in the dark and the silence. I focus on my hunger.

I let the cold stone walls leach the unwanted warmth away.

Chapter Twenty-Seven

Alexandru

"Yowza!" Ms. Renfield's voice sounds from her office.

I set down my book and glance at the moon. It is early for her to wake—just after four in the morning.

Her footsteps sound down her small hall and across the vast marble expanse of the foyer and up the staircase to where I sit in the library.

I can feel her excess of excitement as she bursts in. A smile tugs at my lips as she comes to a standstill at the center of the room, laptop in hand. "You are not going to believe this!"

"Will I truly not?"

She sets the laptop on a side table, and there on the screen is Irina, one of the Renfield half-siblings.

A gap-toothed grin spreads across Irina's face, a harder, sharper echo of Ms. Renfield's. "Well, if it isn't my least favorite person."

"You could not have simply relayed this information?" I ask Ms. Renfield.

"She could have." Irina adjusts her glasses. "But I wanted to let you know that you had better be treating our sister well, or we will be hunting you down."

"Is that so." I do not bother to suppress my smile. The Renfields are nothing if not consistent in their overestimation of human capability.

"I mean it," she says, pointing at me through the screen.

"I would not dream of mistreating Ms. Renfield."

"See that you don't. Anyway, I'll tell you what I told her. Somebody logged into Jerome's computer from an external IP." She ticks points off on her fingers. "Modified files, planted searches, left a back door in the system like an amateur. Well—not an amateur. But not good enough to hide from me."

"So Jerome was telling the truth," Ms. Renfield says.

"That's not the interesting part." Irina leans closer to the camera. "The IP bounced all over—Romania, Brazil, Singapore —but guess where it actually originated?"

"Must I?" I say.

Ms. Renfield watches my face, excited for me to learn this news which she apparently already knows.

Irina leans in. "The hack came from inside InovaSpire."

"InovaSpire?" This is indeed interesting.

Ms. Renfield beams at me, savoring the moment. "Right?"

Irina sits back, looking enormously pleased with herself. "You're welcome."

It is not yet dawn when we reach "The Foundry," a large brick structure perhaps a century old that houses InovaSpire. Ms.

Renfield tells me it was once an actual foundry where molten metal was hammered into tools. Now it is a place where humans sit and tap at glowing screens, and the name is merely ironic.

We proceed up the short walk. There is a coffee shop on the ground floor, but it is dark, chairs stacked on tables behind the glass.

"Such a different world at night," Ms. Renfield observes.

I inhale, savoring the stillness—the absence of that accursed sun and the villagers who clutter the streets by day. The creatures of the night are sleek and quiet and clever. "Far more agreeable," I say.

She draws a card through a small slot beside the door—what passes for a key in this age. "I hope we can nail this before Serena gets here." We head up the stairway to the top floor.

Ms. Renfield greatly admires Serena, though I do not see how this human is in any way superior to Ms. Renfield. "And you are certain she will not be unhappy with your presence at this strange hour?"

"It's not so strange for me. If you recall, I was managing your European empire all winter. I was getting here at three in the morning all the time when I was doing both jobs."

We reach the top floor and move silently past the warren of offices all the way to the front with its large windows framing the Silverton River, black under a sliver of moon. Ms. Renfield settles into the small desk and sets down her electronic ledger which again shows the face of Irina.

Irina waves. "Hi again, Grandpa!"

"You would do well not to address me thus."

"What are you gonna do? Throw me in a bone pit?"

"Come on, guys. Let's go." Ms. Renfield shifts the angle of the screen so that Irina can read it.

"Pull up the network admin console—Tools, then Connection Logs."

I wait, keenly aware of my growing hunger.

"I'm in," Ms. Renfield says. "Now what?"

"Filter for outbound connections to Jerome's IP address. I've got the timestamp from the intrusion..." Irina rattles off various nonsense. "We're looking for which internal machine initiated contact."

Ms. Renfield types. There seems to be some problem that requires them to access something called "archived logs." Irina gives her instructions and Ms. Renfield types away

I wander along the window, focusing on Ms. Renfield's heartbeat from across the room, steady as a metronome.

I thought I had settled this. I stood in the darkness of the dungeon and reminded myself what I am. The predator who sees when others cannot.

Not the fool who sits by a fire and feels his chest turn at a woman's gratitude.

Thank you. For believing in me. It means a lot.

I cannot stop thinking about her revelation about James. This loss she endured, and the way she blames herself. Ms. Renfield is so outrageously conscientious. To have lost her brother in such a way—I can see how it would have pained her. It makes me want to hunt.

No. I do not like this. I do not like any of it.

Who took James, if not this Cuyahoga Killer? Or did he indeed wander off? Could he truly be alive?

I look over at her, typing away, face lit by the screen,

animated by the hunt. I find I want to be beside her. To share in the thrill of the hunt.

"It means a lot."

I gaze over the brightening countryside, feeling pleased about that fact. Even more.

And that is when I grip the steel frame that separates one massive swath of glass from another. Good God, what am I doing?

She is a human! And not just a human, but a Renfield! A Renfield of all things.

The memory rises, slow and foul.

The ritual chamber. The taste of blood and iron still on my tongue, my body strange and new and terrible. I had done it for Elisabeta. For her kingdom, her people, and mostly because she asked me to.

Because I loved her.

I looked up, expecting...what? That she would touch my face? Gaze upon me with warmth and affection?

Instead, something like triumph moved behind her eyes. She looked at me the way one might look at plundered jewels.

I told myself I was wrong. The torchlight. The shock of transformation. My own disorientation.

I did not yet understand that I had seen her true face. I did not yet know the horror that was coming.

I turn from the window.

Twenty-three days since I last fed. Diverting as these mysteries are, I cannot wait much longer.

I focus on my hunger. That, at least, is familiar. That, at least, is *mine*.

On the upside, we could find the killer today. I could drain somebody's blood today. Warm and nourishing.

I move along the row of desks, considering who I would drain if Ms. Renfield were not so tediously ethical about such things. I would start with Officer Maverick Cooper, naturally. And then there was the man in the minivan who ran a stop sign and nearly struck Ms. Renfield some weeks back. I naturally made a mental note of his face. I would very much enjoy feeling him squirm as he recognizes that a superior predator has taken him.

Ms. Renfield's conversation with Irina drones on—something about a bounced connection.

I stroll to the far window, thinking about the Snag Tooth Riders. Ms. Renfield hates how loud their motorcycles are. I would pick them off one by one, perhaps the one with the loudest motorcycle first. Some of the members of this gang are quite beefy. They would provide me with rich blood.

The sky outside is beginning to lighten at its edges. How long have we been here?

"Try filtering by the subnet," Irina says.

A dark curl has escaped one of Ms. Renfield's hair clips, and it hangs down, kissing her cheek bone. Her pulse has quickened slightly. Frustrated.

I turn back to the window.

There is also Harlan Delmere, the land developer who recently plotted to build upon Ms. Renfield's favorite park, much to her distress. I remember how Ms. Renfield let her jaw hang open, as if to demonstrate the horror she felt.

There is also whoever shot at us when we were investigating the wedding killer mystery. They wore a mask, and we never did find out who it was, but they must have some idea what I am. That is never good.

And there is Sloane, who owns the stationary store, but I am not so sure Ms. Renfield would want her dead. They feud, it is true, but Ms. Renfield calls her "frenemy" which is a mix of friend and enemy...

"Alexandru!"

I turn to find Ms. Renfield behind me. "Did you not hear me come up?"

"I was ruminating."

Her red lips quirk up at the side, and I turn back to the view. The horizon has gone fully pink now. "Do you have a result yet?"

"No. Something's still processing, but it's almost seven. People will start coming in soon. I'm honestly surprised Serena isn't here already. When she does show up, I'm sticking to the truth—that I updated files, which I did, and that we're doing deeper research connected to the case. If she asks anything beyond that, I plan to be vague. I suggest you don't contribute."

"And I suggest you worry less about appearances and more about how little time remains."

"We're working as fast as we can."

I turn to her. "Do you think it could be Serena behind all this?"

"I seriously doubt it. But when it comes to true crime, you learn pretty quickly that you never say never." A chime sounds from her workstation, and she rushes back over.

I press my palm flat against the cold glass.

Twenty-three days without food. I can feel the feral rising. My thinking is fragmented. Jagged.

It is rare that I endure these long periods of hunger, but it has happened, most recently last month, when we were foiled in our quest to find the wedding killer.

The elevator hums. "They come."

Ms. Renfield startles at my voice. "Okay! Thanks." She nods and keeps working away.

"Harriet! Alexandru! You two are here early!" Serena strolls over in a cloud of chemical scent.

Ms. Renfield smiles. "Just had to jump on here really quick and then we're gonna go out for a coffee." The two of them have a brief conversation. Serena finds nothing amiss.

"You are very patient," Serena says to me.

"Who's patient?" Malik strolls in alongside KC and some of the others.

"Poor Alexandru's patient. Harriet dragged him over here on the way to coffee."

"Special mystery project?" KC asks.

"All my projects are special mystery projects!" Ms. Renfield says. I cannot help but notice she has removed Irina's face from her electronic ledger.

Malik thanks her for something called a 982 doc, and KC jumps in with some suggested tweak on something.

I observe the group of them, Serena with her tightly wound brightness, Malik, driven and intensely private, and KC, hyper competitive and eager to show his talent.

The group of them drifts away.

Moments later, I feel her pulse kick.

I go to her, arms folded. "You know who. Tell me."

She looks up at me. In a low voice, she says, "It traces back to Varla. You met her—the woman who has my old office. One of my replacements along with Malik."

"The one who does not like you."

"Could be that she doesn't like a lot of people."

I lower my voice. "Alive."

"Maybe?" she whispers.

"We must talk to her."

"I haven't seen her come in yet." She puts her things into her satchel. "Let's ask Serena if she's around."

It smells like candy lemons in Serena's office.

"All done for the day?" she asks.

"Mostly, but I really do want to follow up with Varla on something."

"She's not here yet?" Serena says. "That's weird, we have a meeting with Singapore in ten."

"Is it usual for her to roll in at the last minute?" Ms. Renfield asks.

"Very weird!"

Ms. Renfield furrows her brow. "Well...is there anything I can do?"

Serena raises an eyebrow. "Short of cutting the prince here loose and coming back on staff with me?"

"Hah." Ms. Renfield's laugh comes out strange. "I don't think that's in the cards."

"No," I say.

KC comes up beside us. "Singapore is happening in ten and Varla's gone dark. Sorry to interrupt, guys."

"No, we were just leaving!" Ms. Renfield pulls me out of

there. "I found it," she whispers. "While you were busy being insulted by Serena—the connection logs traced back to Varla's machine."

"Your Serena is indeed not shy about voicing her displeasure with me," I say once we are in the car. "She is lucky she is on your 'do not drain' list. Especially now."

"Don't worry, Count Chocula, your meal might be at hand. Varla Sims rents a farmhouse up in the hills."

"*Count,*" I sniff. "I am sovereign heir to a principality. A count would bow to me."

"It's settled, then; Count Chocula will bow to you and not the other way around. Anyway, I grabbed Varla's address once I saw it was her doing the hacking."

"You believe she is the Crossbow Killer."

"The hack on Jerome came from her computer. Man, I didn't give her enough credit for her technical chops. She was even giving Irina a run for her money with her clever concealment."

"Varla did not like you. I will enjoy taking her blood."

"Well, I envision speaking with her first. I want to ask her about these murders and see if she has an alibi, and maybe you can try and get a read on her. Ideally, she'll confess the way Bo the wedding killer did."

A growl rumbles deep in my throat. "Things will not proceed so far as *that,* I promise you." The memory of Bo Richardson's blade against her tender throat is still too vivid.

The road winds through early spring trees and open farmland. I adjust my hat to shield my eyes from the biting sun. We reach the top of a hill; a small farmhouse sits in the valley below, awash in blue and red flashing lights

"The police! No! How did they figure it out?" Ms. Renfield says. "No, no, no. This is bad."

My sentiments exactly.

If the police have Varla in custody, I can hardly drain her blood. Not without additional inconvenience.

Chapter Twenty-Eight

Alexandru

A police officer is posted at the door of Varla Sims's house. I have never seen him, but Ms. Renfield seems to know him. "That was fast," the officer says.

"What do you mean?" Ms. Renfield says.

"Maverick left a message with you just a few minutes ago."

Ms. Renfield pulls out her phone. "Oh, I had it on do not disturb."

The officer shouts into the house, and Maverick comes out. "That was fast."

"Uh, we were just over at InovaSpire, and everybody was wondering where Varla was and we were heading this way anyway so..."

Maverick squints, chewing his gum. Suspicious we arrived so quickly.

"Why did you call her?" I demand. "What's happening here?"

Maverick exchanges a dark look with his underling and addresses Ms. Renfield solemnly. "Thought you should get a look at this before it's on the news or the Hardware Sam crew goes crazy with it."

I can feel the fear and ice settle into Ms. Renfield's veins. "What's going on, Maverick?"

"Come with me. *He* stays out there."

"I will do no such thing," I say.

"Maverick, please. Whatever this is, I'd like Alexandru to come."

Maverick grumbles his assent and leads the way through a tidy and Spartan living room and on into a small kitchen.

Ms. Renfield gasps.

There at the far end of the kitchen is Varla Sims, laid out on the floor, a rope still attached to her neck. She's wearing overalls with a hole in the left knee.

Just like the Cuyahoga Killer!

"She hung herself? Wearing overalls like that?" Ms. Renfield gusts out.

"Yup. That's how we found her. Got a wellness check call for her from someone she was supposed to bike with this morning and..." Maverick gestures at the body. "There she was, hanging in the kitchen. Regarding the overalls...I don't know what's going on here. She would've been kids like us at the time the Cuyahoga Killer was operating. I mean, it could be a coincidence but..."

"I don't understand," Ms. Renfield says.

"You're telling me you worked with this woman?" Maverick says.

Ms. Renfield speaks without looking away from the body. "Sort of. She was one of my replacements at InovaSpire. She was never my biggest fan but... I don't understand this."

Maverick says, "It looks like a suicide. We won't know for sure until the ME gives us a final pronouncement, but the way the ligature marks look, I wouldn't call it a strangulation at first glance."

Ms. Renfield grips my arm. It is... unexpected. "It doesn't make sense."

Maverick squints. "You're saying she wasn't your biggest fan. That she replaced you at work. Maybe fixated in some way? Lotta troubled people out there."

"But to do something like *this*..." Ms. Renfield waves a hand in the direction of the body.

The scent of this is wrong.

Ms. Renfield lets go of my arm and wanders to the counter to stand over a carton of fries sitting upon a flower plate. Her pulse beats a bright staccato. She has seen something.

"What the hell," she whispers.

"What is it?" Maverick asks.

Ms. Renfield just stares at the food. "This is a Cuyahoga Killer thing. The fries on the flowered plate."

"It is?" Maverick says.

"It's a small detail that you can see if you blow up the photos of his kitchen where he killed himself. It was never seen as that significant, and it's not anything anybody would really remember. Well, unless you're on the Northern Ohio True Crime forum."

"The Northern Ohio True Crime forum?"

"Yeah. There was this long discussion thread at one point about why the Cuyahoga Killer hadn't eaten his fries before hanging himself. It was a really upsetting discussion, like making a parlor game out of this stupid detail. I tried to get the moderator to close the comments, but he wouldn't. One forum member in particular just wouldn't let it go, almost maliciously. Wait a minute... Wait a minute."

"What is it?" I say.

"This is so crazy." She turns to Maverick. "I know this is probably not at all protocol, but did you find any kind of computer or tablet around? I'd just like to see one thing."

Maverick frowns. "I'm not gonna be letting you onto her devices."

"How about if I tell you about a really important clue from the crossbow murders investigation?"

Maverick lowers his voice. "How about you tell me what you know about the crossbow murders, or I take you in for obstruction?"

I have had enough. I step close to Maverick. "This woman staged her death for Ms. Renfield's benefit, and you choose to threaten her?"

"You might want to rethink crowding me, Prince."

Ms. Renfield settles a hand onto my chest. "I'm good, Alexandru." To Maverick, she says, "I was just at InovaSpire where I found evidence that Varla here hacked Jerome's computer to make it look like he is the Crossbow Killer."

Maverick squints so hard, his entire face wrinkles. "You're telling me you have evidence she framed Jerome?"

"Yes."

Maverick looks at the body. "You're not telling me this woman did those murders, are you?"

"It might be worth checking her whereabouts," Ms. Renfield says.

Maverick chews his gum in disbelief. "And then she framed Jerome, and then strung herself up like this?"

"Yes, and she went through great pains to hide it. Alexandru and I were swinging by to see what she had to say about it."

Maverick seems about to say something, no doubt about interfering in his precious investigation, but just at that moment, another officer comes bounding in holding a flattened cardboard box with a picture of a crossbow on the side of it. "This was in the bedroom. It's the right kind, boss."

Maverick examines the box, paying special attention to a sticker on it with a price and some other bits of writing. "Good work. Check around and see what else you can find. This entire property is now a crime scene. Back everyone off."

Chapter Twenty-Nine

Harriet

Maverick makes a few calls.

I keep staring at the kitchen counter with the fries and thinking about the one forum member who kept that whole fries thing alive. The one person who seemed to have it out for me.

Sherlocksmith.

Maverick strolls over. "Okay, Harriet. What do you think you're gonna find on her computer or whatever that you want to take a look at?"

"I think I'm going to start typing in the true crime forum URL and see it autofill. And I think I'll see the username and password autofill. And I think that username is going to be Sherlocksmith."

"That's a forum member?"

I nod.

"You think Varla is this Sherlocksmith."

"Sherlocksmith has antagonized me for years and was also obsessed with that french fry detail. Like they would hammer on it, even after I asked for people to stop discussing it."

"Are you saying the crossbow murders have something to do with you?"

"I don't know. All I know is this scene has a whole lot to do with me. And I have proof that Varla framed Jerome."

"We'll take a look at her laptop together, and then you'll give me your proof and get out of here." Maverick leads the two of us to a side room that seems to be an office.

"The proof is very technical, but I'd be happy to send it over."

"And you'll cease and desist your investigation."

"This investigation no longer holds interest for us," Alexandru puts in.

Maverick holds out a pair of latex gloves. I put them on and sit in front of the computer, waking the machine up. I start to type in the forum URL. I don't have to get very far before it auto-fills. I hit return and it all comes up.

"Sherlocksmith," Maverick says.

"How long was this Sherlocksmith antagonizing you on the forum?" Alexandru asks.

"At least seven years, I'd say. A real bully. I always thought it was a dude."

"Did you have any kind of relationship with any of the three murder victims?"

"No, I didn't know any of them," I say.

Maverick looks thoughtful. "If Varla was a forum peer, she knew you'd be investigating. Is it possible she thought that this was a clever puzzle to construct?"

"A nesting doll of culprits," Alexandru says, almost to

himself. "Dooley Brogan, then Jerome, then the puppeteer herself—each shell cracking open to reveal the next. Theatrical, however inelegant."

"Right?" I say. "If this is supposed to be some masterpiece puzzle, it's just not that clever."

"Not clever?" Maverick barks out a laugh. "Harriet, this woman is quite possibly a serial killer, and serial killers aren't clever. Jeffrey Dahmer kept body parts in his freezer. Ed Gein made lampshades out of skin."

"An interesting décor concept," Alexandru puts in unhelpfully.

"We got a crime scene crew on the way, and I don't want you two contaminating things any more than you already have. You got my email address. Pull together everything you know and forward it to me. I'll be in touch."

My mind is spinning as we head to the front door. Was this whole thing about me somehow? Three people dead to taunt me?

Maverick swears softly when he sees the crowd out there.

Suddenly I think of one more thing. "What color is Varla's car?"

"Is that important?" Maverick asks.

"It might be."

Maverick leads us around the drive to the garage in back. A uniform officer is coming out the side door.

"Is there a car inside there?"

"Gray Subaru," the officer says. "Four-door. Maybe five years old."

Maverick looks over at me. "That important somehow?"

"Alma Washington told me that somebody in a smallish

gray car was sitting and watching Dooley Brogan's house before the murders even started."

"Oh yeah, we heard all about that," Maverick says.

"Right, she thought it was one of you. Somebody wearing a ball cap in a gray car."

Maverick grunts. "Alma Washington is not exactly known for her thorough descriptions. We'll get a picture of the car and talk to her."

"Alma lives at that home up on Kempton Street."

"Right near the Brogan residence," Maverick says. "Okay, then."

A white Porsche pulls into the drive, and Serena, Malik, KC, and Jeb the salesperson all jump out.

Serena rushes up to me. "Harriet! What's going on? Is Varla okay?"

"She is dead," Alexandru says.

Serena's hand goes to her mouth. She looks stricken.

"No," KC whispers. "No. What happened?"

I tell them about Varla hanging herself in the kitchen. I don't add the part about the overalls with the hole in the left knee or the carton of cold fries on a flowered plate.

Serena's eyes are bright with tears.

KC steps closer, his face a mask of concern. "She hanged herself? That's...God, Harriet. You walked in to see that?"

Something in his tone makes me hesitate.

Alexandru's hand closes around my elbow. "We must go."

"Why would she do that?" KC says.

Alexandru's voice is a growl. "How is she to know what is in the mind of this woman? Such questions serve nothing." His grip tightens, steering me away from them.

"I was just—" KC calls after us.

But Alexandru is already walking me toward the car, his stride long enough that I have to half-jog to keep up.

"What was that about?" I ask once we're out of earshot.

"I do not wish you to perform your pain for the entertainment of others."

I glance up at him. "They just wanted to know."

He makes a rough sound in the back of his throat—not quite a denial, not quite agreement. "KC's questions were prurient. Ghoulish. You do not owe him an accounting of your distress."

"You're protecting me," I say.

"I am not."

"Thank you."

He releases my elbow as we reach the car, and I catch a glimpse of his expression before he smooths it away—something old and feral.

His hunger.

The bell over the door of Mrs. Morgan's Curios jingles as I walk in. The familiar smell of wood polish and old books comforts me, even though my mind is spinning with the darkness of that scene with Varla.

Mom looks up from behind the register, where she's sorting through a box of what looks like estate jewelry. "Back so soon? To what do I owe the pleasure?"

I take a taffy from the bowl, unsure where to start.

"Something happened, and I wanted you to hear it from me

before it hits the news." I look up and meet her gaze. "They found the woman who took my job at InovaSpire dead."

"Dead?"

"Presumed suicide. But the way she did it..." I pause, not wanting to say the rest.

Mom frowns. "What way did she do it?"

"She hung herself wearing overalls. With a hole in the left knee. In her *kitchen*. And there were other random details in that scene just like—" I don't have to finish.

Mom's expression turns serious. She sets down a tarnished brooch.

I rub the side of the candy, rubbing out the bulges. "It's looking like she was the Crossbow Killer, too. They even found a crossbow over there."

"I don't understand. The Crossbow Killer was your replacement at InovaSpire? And what do the crossbow murders have to do with..." The Cuyahoga Killer, she means, but she doesn't have to say it.

"I'm afraid the connection might be me."

"In what way?"

"We're still piecing it all together, but I was able to get a look at Varla's computer, and it turns out that she's this person named Sherlocksmith who's been a jerk to me on the forum for years. So Sherlocksmith gets hired for my old job, kills somebody right in front of our store here knowing I'd investigate, she frames Jerome, an old friend of mine, kills that retired teacher, and then hangs herself like that."

"All to antagonize you?"

"That's what it looks like. It doesn't make a lot of sense."

"Did you know the retired teacher?"

"Nick Lernov? No."

"What was this woman like to you in person?"

"She seemed friendly and professional in the interviews, but later on she seemed to have a grudge. I never understood why."

"Sherlocksmith," Mom says. "Did she see herself as some kind of Moriarty to your Sherlock, do you think?"

I snort. "I'm not much of a Sherlock."

"You're better. You are a brilliant, inquisitive young woman, and you're always there when somebody needs help. It's one of the beautiful things about you, and I'm sorry that this sick young woman took advantage of that. And I know I shouldn't say this, but I'm glad she's dead. She saved the justice system the trouble of putting her away."

"I sent all the evidence that I have to Maverick, and hopefully he can make sense of it. He wasn't thrilled with my investigation, I'll tell you that." I stare at the taxidermy weasel behind the register. "Still. Why the retired teacher?"

"I'm sure Maverick will work it out. He thought that the ligature marks looked like suicide, but that can be faked."

"Harriet!" Mom scolds. "Sometimes things are what they appear. I know that's not as interesting—"

"I'm just saying it doesn't all fit together that well. The retired teacher..."

Mom lets out a soft sigh, and there it is: that look of pity and concern. The same as when I told her I thought James wasn't taken by the Cuyahoga Killer, and that the black car had to be significant somehow, and how the man Alma saw maybe had something to do with it.

"Doesn't make sense. Just saying."

"I know, honey. But this young woman was trying to torment you, and I don't want to see her succeed."

"It's just, what kind of pattern is it, even? It's just so off in so many ways! Maybe there's something I'm not seeing."

"Hey." She reaches across the counter and squeezes my hand. "I should've been there that day. Walking him home from school. I put my responsibilities on a little girl."

"No, don't say that."

"I am saying it. I won't stop saying it."

"Twelve years old is not little."

"You were a little girl, and I was the mother. I could've walked the six blocks up there. I had Granabelle here to watch the store. I leaned on you far too much when it came to James."

"As you should've!" I protest through my tightened throat. "If I was old enough to babysit, I was old enough to walk him home, but what did I do? I left him there because I was more interested in boys and ice cream."

"Stop! You were supposed to be interested in boys and ice cream at that age."

"Please, I don't want to do this, Mom."

She comes around the counter and gives me a hug.

I squeeze her tight. "I might be getting taffy in your hair."

She pulls away and fixes me with a harsh look. "The only person responsible for James disappearing is the one who took him."

Her saying "the one who took him" instead of "the Cuyahoga Killer" is a concession to me.

"I love you," I say.

"Back atcha. Just keep that taffy out of my hair."

I say my goodbyes and head down Commerce Street, past

Gable's Grocery and the barber shop and Gazebo Park, feeling uneasy about the whole thing. I tell myself it's just the shock of seeing Varla's body like that. Obviously, it would bring up all kinds of dark feelings.

And what am I going to do about Alexandru? We are four days until he's full-on feral beast. Who is Alexandru going to drain now that the Crossbow Killer is dead? I fear he'll go for Dooley.

I'll figure it out.

I pop into Berky's bakery and make a beeline for the front counter. I decide to go for a semi healthy giant muffin instead of the full-on cookie breakfast that I deep down want. I add on a giant cup of coffee.

"Harriet!" Josie's waving at me from a table. She's with her little boy.

I grab my stuff and go over.

"Honey!" She hugs me. "I heard about that woman—" she glances down at two-year-old Angus and lowers her voice, "doing what she did like she did... what the h-heck?"

"I know." I sit and tear apart the muffin, wishing I'd ordered a cookie instead, because I sort of deserve it.

"What the heck?" says Angus in his cute little-boy voice.

Josie frowns. "I don't get it. Did she have some weird obsession with you or something?"

"That's what it looks like. She was kind of a jerk to me on the internet, and she took it into real life."

"Exactly what you don't want," Josie says.

I pop another bit of my healthy muffin into my mouth and think how mad I'll be if it has the same exact amount of calories as a chocolate almond Berky Bomb. Which it probably is.

"The whole thing doesn't entirely sit right, if I'm being honest."

"Harriet. What's going on? Do you not think it's Varla?"

"No. I don't know! It doesn't sit right is all I'm saying."

"Look. This is just between us, but the city council got a briefing from the police a little while ago. They interviewed your old boss and a few other people at InovaSpire, and this woman's absences from the office coincide with the murders."

"Okay. But that is circumstantial."

Josie makes a face.

"No, I know," I say. "Of course all the evidence is pointing to her."

"Maybe they'll find journals or ramblings or something that explain a bit more of her thinking."

I gaze up at the bright French menu on the chalkboard. "If she really is the Crossbow Killer, thank goodness that's over."

"Have you seen your mom yet?"

"I told her just now. She was pissed on my behalf more than anything."

"Your mom is a tough cookie."

"Tough cookie!" Angus says.

Chapter Thirty

Harriet

I head to my office and spend some time on my stepped pyramid made from small stacks of quarters.

It helps a little, but not that much. Alexandru's hungry. Is he going to go for Dooley tonight?

I go up to the grand library and flop down in the newly appeared second chair in front of the fireplace. Alexandru is, as usual, in his normal chair with its weirdly curved handles.

"You are distressed."

He's right about that. "You never said where this chair came from. I think you put it here just for me."

"You are always telling me to blend in with humans. Is it not the way of humans to have a furniture grouping?"

"You need a chair for Gregor, now."

"Gregor does not use chairs."

I squint across the room toward the corner where I can just make out Gregor's form in the gloom. "Maybe it might be nice to ask him."

"I do not want a chair, milady," Gregor says.

"You see?" Alexandru says.

I lower my voice to a whisper. "You know he said that because he thinks you don't want him here. Gregor is an interesting person with a lot to offer. Did you know he's an expert woodworker?"

"The subject is closed."

"I personally would enjoy sitting with Gregor."

Alexandru sighs wearily.

"I'm sorry, am I being tedious? Because you know what I find tedious? Being punished for something my ancient ancestors did that I have nothing to do with. Is that what you're doing to Gregor, too?"

A voice from the corner. "I am pleased to serve, milady."

"I think he's punishing you for something."

Alexandru turns a page. "I am beginning to regret this furniture grouping."

Clearly, I'm not going to be getting any answers here. I turn my attention to other matters. There are just so many. "You can't drain Dooley."

"Would you prefer I drain one of the Snag Tooth Riders?"

"No."

"Somebody else, then? Either you pick or I do."

"I can't pick."

"It as an honor to sacrifice oneself to provide life force to a superior being such as I."

"Gag," I say.

"We will catch a murderer next month."

"I know you're going to say this is wishful thinking, but Varla being Sherlocksmith...I'm having a hard time with it. I'm questioning it."

Alexandru looks interested. "Say more."

"I don't know. Does something feel off to you?"

"I'm more interested in if something feels off to you. If something feels off to you, that is worth considering. You have known Sherlocksmith for a number of years. Tell me about this person."

"Well, Sherlocksmith always acted superior to me in every way and always had a better solution to everything than whatever I'd put forth. Through the years, whenever I'd make any kind of assertion, Sherlocksmith would be the first to jump in to argue. Always wanting to be superior."

"Sherlocksmith liked to best you."

"Yes. And with that french fry thread where the Cuyahoga Killer didn't eat his fries before hanging himself? Like I said, Sherlocksmith would pound on that so much, I felt like they wanted to keep reminding me of what happened, just to taunt me."

Alexandru growls. "Sherlocksmith enjoyed distressing you."

"And getting the last laugh. Getting the last word on any exchange. That doesn't feel like Varla."

Alexandru considers this. "Varla did not like you, but what I sensed from her was more defensive than offensive."

"Yes!"

The planes of Alexandru's face look stark in the firelight. "I have known devious people; some of them quite well. One thing they have in common is how they revel in their malicious handiwork."

"Yes! And you can't revel in your malicious handiwork if you're dead."

"Nor have the last laugh."

"No," I continue. "The Sherlocksmith I know would keep going until they couldn't. Even if they got arrested, they'd keep on, living for the chance to force me to testify. They'd happily and gleefully taunt me from jail."

"Such a one would not provide a convenient death."

My mind spins. Suddenly, it's all making so much sense. "So what if Sherlocksmith figured out a way to make the murder look like hanging, like maybe drugging poor Varla and hoisting her up there or something. Could be just a matter of time before the medical examiner figures it out." I stand. "We have to solve this mystery before the police get to the real culprit!"

He looks at me the way he does sometimes, like he hasn't quite figured me out yet. "You, my dear, have a nemesis."

"No," I say.

"I should know."

"I am so not the type to have a nemesis."

"Welcome to the club, as they say."

"Wait. The club? Are you saying that you have a nemesis? Somebody who revels in their malicious handiwork?"

Alexandru sets aside his book. "He is of no concern to you."

"So you do!"

"I grow hungry, Renfield."

"Right." I pace up and down in front of the fire. "I have to think Sherlocksmith was at the scene. And we know they have some access to InovaSpire. Also, why frame Varla?"

Alexandru says, "You once told me that murder victims aren't ever random."

"Right. Not for a methodical killer, anyway. Somebody

obsessed enough to stalk me on a forum for years, to study every detail of the Cuyahoga case, to stage this entire elaborate trap... that kind of methodical person is incapable of doing anything random. Every decision relates to something larger. Is there some way in which Varla represents me? Or is she connected to Sherlocksmith? Does Sherlocksmith work at InovaSpire? Did Sherlocksmith seek her out and maybe even befriend her after she took over my position? The first victims, Razor Johnny and Milo, were there to implicate Jerome. But what about Nick Lernov, the retired teacher? I never did do a deep dive on him."

"Perhaps it's time to know more about both of them."

I grab my tablet and do a quick search on Nick Lernov. The first thing that comes up is the fact that his memorial service is being held this afternoon.

I turn to Alexandru. "I'm assuming you have a black outfit?"

"Indeed I do."

"We're going to a funeral."

Chapter Thirty-One

Harriet

The Brennan Family Funeral Home is a two-story brick building with the doors propped open. We weave between people who've spilled out onto the front stoop. Inside is just as much of a mob scene, with people everywhere dabbing at eyes and speaking in hushed tones.

As usual, Alexandru draws stares. The teenagers nearest the door stop mid-sentence. An older woman touches her pearls. It's not his charcoal suit—it's a funeral, so he's not over-dressed for once.

It's more that Ashwood does not produce men who look like this. Neither does anywhere else, exactly.

The viewing room is lined with photo boards that show Nick Lernov as a young man with a full head of hair and a skinny tie. Nick Lernov at a chalkboard writing something about the industrial revolution. Nick Lernov holding a trophy, surrounded by beaming teenagers.

A lot of the photos feature teenagers, actually. And trophies.

"Quiz Bowl," Alexandru reads from a banner in one of the photos. "This is a sport?"

"Sort of. Teams compete to answer questions about a range of subjects, like history, science, literature, math."

"You participated in this?"

"No. I was a different sort of nerd." I lean closer to a photo from what looks like a state championship. The kids hold up a massive trophy, and Nick Lernov stands behind them, beaming. "This team did really well."

We drift along the photo boards, eavesdropping on the mourners. "...never talked down to us." "Strict, but not in a power-mad way." "...helped me so much that year..."

A baby begins to wail loudly.

"Lots of prey and emotions in a small space," I say quietly. "How are you holding up?"

He gazes down at me like it's so strange and bizarre that somebody would ask him how he's doing. "I will survive."

I study a photo of Mr. Lernov at his retirement party. It's the most recent one on the long table.

Alexandru touches my elbow. "Look." He points at a team photo from maybe twelve years ago. A group of teenagers in matching polo shirts holds a banner. Mr. Lernov in the center.

And on the far left, younger but unmistakable—

KC.

"What?" I grab it and study it more closely. "KC!"

"Yes."

"I guess KC is from Creighton. But... I don't know, is this a coincidence?"

"Perhaps."

KC knew Mr. Lernov. And he knew Varla.

Mind racing, I whisper, "KC *is* always trying to get me to use his apps and workarounds, trying to show me better ways of doing things. I always thought he was eager to impress me or something, but...wow, could it be?"

We look around for other photos from that school year. There aren't any. "They went to state. It seems like every year except the year KC was on the team."

"A poor player," Alexandru observes.

"If he was a truly poor player, he'd be cut from the team."

"Ah. You do cull your weak, then."

"We cull them from *teams*, Alexandru. Not from existence. People help those who need it; they don't kill them. It's a little thing called human civilization."

"Human civilization." Alexandru's words drip with disdain, showing exactly how he feels about *human civilization.*

He plucks the photo from my fingers and turns to a nearby trio of women crying over photos from the year before. "Tell me what you know of this man." He points to KC's face.

Instead of looking at the photo, they just stare at him, dumbstruck. One woman has literally stopped crying mid-sob, like Alexandru's outrageous hotness knocked the sadness right out of her.

A thrill skitters up my spine, watching him in action out in the wild. It's not the place, not the time, but sometimes he takes my breath away.

"This male. You three are pictured on the team with him. What can you tell me about him?"

I raise my brows; I didn't know his raptor-like vision extended to photos.

One of the women takes the framed photo and scowls at it. "Oh yeah, that's KC Hawkins."

The tallest of the three makes a sound of disgust. "That jerk. He got the whole team banned from state one year. It was awful."

I move in next to Alexandru. "What happened?"

"He hacked into the competition coordinator's email and downloaded the question database for regionals," the first one says. "He was telling kids on the team which topics to focus on, sneaking in his own flashcards, and it was very suspicious how right he always was."

"Yeah, and Mr. Lernov busted him. He could tell the team's accuracy was too high," the tallest one puts in. "The school made KC turn over his laptop, and the proof was all there."

I glance at Alexandru. He raises one eyebrow a fraction of an inch. We've got something. I want to grab his arms and yell Dude! and swing him around or something.

"Mr. Lernov got the Quiz Bowl people involved, not to mention the principal and his parents. KC was acting like Mr. Lernov was this bad guy for reporting it and ruining his college prospects, but what about us? We had to forfeit all our regional wins. We didn't get to go to state. The following few years, everybody looked at us like we were cheating if we did well."

"Did KC get kicked out of school?" I ask, trying hard not to look at Alexandru because I feel like he'll make me smile.

The women look at each other. "I feel like he got suspended for a pretty long time," the tallest one says, and the others nod in agreement. "Such a loser."

"Mr. Lernov didn't deserve that," the first one says, protective. "KC made him out to be the villain when he was just doing his job."

I nod solemnly, like I'm commiserating about the injustice to Mr. Lernov. Which I am. But also: we need to get out of here so I can properly freak out about this lead.

Chapter Thirty-Two

Alexandru

They're about to cry again.

"That will do." I take Ms. Renfield's arm and drag her away.

"Sorry! Thank you!" she calls to them, and then we're in the other room. She grabs my suit coat, eyes shining with excitement. It's the thrill of the hunt. The thrill of closing in.

The pulse at her throat has quickened.

I cannot look away.

I am acutely aware that this is not hunger. Not entirely.

I want her mouth. It is absurd. Inexcusable.

It cannot be.

But the beat of her heart is relentless. Intoxicating.

"Seriously, I mean, KC?" she's saying. "Right under our noses the whole time? But it makes so much sense!" And then, "Earth to Alexandru!"

"What now?" I growl.

A chime rings out. A man in a black suit gestures toward the next room. "The service is about to start."

"Thanks! Be right there!" Ms. Renfield grabs my arm and pulls me against the flow of mourners shuffling into the service. "In here!"

We duck into a curtained vestibule—lamp, velvet chairs, high table.

"I don't want to be roped into sitting through the service," she explains, pulling out her phone. "We have to figure this out." And then, "Serena? Hi! It's Harriet."

I should be paying attention to the call. I am instead watching the way her lips shape words. I have not fed in twenty-seven days. It is affecting my judgment.

"Can you tell me," Ms. Renfield says, "what was Varla's relationship with KC like?"

Her eyes sharpen as she listens. She paces three steps and turns, a hunter circling prey. I have seen this look on military commanders. Dangerous courtiers.

Her pulse drums faster beneath the edge of her jaw. I imagine pressing my face to that warmth, breathing her in.

She casts a glance in my direction and a pink flush climbs her throat. I find myself cataloguing these things the way I cata-logue vulnerabilities—involuntarily. Precisely.

Her lips would be soft. Unbearably so.

"Who's getting Varla's job now?" she asks Serena.

Serena answers. Again Ms. Renfield lifts her gaze to mine and something passes between us. The pieces are falling into place behind those clever eyes.

"So KC is taking over Varla's role," she says slowly. "No. Yes. I'm sure he's more than capable."

She makes excuses and hangs up, practically vibrating. "Dude! KC applied for my job when I left. He resented Varla getting it. He's been *helping* me investigate, positioning himself..."

On she goes. She's magnificent like this. Alive with the hunt. Speaking rapidly, utterly focused. Pure perfection.

She is more intoxicating than blood.

My hands reach out to curve around her waist, fingers digging into flesh.

"What are you doing?"

I lift her onto the table and set her there. "Setting you at a convenient height."

Her heart beats, a bird fluttering wildly against the bars of its cage. Her eyes gleam with defiance and something like pleasure. "Convenient for what?"

I lower my voice. "To kiss you, Ms. Renfield."

She sucks in a shaky breath. "This is the twenty-first century. You can't just kiss a woman."

I go very still. A hunter does not lunge; a hunter makes the prey come to him.

I trace her jaw, feather-light. "Then you will kiss me, Ms. Renfield."

"What?" she breathes, heat rising in her skin, her pulse spiking against my fingertips.

I lean in. My mouth hovers a hair's breadth from hers. I am aware of every point of warmth between us. The soft rush of her breath. Her hands motionless on the table edge, white-knuckled, as if she is fighting herself.

"Do as I say, Ms. Renfield."

"You can't command such a thing," she says. But she has not moved away.

Heat rolls off her skin, as if she's burning from the inside. I brush a curl behind her ear. My fingers linger on the soft skin behind her ear.

A shiver rattles through her.

I grate out, "I would like to kiss you now."

Her breath comes in light pants. "That is a declaration; not a question."

I growl.

Her fingers close over my lapels.

She leans in and presses her hot, soft lips to mine. "You are the worst."

I feel the shape of each word against my mouth. It is a kiss and an insult.

So very Ms. Renfield.

"I am the worst," I reply, lips brushing hers right back. "Do not forget it."

My mouth finds hers again, harder this time. Her pulse hammers against my chest. My fingers slide into her hair, tangling in the curls at the nape of her neck.

She makes a small sound.

It hits me like blood.

I pull her closer, until there is no space between us at all. Her body is warm and alive and furious with breath. I can feel the rhythm of her heart everywhere—her throat, her wrists, the frantic beat where she presses against me.

Every instinct I possess is awake.

Not for blood.

For her.

A name rises in my mind from twelve centuries back.

I crush it.

She gasps against my mouth and clutches my shoulders,

fingers digging into muscle as though she might anchor herself to me.

My hand tightens in her hair and I deepen the kiss. I am twelve centuries old and I have forgotten how to be gentle.

Another breath escapes her, half protest, half something else entirely.

Madness.

That is what this is.

The hunger is making me reckless.

A groan escapes her. She squeezes my shoulders, fingers curling into flesh. I can feel her pulse everywhere—her throat, her wrists, against my chest. Every predatory instinct I possess is screaming—and for once, not for blood.

"Wait." She pulls back, dazed, lips swollen, heart hammering. "What—we can't do this."

"Can we not."

"No! We have a killer to catch. Also..." She seems to shake herself clear of something. "Also you're a murderous vampire who thinks humans are only good for foodstuffs."

I trace my thumb across her lower lip. "I have never once thought of you as foodstuffs, Ms. Renfield."

I mean it. That is the problem.

She grabs my wrist. "But you think of everyone else as foodstuffs!"

"They *are* foodstuffs."

"Okay, okay." She shoves me away and jumps off the table. "And there we have it, folks, exhibit A–Z of why *this*"—she points to me and then to herself, and then to me, and then to herself again—"will not be happening."

"Fine. We will locate this KC and I will drain him."

"All signs do point to him." Her eyes go distant, that look she gets when the pattern clicks into place. "He creates a puzzle for me, starting with a murder right outside my family's antique store. And it's the Russian dolls, one on top of another. Dooley looks guilty. Then Jerome looks guilty. Then Varla looks guilty. And that horrible reenactment of the Cuyahoga Killer suicide...he knew that would get to me."

I say nothing. I am remembering the taste of her.

"And meanwhile KC enjoys watching us drawing the wrong conclusion, and then he swoops in and takes my job, laughing all the way. Now *that* is Sherlocksmith." She pulls out her phone.

"What are you doing?"

"Being sure." She hits a button. "Serena? Hey, me again—I know, I'm sorry. Quick question: is KC still there? He is? Good. No, no reason. I forgot to give something to him earlier. No, don't grab him, it's not urgent." She gives me a mischievous look. "Don't tell him I called. It's a surprise."

She hangs up. "He's there, enjoying his shiny new job. Which means his house is empty."

"You wish to search his house."

"I wish to confirm." She's already moving toward the door. "And if we happen to find a crossbow or some incriminating files or a shrine to my spreadsheet methods? All the better."

Chapter Thirty-Three

Alexandru

KC Hawkins lives in a low, flat dwelling—a "ranch house" Ms. Renfield calls it —on the outskirts of Creighton. There's a lot of forest around here, but KC's grass is an unnatural green, and the hedges are trimmed into rigid geometric shapes.

"Huh," Ms. Renfield says.

"What?"

She studies the house with her usual analytical gaze. The gaze that precedes a spreadsheet. "Just... kind of outlandishly controlled."

She produces a small kit from her bag and has the back door open in under a minute. I raise an eyebrow.

"Granabelle," she says by way of explanation. "Don't ask."

Inside, the neatness continues. Humans usually clutter their nests with ridiculous items—photographs of loved ones, trinkets from travels, cards, and the various appliances and junk they seem to collect. This house has none of it.

She moves through the space with her usual focus, opening

drawers, checking cabinets. I watch, remembering the feel of her mouth under mine. The dazzling scent of her blood.

"Bedroom," she says, heading down the hall.

I follow.

The bedroom is more of the same—neat, sparse. She checks the closet. I check under the mattress. Nothing.

"He's smart," she says. "He wouldn't keep anything obvious."

She crouches to look under the bed, raven hair spilling forward, and I am struck by the fierce concentration in her small frame. So one-pointed, this woman. So carefully controlled.

I could reach down and fist that dark hair and pull her back up, pulling her face to mine, her mouth to my mouth. Or perhaps I would push her onto the bed and kiss her elsewhere until that magnificent control shatters entirely.

I look away.

My mind is warped with hunger.

That is the only explanation for this fixation on a Renfield. We return to the living room. She's running her hands along empty bookshelves—why? Checking for hidden compartments? I open a closet and find it contains only a vacuum cleaner and a single coat.

"Is this part of the game? To have a home that defies investigation?" She presses her fingers to her temples. "Uhh!"

But it is not the search that bedevils her. She is reliving the kiss—it's in her scent, the increased heat on her skin. Her spiking pulse.

I am, after all, exceptional.

"Alexandru..." But then her gaze falls on something in the

corner. "There's a laptop!" She flies to it and opens it up, taking a seat on the bed. "Password, password. What do you think of Sherlocksmith?"

I open the small wooden box next to the computer. Inside, newspaper clippings, all of them about the crossbow murders. Arranged. Waiting.

For us.

One second too late, I understand.

The first bullet takes me in the shoulder.

The second and third follow before I can turn. The fourth catches my throat. I hear Ms. Renfield scream as if from a great distance.

Fifth. Sixth. Seventh.

I stagger backward. This is not pain, precisely, but there is damage and a great deal of concentrated force. My body requires a moment to process it all.

More bullets. I lose count. The wall behind me explodes with plaster dust.

I go down.

Chapter Thirty-Four

Harriet

Alexandru slams against the wall and crumbles to the floor.

I've never seen him fall before.

My ears ring. My head spins.

I didn't think he could fall.

"Don't look at him."

KC stands in the doorway. He's holding some kind of a giant gun with a silencer, and his eyes are too bright. Too wide.

"What have you done?!" I go to Alexandru and kneel beside him. He's like a sleeping prince from a painting, lashes like dark crescents against pale skin. His beautiful charcoal suit is torn through in a dozen places, and you can see his ripped-up skin underneath, but there's no blood.

"Hey." I touch the sharp line of his jaw, willing him to open his eyes.

He remains still. Not his usual deadly-predator-waiting-to-strike stillness, but something worse. Something final. Can enough bullets kill him? Does he need time to heal?

I fold his cool fingers closed in mine.

"I don't think he's coming back," KC says. The smugness would enrage me if I had anything left for it.

I squeeze Alexandru's hand. How many times have I wanted him dead? I can't count them. But I would give anything right now to feel his fingers tighten back.

Something hard presses into my back. The point of KC's gun. "Up."

I stand and spin around. "What have you done?"

He makes a tsk-tsk sound. "I'm going to consider that a rhetorical question." He gestures for me to move away from Alexandru's crumpled form.

I comply, ears ringing. It's like I'm operating through a layer of gauze. My eyes keep darting to Alexandru. No movement. No blood either, but KC hasn't noticed that yet.

"Umm..." Keep him talking—that's my idea here. Alexandru needs time, that's all. "How did you know I'd be at the funeral?"

KC's face lights up. "Oh, I didn't. But I knew you'd stumble into *something* eventually. You're predictable that way. Once I realized you were going there, I knew this would be your next stop, so I hid and waited." He tilts his head, studying me. "I actually admired your thought processes on the forum. Until I realized it was all just luck. You stumble on things while you organize random facts into your little rows and columns."

"The different suspects." I force the words out. "You really thought it through."

"*There* she is." He sounds almost proud. "I wanted you to see the pattern. And now they're data points in something *meaningful*. Most murders are just... noise. Random violence by random idiots. But this? This was architecture. The forum's going to love it."

KC smiles. There's something behind his eyes that wasn't there at InovaSpire—a brightness that has nothing to do with intelligence.

"What? Did you not think I'd have an endgame? This is me we're talking about."

I glance down at Alexandru. Still nothing. He has to be okay. He has to be.

KC continues, "The only thing I can say about you is that you realized you were out of your depth at InovaSpire and took a lesser job. I never quite understood it until I saw the way you looked at that supposed prince that one day when you were researching Milo. God, the way you looked at him. And he just... tolerated you. A useful little pet who organizes his receipts."

My jaw tightens. "You're going to frame us." The pieces click together. "You'll make it look like I shot him, he shot me."

"That's right! Mutual destruction. You really unloaded on Alexandru. Anger issues." He motions at the spot in the doorway. "You're going to need to stand there."

"I won't." I take a step back toward Alexandru. My best move right now is to ruin his forensics.

"I gave you an order."

Then his face changes. The smile drops. His eyes go to something over my shoulder and just... stop.

"Wh-wh—" He doesn't finish it.

A voice, dry as dust: "Ms. Renfield can be rather defiant."

I spin around.

Alexandru is standing. His gaze moves over me. Something in my chest unknots.

"Ms. Renfield—"

"I'm fine."

It's all he needs. He steps past me like I'm not there.

Behind me, KC makes a sound I've never heard a person make. "I shot you. I shot you. Where's the—" A scramble of footsteps. "Where's the blood?"

"It seems your architecture has a flaw."

"What are you?"

Alexandru gives him a smile that has nothing to do with warmth. "I'm the variable you failed to account for."

One stumbling step back. "Please. Please, no."

The gun hits the floor.

Alexandru's hand fists in his hair, the other gripping the front of his jacket, and he brings KC's throat to his mouth.

With a sound that is not quite human, he bites in.

KC struggles in his arms: helpless, genuinely helpless, which is something I've never seen KC be. Alexandru feeds with savage focus, chest is visible where the bullets went through. Pale, hard. No wounds. Just him.

As if he feels me watching, he looks up.

He doesn't stop. He just looks at me. Feeds and looks at me, and the intensity of it pins me where I stand like a moth to a board.

It's brutal and violent and ancient, and it does something to me I'm not going to examine.

I back up, nearly stumbling over an overturned chair, unable to look away.

Alexandru tears his mouth from KC's neck. His lips are

red. His fangs are white and exact, and he's holding KC like he weighs nothing.

"Go," he says. His voice is rough and strange and not quite his.

I can't look away. I need to look away.

No, no, no, no.

I turn and I run.

I don't remember getting to my car. I don't remember starting the engine. I just drive, because driving is something I know how to do, and right now I need something I know how to do.

Chapter Thirty-Five

Harriet

I lie awake for hours, staring at the ornate plaster molding on the ceiling of my bedroom at Kingston Manor, replaying the same images over and over.

Alexandru's elegant hands gripping KC's hair, cufflinks glinting in the light, his torn suit jacket falling in perfect lines across his shoulders.

His beastly fangs plunged into KC's neck, lips red with blood. The growl he'd made as he began to feed—low, guttural, satisfied.

A dangerous predator sating itself.

I press my palms against my eyes, but the images don't stop.

Those same hands I'd watched gesture with weary aristocratic disdain and sexily don gloves. Those lips I had kissed so eagerly.

I couldn't look away.

It was like a Renaissance painting—all gore and gorgeousness.

And what did he do with the body? Will KC mysteriously go missing like the last murderer we caught?

Somehow, I drift off. I wake at seven in the morning feeling like a shell of myself. I wander into my office where I take a couple gulps of yesterday's coffee, because no way am I going in the kitchen or even leaving my wing. Maybe I'll never leave. I don't know how to face Alexandru. I don't know how to even look at him.

What I saw last night...

I roll my chair over to the sturdy table against the far wall of my office, the smooth white expanse and the half-finished quarter pyramid.

It feels like a lifetime ago that I started it.

I grab the bowl and continue working on it. I lose myself in arranging the coins, sometimes making micro adjustments with toothpicks to get them to perfectly line up.

It's helping.

I'm making progress, getting to the top, feeling hopeful. This old house is so thick and stable and I'm on the ground floor. Back at the antique store, I would build these and inevitably a truck would roll by, or a door would slam and the thing would come tumbling down.

The higher and stronger I build it, the calmer I feel. I have this one thing perfectly under control, coins in perfect order.

So pointless, but I just need it. I need this one thing to be perfect.

I need that right now.

My phone buzzes. A text from Josie.

OMG did you hear about the fire at that house on Miller

Road? They just confirmed the body was KC Hawkins. Dental records. So horrible.

I stare at the pyramid, shining in the morning light.

Alexandru set that fire. He's been feeding on people for centuries. He knows how to deal with bodies.

I should feel something. Horror, maybe. Guilt. Alexandru killed a man and then he burned down the house to cover the evidence, and now I'm sitting here building a coin pyramid like that'll solve things.

I carefully set another quarter on top.

I'm back at the funeral home, remembering the confidence of his hand as he lifted me to the table. The feel of his hands in my hair, his lips on mine.

I am the worst. Do not forget it.

I got a firsthand reminder last night at KC's. And I couldn't look away.

Well, people rubberneck at all sorts of awful things, like accidents on the side of the highway. It doesn't mean the person likes looking at it.

I pick up another quarter and force myself to focus. Line it up. One and then another.

There's a soft knock at the door.

"Come in," I say.

Gregor enters, carrying a coffeepot and cup. His movements are careful and precise as he sets the tray on the corner of my desk.

"Thank you, Gregor. Is everything okay?"

"Yes." His eyes flick to my coin construction. "You are building again, milady."

I stand back and smile, feeling halfway serene. "What do you think?"

Gregor shows no emotion. "Impressive, milady."

"I don't know about impressive, but it saves my sanity to look at it." I turn to him. "You've been with Alexandru for what, five hundred years?"

"Around that, milady."

"Do you ever imagine doing anything else? From what I saw the other day at the antique store, you could have a pretty amazing livelihood as a carpenter or something. People were impressed with your knowhow."

"I would not wish it."

"So *this* is what you wish? Serving Alexandru?"

"This and nothing more."

"But no one deserves to be treated the way he treats you."

"Milady is kind." He starts backing toward the door.

"I mean...just think about it."

He nods and leaves, and I turn back to my coin tower.

I work for another hour, building it higher than I've ever built a coin tower before. Finally it's done.

I dig in my drawer and find a silver disk I sometimes use for these things and set it on top and then I put a tiny little owl figurine on the very tip-top.

But even a perfect pyramid made of quarters doesn't blot out the memory of our kiss. And the feel of his eyes on mine as he fed.

Chapter Thirty-Six

Alexandru

The storm arrives in the late afternoon, rolling in from the west. Rain lashes the windows of my study. Thunder roars in the distance.

A book is open in my lap, but I am not reading it.

I keep reliving the kiss. Hearing the soft sounds she made. Feeling her heartbeat against my chest.

When I know better than anybody what the bloodline she carries is capable of.

Humans have pathetically little inkling of the true power of ancestral lineages and tendencies. They think what their great-grandparents did or were capable of has nothing to do with them.

The naïveté in this is staggering.

How desperately did I dream of making the Renfields suffer? The rage of it sharp even now, even after all this time.

And not only have I been lenient with this one, but I kissed her.

I force my mind back onto the book, an account of Trajan's

campaigns in Dacia, but I find my mind wanders. I extend my awareness through the manor. Ms. Renfield is gone. I felt her leave some time ago, her presence fading as she drove toward town.

But Gregor is here. I find him in—

I go still.

He is in her office. In Ms. Renfield's private space. And what I feel from him is not the usual gray fog of his endless penance.

It is a hot, tight knot of resentment.

Truly?

I am on my feet before I consciously decide to move.

The walk from my study to her office takes less than a minute. My footsteps making no sound on the marble. The door is ajar.

Gregor stands in the center of the room, his back to me. On the small table where Ms. Renfield works on her coin towers, there is nothing but scattered coins.

He destroyed it.

Deliberately. I can feel the satisfaction in him, the vicious pleasure. Something that brought her peace.

"Gregor."

He turns. His face is blank, but I can feel the defiance beneath it. "Overlord."

"You will rebuild that. Exactly as it was."

He says nothing. Does not move.

"Now."

Something flickers in his eyes. For one moment, I think he might refuse. That would be interesting. That would give me an excuse to remind him what I am capable of.

But he is not that foolish. He never has been.

He moves to the table and begins gathering the coins.

"When you have finished," I say, "you will go to the roof. The gutters require cleaning. You will use a spoon."

Lightning splits the sky as if on cue, followed by a crack of thunder that rattles the windowpanes.

"The storm, overlord—"

"Do I stutter? You will clean every gutter on this manor. You will use a spoon. And you will not come down until you are finished or I grant you permission."

He bows his head. "Yes, overlord."

Good. Never before has he moved against a Renfield. I will not have him start now.

"Begin with the reconstruction. I want it completed within the hour."

With that, I return to my study.

I stand at the window, watching the rain, listening to the distant sounds of Gregor's careful work. The small clicks and taps of coins being assembled.

Later, I hear the creak of the roof access door. The scrape of his footsteps on slate tiles. The howl of wind.

Even this does not calm me.

How could I have kissed her?

I am a thousand years old. I have bedded duchesses, courtesans, and warriors. I have felt nothing for any of them beyond the momentary satisfaction of appetite.

But this Renfield.

Outside, Gregor scrapes at the gutters with his spoon.

Good. Let him suffer. Let us both suffer for our foolishness.

Chapter Thirty-Seven

Harriet

Something is wrong with my spiral coin tower.

I noticed it the moment I walked into my office— my perfect spiral sitting on the window table where I left it.

I set down my bag and move closer, studying it.

The coins are there, but they're not lined up. The spiral is sloppy. Did I just *think* I lined them up, but I really didn't?

Was I way more upset than I thought?

I sink into my chair and stare at the wrong little tower, unnerved. What's going on? Did the stress of seeing Alexandru drain KC affect my perception?

Good grief, am I starting to go buggy like my father?

No. No way.

I take a breath. Then another.

Still, I don't know what to think. Somebody would've had to knock it over and start again to get this sloppy look. Who would do that? Not Alexandru, and surely not Gregor.

Is it me?

Right then, a familiar urge rolls over me. It's the urge I've been getting lately whenever I'm faced with something difficult.

The urge to find the black ledgers. To resort to them, as if they have some wisdom, somehow. As if they'll put the world right in a way that all the coin sculptures, spreadsheets, and databases never could.

I tell myself I don't want them. I saw my father, all muttering and weird, poring over those ledgers. I refuse to end up like that.

And this attraction to Alexandru needs to end. I know what he is—how can I dream of kissing him again? How could I have watched him kill and feel something other than horror?

No.

And I'm not going to go and find the ledgers.

And I'm not going to sit here like a victim. I need to take control of the situation. I need to figure out a way to get free of him. Neutralize him. I can't imagine it, but wouldn't it be justified in terms of how many lives I would save? How did I ever think he might change?

It's a moot point. I don't know how to kill him, or even if he's killable. I need more information. I need to make a plan.

And in the meantime, Alexandru and I need to set some boundaries.

Whatever is happening between us has to stop. Now.

I find him in his study.

He's standing at the window, watching the storm, his profile regal against the gray light. He doesn't turn when I enter, though of course he heard me what with his bat-like sonar hearing.

"Ms. Renfield." His voice is cool and distant. "I trust your excursion to town was restorative."

"We need to talk."

He turns, expression unreadable.

I force myself to hold his gaze, even though every instinct is telling me to look away. "There's something... happening between us. And we need to discuss it."

For a long moment, he just looks at me. "Something happening between us." Then, ever so slowly, his lips curve into a smile. "You Renfields. Always so dramatic."

Heat suffuses my cheeks. "I don't believe I'm being dramatic."

With a sigh, he moves away from the window, ambling along the rows of books with his usual predatory grace. My pulse quickens, just watching him. "What is it, then?"

"You kissed me, and the kiss was, as I recall, pretty intense."

"For you, perhaps."

The words hit like a slap. "Excuse me? No way, it was intense for you, too."

His chocolate-dark eyes sparkle in the gloom.

"Dude. Don't even deny it. I may not have vampire empath voodoo, but I was there. You were into it."

"I was hungry. And you, Ms. Renfield, smell very much like food."

My belly does a sad little flop. "Well," I say, "let's not let you get so very hungry ever again."

"Let's not."

"Like ever, ever, ever again," I bite out.

It's here that I hear the scraping sound. Faint but persistent, coming from somewhere above us.

I stop. "What is that?"

Alexandru's expression doesn't change. "It is Gregor."

The scraping continues. Metal on slate. I move to the window and peer upward into the storm.

A figure is on the roof. Dark coat whipping in the wind, rain plastering his hair to his skull. He's hunched over the gutter line, and in his hand—

I spin around. "Gregor's on the roof? In this storm?"

Alexandru settles into his chair with the air of a man perfectly at ease. "He is cleaning the gutters. With a spoon."

"It's a thunderstorm!"

"Gregor is heartier than he appears."

"With a spoon?" The horror of it crashes over me. "He's on a slate roof in a lightning storm, cleaning gutters with a spoon?"

"The gutters have needed attention for some time."

"Don't you even care about him?" The words burst out of me, raw and angry. "He could fall! He could be struck by lightning!"

"His welfare is not your concern."

"I'm making it my concern!"

Alexandru's eyes snap to mine, and for a moment, something dangerous flickers there. "Be careful, Ms. Renfield. You remain in my household at my pleasure. I can still banish you to the cellar to count rice in the dark."

"Why?" I demand. "What did he do to deserve this?"

"He displeased me."

"That's not an answer."

"It is the only answer you will receive." He leans back in his chair. "Now. To business. You may take a respite from hunting.

I will simply drain Dooley Brogan next month when I feel the urge to eat. You will continue to attend to my empire."

"What? No. Dooley could very well be innocent!"

"Your society has labeled him a murderer."

"But they changed their mind! Sort of."

"It is decided."

Of course he doesn't care. He's a monster who sends his servant onto a roof in a lightning storm.

"I'll find you someone else," I say. "A real killer. Give me time."

His gaze drifts back to the window, dismissing me. "Close the door on your way out."

I leave without a word.

But all night, as the storm rages on, I hear the scraping of Gregor's spoon against the gutters. And I wonder what kind of life I've stumbled into.

And if I'll ever find my way out.

Chapter Thirty-Eight

Alexandru

She has been avoiding me for three days.

Not overtly. Ms. Renfield is too professional for that. She still appears at the appointed times to deliver her reports. She still maintains the business ledgers and correspondence and the administrative work that she so excels in.

But she no longer lingers, regarding me with that mix of exasperation and reluctant fascination.

She no longer engages me in chit-chat.

She has learned her place, I suppose.

Tonight, after she delivered her evening report in that new, clipped tone of hers, she retreated to her quarters. I heard her footsteps on the stairs. The slam of her door. The soft sigh she sometimes makes as she sinks into a chair. Her discourse with Liz, her plant. Sometimes the clip of coins as she builds a new tower.

I wander to the far end of the mansion and climb the stairs to the turret room, lost in the memories of home and hunts gone by, but it is not the solace it used to be. My mind roams to darker things.

A few decades after the binding. There was a woman in a village below the castle who had done nothing... nothing, that is, except exist in a way that inconvenienced the Renfield of that era, Elisabeta's grandson.

He held the amulet and smiled at me the way a child smiles at a trapped thing.

I watched myself trudge down through the snow toward the village lights, knowing exactly what I was going to do and unable to stop a single moment of it.

My hands did what they were told. I have never forgotten her bewildered expression as I crushed the life from her.

There were others. There were always others. I have forgotten none of them.

Some hours later, I go down to the great hall where Gregor has built a fire in the hearth.

Ms. Renfield's book lies abandoned on the table. A half-empty cup of tea has gone cold. An empty bowl that once held her Bugle snacks.

It is here that I spot it: her sweater hanging over the chair. It's one of her usual sweater jackets, this one gray with pockets on either side. She was wearing it this morning.

I go to it, run my finger over the fabric. And then, without thinking what I'm doing, I bring it to my face and breathe her in.

I breathe her in.

And then I lower the cardigan.

But I do not put it down.

Epilogue

Harriet

The clock has started again. I've been working every angle I can think of—a hit-and-run outside Creighton, a body pulled from Lake Erie—and hitting the same dead ends as the police. Three days of minimizing contact with Alexandru means three days of doing this alone, and it shows.

I'm staring at a spreadsheet that isn't telling me anything when the knock comes. Gregor is out. Alexandru is, as ever, constitutionally incapable of answering a door. I hoist myself out of the chair and go pull the heavy door open.

Standing there is one of the most breathtakingly beautiful men I've ever seen: honey-brown hair, sparkling blue eyes, a smile that lights up the night. He's wearing a three-piece suit of cream linen, like he's maybe on his way to a garden party at Buckingham Palace.

"Can I help you?"

"I do hope so." He looks past me into the foyer, curious. Appraising. "I'm a friend of Alexandru's. Is he in?"

Alexandru has friends?

He walks in without being invited and then turns around, regarding me with a pleasant expression. "I'm sorry, where are my manners?"

"I wouldn't know."

He laughs—genuinely delighted. "I like you already." He extends a hand. "Algernon. Duke of Densmere. But my friends call me Nero."

"I'm Harriet. Harriet Morgan." I shake his hand, mesmerized.

Alexandru's voice comes from behind me, cold and flat. "Step away from him, Ms. Renfield."

Alexandru stands on the bottom step, perfectly still, perfectly deadly, like he's carved from the darkness itself. He is the most frightening thing in the room—more frightening than I've ever seen him.

Algernon smiles straight at him.

I don't know what's happening. I don't think I want to.

"Ms. Renfield." Quieter. "Step away from him."

Nero's smile doesn't waver. "Ms. Renfield? I do not believe that's her name."

Thank you for reading! I hope you enjoyed Alexandru and Harriet's latest mystery.

But wait—what about that time in the middle of the book when Alexandru and Gregor and Harriet went to dinner over at Harriet's mother's?

What exactly happened???

Did Alexandru actually eat something? What about Gregor with his gruel? What did Granabelle wear? What happened??

It's all in the newsletter subscriber bonus scene, my friend! You can get it here>> https://geni.us/Rnde

Will Alexandru and Harriet be able to find YET ANOTHER murderer before Alexandru goes all beastly and feral?

Don't miss the next book, out September 22, 2026!

Find links here: https://geni.us/Renfield3

(or just go to my website: annikamartinbooks.com and poke around in the books area)

This book is part of the Immortal Boss series of Vampire Mystery books. The books can be read as standalones, available widely in print and audio, and in ebook through Amazon.

Also by Annika Martin

Find a complete list of books and audiobooks at
www.annikamartinbooks.com

About the Author

Annika Martin is a New York Times bestselling author who lives in Minneapolis with her husband; in her spare time she enjoys taking pictures of her cats, consuming boatloads of chocolate suckers, and tending her wild, bee-friendly garden.

newsletter:
annikamartinbooks.com/newletter

Facebook:
www.facebook.com/AnnikaMartinBooks

Instagram:
instagram.com/annikamartinauthor

website:
www.annikamartinbooks.com

email:
annika@annikamartinbooks.com